"With her sparking new voice and endearing love for Fire Island, Becky Chalsen has a forever fan in me."

—Jane L. Rosen, author of *On Fire Island*

"Sun-soaked, breezy, and charming, this book deftly reminds us that while romances may come and go, some of life's greatest love stories are our long-term friendships."

—Mikki Brammer, author of *The Collected Regrets of Clover*

"Chock-full of joy and drama, humor and heart, *Serendipity* reads like a bright, balmy weekend spent on Fire Island—Rocket Fuels and all. With a charming cast of characters and a perfectly summery setting, Chalsen has once again crafted the quintessential beach read, capturing the all-too-relatable highs and lows that come with ushering relationships into adulthood (romantic or otherwise). It's a sunny celebration of love in all its forms; I savored every word."

—Genevieve Wheeler, author of *Adelaide*

"Moving and insightful, *Serendipity* perfectly captures the complexities of long-term friendships and romances. Chalsen's charm sparkles in this perfect summer read with enduring resonance."

—Emily Wibberley and Austin Siegemund-Broka,
authors of *The Breakup Tour*

"*Serendipity* is as unforgettable as the perfect beach rental. Absorbing and deeply relatable, this book sparkles with the textured truth and complications of long-held relationships. A coming-of-age, romantic comedy, and dazzling ode to friendship all in one. As to be expected with Chalsen, this book is a thoughtful meditation on the choices, pain, and love that come for a person in their twenties, wrapped up in a radiant, beachy sweetness. The Serendipity House gang will stay with me for a long time."

—Cat Shook, author of *If We're Being Honest*

"Ocean Beach comes alive on the page like a sun-bleached postcard; a dreamy and vivid story about a group of old friends looking for a summer of fun but finding so much more. I adored Maggie—a very relatable creative woman whose life hits the rocks, and she comes back to her roots to face her past and find her purpose again. Becky's writing is so rich and vivid, and this book is totally transportive. *Serendipity* is all heart; a glorious page-turner, the perfect summer read—absolutely magic."

—Lizzy Dent, author of *The Summer Job*

"*Serendipity* is a sun-kissed love letter to old friendships and new adventures, to making mistakes and growing up, to dancing with your friends until your feet hurt. Reading it feels like framing a photo from your favorite vacation and smiling at it every morning. Chalsen writes with the tender pen of someone who cherishes true friendship, the bonds that survive beauty and heartache, sun-filled days and rainy ones, knowing the clouds will open up again. *Serendipity* made me dream of sandy skin, sunscreen, and soulmates."

—Taylor Hahn, author of *The Lifestyle*

"Becky Chalsen absolutely delivers with her sophomore novel! I devoured this book in one sitting—it is a perfect beach read! Chalsen deftly weaves together a realistic coming-of-age story about friendship, growing up and growing apart, and what happens when old friends come back together. I fell in love with each of the characters and with the gorgeous summer setting. Move this one to the top of your summer TBR!"

—Falon Ballard, author of *Right on Cue*

"This warm and witty novel about the people and places we choose to call home is the perfect beach read. Chalsen mixes light, sparkling summer fun with profound meditations on that period in our lives—usually mid-to-late twenties—when our childhood expectations fall apart, and we're forced to reinvent who we are and what it takes to make us happy. Fans of Emily Henry's *Happy Place* will fall head over heels for *Serendipity*'s gorgeous second-chance love stories between a group of friends, set against the alluring sun and surf of Fire Island."

—Ashley Winstead, author of *The Boyfriend Candidate*

Serendipity

A NOVEL

BECKY CHALSEN

DUTTON

DUTTON

An imprint of Penguin Random House LLC
penguinrandomhouse.com

DUTTON and the D colophon are registered trademarks
of Penguin Random House LLC.

LIBRARY OF CONGRESS CATALOGING-IN-PUBLICATION DATA
Names: Chalsen, Becky, author.
Title: Serendipity: a novel / Becky Chalsen.
Description: [New York]: Dutton, 2024.
Identifiers: LCCN 2023044803 (print) | LCCN 2023044804 (ebook) |
ISBN 9780593474723 (trade paperback) | ISBN 9780593474730 (ebook)
Subjects: LCGFT: Novels.
Classification: LCC PS3603.H336635 S47 2024 (print) |
LCC PS3603.H336635 (ebook) | DDC 813/.6—dc23/eng/20231222
LC record available at https://lccn.loc.gov/2023044803
LC ebook record available at https://lccn.loc.gov/2023044804

Printed in the United States of America
1st Printing

BOOK DESIGN BY ELKE SIGAL

To the group chats we'll never put on mute,
with the people we'll always call home.

For my quadruplet sisters, Joanna, Maggie, and Lizzy,
the best friendship I've ever known, my very favorite text thread.
I'm so grateful to be a quarter of our story.

It's a funny thing coming home. Nothing changes.
Everything looks the same, feels the same, even
smells the same. You realize what's changed is you.

—F. SCOTT FITZGERALD

That's showbiz, baby.

—UNKNOWN

Serendipity

Prologue

Cornerstone Crew

Tuesday, June 6 @ 3:17 AM
Georgie: Friends, the time has come.

Georgie has named the conversation "Ocean Beach Buds"
Georgie: Ocean Beach Weekend 1 is almost here. As a reminder,
we have the Fire Island house for June 9–11, July 7–9, and
August 11–13 this summer. (But if these dates aren't already in
your calendar, I'm offended.) Let's chat grocery order and room
assignments in the AM? Still can't believe Mac found the same
place as after prom! Feels like a great sign for what's to come.
Georgie: House details: www.fireislandrentals.com/oceanbeach
/the-serendipity-house
Georgie: I really need a beach day.

Tuesday, June 6 @ 7:35 AM
Mac: Dude, what you really need is to quit your job. Or at least
be quieter when you come back home. I'm buying you less
squeaky shoes for your bday haha

Mac: But yes, friends, our Ocean Beach return will be epic. Can't wait to get out there!

Liz: I'm not over this 3:17 AM time stamp. RT quitting your job. But Cam and I can't wait! xx

PJ: These weekends are truly the only events I care about in my calendar. Here we go, OB! Thanks again for the invite.

Brenna: Guys I just got a Facebook memories notification that we graduated seven years ago exactly! And now we're headed back to the Serendipity House!? This is officially our 7-year high school reunion. It's decided.

PJ: . . . Can I still come then?

Brenna: Of course! East Meadow High welcomes all.

PJ: Awesome. Go Jets! I'm fitting in already.

Quinn: We didn't graduate seven years ago. Time is a simulation. Graduation is a construct. We are ageless.

Liz: Agreed ^

Quinn: Also, seven-year reunions really aren't a thing.

Mac: No, I'm with Brenna. Let's make 'em a thing.

Cam: Btw Liz and I just started a grocery list on Google Docs. Shared with you all. Check and add whatever!

Brenna: Perfect! We can use that grocery service again that delivers via ferry. I've still got their info saved!

Georgie: And then let's just plan to circle back re: Friday ferry times later in the week?

Quinn: Booo "circle back." We get it, you work in Big Law. But yes. Circle, we shall.

Mac: Oh, also everyone, Robyn is officially in, too. Sorry for last-minute notice!

PJ: Sounds good!

Georgie: (Quinn, I'm actively ignoring you.)

Brenna: I wish I had a boyfriend to bring. ☹️

Quinn: B, can you hear me playing my tiny violin from the kitchen?

Brenna: Ooooh. Meet you in the kitchen.

Georgie: Back to Serendipity. The rental house has 4 bedrooms, so let's do Cam/Liz, Mac/Robyn, Quinn/Brenna, and then me and PJ, if he'll have me as a roommate?

PJ: Sir, it would be an honor to be your Ocean Beach roommate.

Brenna: OH! So! Speaking of roommates . . .

Quinn: Remember how Maggie called us yesterday . . .

Brenna: She's moving back to New York . . .

Brenna: And taking the third bedroom in our unit—moving in on Thursday! She'll sublet through the end of our lease, which is up in September anyway.

Quinn: (And yes, Princess Karla FINALLY moved out yesterday . . . thank you, universe.)

Brenna: As such . . . we are anticipating that it might be suuuuuper awkward if we don't invite Maggie, too? Since she'll be literally living with me and Quinn? We don't want to start summer off on the wrong foot.

Quinn: An awkward, rude, no-invite sorta foot.

Brenna: She's so much fun. It'll be like old times! Promise. Is it okay if we ask her to join?

Georgie: Fine by me! We can readjust the per portion rental charge if she's down.

Brenna: Yay! More = merrier. (And less $$ for all, hehe.) Everyone else?

PJ: I've never met her but fine with me haha

Cam: Lol, only if she doesn't write a movie about us afterwards . . .

Brenna: . . . That would be kinda awesome though!!!

PJ: Woww I've never met a screenwriter before. Should I be starstruck?

Liz: I think she's technically just an assistant or something.

Liz: But yeah, fine with us if she comes.

Quinn: Thank you! Mac?

Brenna: Please, Mac?

Mac: Oh, I didn't realize she was moving back home. But yeah, sure.

Brenna: Yay! Asking her now. I'll add her later if she says yes!

11:45 AM—Maggie was added to the group chat.

Maggie: Hey guys! Thanks for including me. Omw back to NY now. Can't believe we're going back to Fire Island! Time to have some fun. x

WEEKEND ONE

~~~~~

June

Chapter 1

A fter six years in California, Maggie was surprised. She
didn't expect to feel so charmed by the beach.

Surprise was an all too familiar feeling for Maggie these
days, though. Recently, it seemed all her would-be plans had
stood up and flung themselves out the window, leaving rushing
emotions in their wake. She rotated between bemusement and
bewilderment, shock and fear, and hope and panic. But Maggie
was a writer, a master of spin, so the word she chose to encap-
sulate it all was simply *surprise*.

It had a better ring to it.

For instance: In the past week alone, Maggie had chosen to
feel not *depressed* but surprised as she handed in her security pass
at the studio lot, saying goodbye to the Melrose office she'd spent
more time in than her own home while working as Kurt's assistant for the past two years. She was not *ashamed* but surprised

as she packed up her month-to-month rental in Los Feliz afterward, throwing what few belongings she had into cardboard boxes and old suitcases, loading the luggage into the trunk of her bright blue Ford Escape. Its bumpers were still scratched and peeling from Los Angeles parking mishaps. (She never quite mastered the art of the parallel park.) Maggie was surprised, and definitely not *regretful*, as she pulled out of her driveway for the last time and made her way onto the darkened highway headed east, leaving visions of moviemaking glory in her rearview for good, like roadkill on the 405.

No, she was none of those things, those misfortunate mindsets. She couldn't be. She was simply surprised.

And well, perhaps the biggest surprise of all was happening right now. Maggie, sitting at the edge of the Atlantic Ocean, toes in the sand, as the sun began to set on the first evening of an extraordinarily unexpected weekend on Fire Island, New York.

Talk about a plot twist.

A return to Ocean Beach had no place in Maggie's original summer plan, so how had she gotten here?

Technically, she'd taken the Long Island Rail Road from Penn Station to Bay Shore, followed by a five-minute shuttle bus to the docks and a half-hour ferry to Ocean Beach, her favorite of all the Fire Island towns.

Metaphorically, she'd made a thousand wrong turns until the universe somehow brought her back to where it all started.

Back, against all odds, to Long Island.

Brenna and Quinn had been nothing but kind since Maggie

reached out with the news of her sudden LA departure and the announcement that she was moving back home. On that same awful morning, the one when she realized her career was over before it had even begun, she had logged on to Facebook with tears still pooled in her eyes. Like kismet, she saw that Brenna and Quinn had posted with a crowdsourced plea for a subletter to fill the vacant space in their Murray Hill apartment. "*ASAP*, ASAP," the status had read.

The post felt like a billboard for Maggie to follow. She brushed off their numbers in her phone contacts and within hours, a subletting arrangement was formalized. To New York she'd go. Home for the summer—she told herself that it felt like the premise of an early-aughts comedy, hijinks and humor around the corner.

It was a classic rewrite, something Maggie had found herself doing since her teenage years, back when disappointment had started to take permanent root on her parents' faces. She had learned to rewire her emotions, her wants, to preclude failure. Maybe because she had grown up on movies, had practically been raised by love stories like *When Harry Met Sally* and *Sleepless in Seattle*, Maggie developed what seemed to be a perpetual predilection for happy endings.

Even if it meant reframing the plotline completely.

A failure in LA? A week spent sobbing in bed? Who wanted to watch that film?

Not Maggie.

Instead, she used the lonely hours on her one-woman road trip from LA to NY to smooth out her narrative. She decided to see this as a gift from the universe. A chance to start over. To start anew. The better movie, the better life, had to be right around the corner. Right? When Maggie's phone then pinged with the invitation to join the Ocean Beach weekend, she knew she'd been correct.

But now reality had set in, and Maggie ran her fingers through the sand, trying to quell the anticipatory nerves that started unwillingly swirling in her stomach. The travel fatigue was fading, the newness wearing off, and she finally had a chance to ask herself whether this might have been misguided. Not just moving home, but voluntarily trapping herself on an island with old friends who felt a bit like ghosts. No cars on Fire Island meant that the only way back to civilization was via ferry. What if she needed to escape?

It was too late for that type of thinking, Maggie reminded herself. Regrets would get her nowhere. She knew this by now.

Instead, she focused on how elated, truly elated, Brenna's and Quinn's faces had been when they'd swung open the door to their apartment just yesterday. Reunion initiated with music on the Bluetooth speaker backtracking the move-in process, friendship picking up where it had been put down, no matter the time in between. Brenna and Quinn had always been the easiest, the most naturally disposed to goodwill (and for-giveness) of the friend group. The banner her new roommates had hung across the kitchen—*Welcome home, Maggie!*—had been constructed with printer paper and Sharpie, but it still made her lower lip quiver.

Next Maggie reminded herself of the way Georgie had run across Manhattan's Penn Station terminal to greet her mere hours ago, lifting her in his arms like he always used to. He seemed even taller, his face even more freckled, his hair even curlier than she remembered, but his smile just as wide as when they were kids.

From Georgie's arms, she had looked down at the new face of the weekend, PJ, the only member of the trip who hadn't gone to East Meadow High School with the rest. PJ had met the Peters twins, Cam and Mac, at UVA, and then joined their larger friend group after college when he followed the brothers to Manhattan. Maggie had extended her hand from on high (still in Georgie's arms) and noticed how PJ's eyes glistened despite the train station's fluorescent lighting. *Nice to meet you, Maggie,* PJ had said. *So pumped you're joining this weekend.*

The reunions were off to an ideal start.

So why did Maggie's stomach still feel so shaky?

The faces of Mac, Cam, and Liz blipped into her mind.

Right.

She swallowed hard, throat suddenly dry, and opened the Notes application pinned on her iPhone's home screen. Her digital diary. When she was a kid, Maggie's yellow No. 2 had practically been a sixth finger on her right hand. She'd scribble on any spare paper she could find. Words had always been her comfort, and even then she'd known she was born to be a writer. Now, like most mid-twentysomethings, she had replaced her pencil with her phone. She bit her bottom lip and typed:

Ocean Beach. It sounds like it could or should be some sort of oxymoron in name, though it's so enchanting in its essence. Maybe that's why I can't help but feel a bit moronic for being here? Is it too late to run away and hide?

She sighed and deleted those words. Rewrite, rewrite, she reminded herself. Trying again, she typed:

Ocean Beach, I promised to be positive, to pivot like it's no problem at all. This is going to be my summer. This is going to be my chance, to see what might have been if I'd never moved at all. My West Coast experiment has ended. The Hollywood lights let down. East Meadow friends, I'm home again. It's time for a new chapter to begin.

Then her typing was interrupted by a shout:

"Come on, Mags! It's time for a cheers!" Brenna called out, beckoning from the corner of sand where their group had made camp.

"Thanks again for bringing the snack spread of my dreams," Georgie added.

"Nothing better than happy hour at the beach," Maggie replied as she made her way toward her friends. Their towels were now circled around a charcuterie platter Maggie had surprised the group with, as well as a speaker blasting a "Feel-Good Indie Rock" playlist and water bottles filled to the brim with tequila and La Croix homemade cocktails. Ocean Beach had a rather strict "No Alcohol on the Beach" rule (which, as

PJ pointed out, Georgie had reminded them of only *after* they'd paid the nonrefundable deposit for the rental), but when Maggie suggested the good-ol' water bottle trick, everyone agreed.

"To Ocean Beach!" Quinn kicked off, those same water bottles now dispersed and held in the air.

"To Ocean Beach!" The friends echoed the toast.

"And to Maggie finally moving home!" Quinn clinked her drink against Maggie's.

"Thanks for having me," Maggie said with a smile. "Can't believe I've barely been in New York for forty-eight hours and I'm already on Fire Island."

"It's bolted and we love it," Quinn said, a reference to one of their favorite high school terms. Maggie had coined *bolted* as a breakneck decision to do something wild, something fun. It was her favorite behavior, and she was usually leading the charge. Maggie loved eleventh-hour adventures, whether skinny-dipping in Cam and Mac's pool or buying last-minute tickets to the *Scream* marathon on Halloween weekend, with Ghostface masks for everyone that she'd picked up at Party City hours before. On principle, Maggie loved a theme, a celebration. She was the first to bake surprise cupcakes for birthdays or demand cocktail attire to watch the Oscars from the couch. If life was a movie, Maggie wanted hers to shine.

"We're glad you're here." Brenna gave her arm a squeeze. "Glad you're home."

"So, Mags, why the sudden move back? Not that we're complaining," Georgie said.

"Just felt ready for a change," Maggie answered. It wasn't the full truth, sure, but she knew that nobody wanted their first afternoon of a beach weekend ruined by a career sob story. "Plus, when I heard you were throwing an after-prom reunion weekend, I couldn't miss my chance to crash."

"Seven-year reunion! I told you! It's a thing!" Brenna's face lit up.

"It's not a thing," Quinn groaned.

"This feels right," Maggie said, laughing. "So, what else have I missed? Fill me in on everything." She propped herself up on her elbows, letting her arms be anchored by the sand as she listened to her friends share stories. Mac and Georgie had finally gotten rid of the mice in their apartment, just in time for summer cockroach season. Brenna and Quinn were both doing well at their jobs, Brenna in HR and Quinn in software engineering, but together they secretly dreamed of starting a dog-astrology website. A new tiki bar had opened up below PJ's apartment and he'd already cemented a handshake deal with the owner for discount drinks for him and his friends. The updates went on and on.

Maggie grinned through it all. She had forgotten how much she loved the pace of this group's banter, the way they talked over each other while understanding every word. It was like Maggie could have blinked and fallen back in time to their high school days. Even their body language felt the same, and the way they were all sharing towel space and soaking up the sun, ankles crossed over each other's, snacks spread out in the middle. It had the distinctly nostalgic flavor of after-prom on Fire Island.

When Maggie had first walked into the Serendipity House earlier that afternoon, she'd felt similarly flooded by the memories. The same patio where they'd counted stars. The same bathroom where they'd slathered aloe lotion over inexcusably bad sunburns. The living room couch where they'd squeezed as many bodies as physically possible to rewatch the senior class highlight reel Maggie had filmed all year and then played at prom.

It was only when she walked by the door at the top of the stairs, though, that she felt goose bumps explode across her skin. That queen bed was the one she'd shared with Mac, her high school boyfriend. Ex-boyfriend. Their romance had started in the winter of their senior year but climaxed in Ocean Beach, pun very much intended. It had been a season of teenage flirts and daring firsts, but that weekend was when they'd finally slept together. After a night out at the Ocean Beach bars, Maggie lost her virginity to her down-the-street neighbor, one of her lifelong best friends.

She'd spent the rest of that summer loving Mac.

Seven years later, Maggie looked at the bed and could have fainted.

Despite the distance, despite the fact that she'd broken up with Mac a long time ago (for reasons she'd once felt certain of but somehow couldn't remember now), she was shocked to learn that even the thought of him could still conduct the beat

of her pulse. He could make her entire body freeze with anticipation. Mac's arrival was right around the corner. Their reunion, imminent.

They say you never forget your first, and Maggie had spent
hours on her road trip hypothesizing, wondering if this weekend,
this surprising summer spent back home, was the start of a romance of her own. If after years of watching romantic com-
edies, writing stories about falling head over heels, she was
ready for her fairy tale to *really* begin.

Was a second chance with Mac what all these twists and
turns had been leading to all along? To be back in Ocean
Beach, together?

Of course, it wouldn't just be Mac and Maggie reuniting
this weekend. Liz and Cam were set to arrive any minute, too.
Liz was Maggie's very first friend, her kindergarten playmate-
turned-pseudo-sister. Cam was Mac's twin brother, and Liz's
high school sweetheart. The four friends had grown up in the
same part of Long Island, dubbed the Tree Streets for their
arboretum-inspired names, ridden the same bus. The group
formed the backbone of Maggie's youth. While best-friendship
was a tier, it was no secret that Maggie and Liz and Mac and
Cam had a next-level, a family-level, friendship.

Before, of course, it all came crashing down.

Quinn must have read Maggie's mind. "What time are the
others getting in?" She popped a cracker stacked with cheese,
prosciutto, and a spicy Wickles pickle into her mouth.

"I think Liz said they were taking the six p.m. ferry?" PJ
said.

"They really should be here by now, then," Brenna said, biting her lip ever so slightly. "I'll text them that we're at the beach."

"What's the rush? We're on island time." Georgie dramatically took off his watch and tossed it onto the picnic blanket.

"I can drink to that," PJ announced, finishing his drink in one swig, causing the group to laugh. Friday happy hour antics. "Second round, anyone?" He smiled.

"I shouldn't," Georgie groaned. "I have more work to finish up back at the house."

"I'd love another." Maggie let herself exhale. The sun was starting to set, the sky a hypnotizing blend of blues and pinks, and the beach remained littered with tanning tourists glued to their towels or lounging on rusting Tommy Bahama chairs. Even with a few stubborn clouds approaching, there would always be the unyielding determination among beachgoers to make the most out of a vacation. Sunup to sundown spent on the sand.

It was charming. It was unexpectedly calming. Unlike in the hustle culture of the film scene in LA, Maggie felt like she could begin to breathe. She'd barely had time to glance at the beach during her recent years in California, so intense was her workload on Kurt's desk. Now, despite the whirlwind of the past week, despite the exhaustion of her road trip deep in her bones, despite the anxiety of anticipating all that could go both right and wrong this weekend, she felt an unexpected but very welcome sense of peace.

The magic of the beach.

But as PJ turned to replenish a round from the cooler, his body faced toward the beach entrance stairs. "Speak of the devils," he said, and Maggie felt her nerves kick in. "Here they are." Calm replaced by surprise once again.

Only when Maggie saw the sight for herself did she allow the smallest moment of relief. There were merely two figures silhouetted by the setting sun, not three, but from the way their shadows walked with hands interlocked, Maggie knew it wasn't Mac, butterflies be damned.

It was time to say hi to Liz and Cam.

Age had already left its varying mark on so many of their high school class. A few athletes had swapped their sporty physiques for beer bellies, while some of the quieter kids had grown into their features during college and glowed with new confidence.

And yet Cam and Liz somehow looked exactly the same. Young, gorgeous, and madly in love.

Suddenly, visions of the Peters brothers' basement parties and lunches at Applebee's and backyard volleyball games and bus rides from school whirred around Maggie like a slideshow. For so long, Mac and Cam and Liz had been like an extension of herself, of her home.

Only when Maggie moved away, she said goodbye to it all.

Her chest tightened at everything she'd left behind.

Would they really let her say hello again?

Maggie took in the sight of Cam and Liz walking in the direction of the picnic spread. As Liz stopped to slip off her sandals and step barefoot onto the towels, Maggie saw something glimmer.

Her stomach flipped.

Maggie knew then that her homecoming didn't matter; her past transgressions wouldn't be brought up, at least not right now, for the entire dynamic changed when Cam grabbed Liz's hand and raised it toward the sky. "We have an announcement," he sang, his words light and dancing.

Liz blushed. "I said yes!"

The sparkling diamond engagement ring set the group ablaze. *"CongratsOhmygodMazeltovFinally!"* Maggie could barely get a word in.

"This is amazing! Our first friend group wedding." Brenna was practically singing. "Can we help plan? Where will it be? *When* will it be? What will you wear?"

"A dress?" Liz laughed, tucking her auburn hair behind her ear.

"Of course! Well, if you need any spreadsheets or shopping trips or anything at all—"

"B, let her breathe!" Quinn clamped her hand over Brenna's widely plastered smile. "What she means to say is, we are very happy for you. Even though this is literally the least surprising proposal to ever occur."

"Sorry to disappoint you, Quinn." Cam's face remained the picture of joy as a receiving line of sorts formed, each friend taking turns to hug the new fiancés.

When it was Maggie's turn, she found herself suddenly

tongue-tied. She was overwhelmed, excited and nervous and caught off guard. What were the odds that her NY homecoming would so perfectly line up with Liz and Cam's engagement? She tried to recalibrate her reaction to the colossal news, in honor of the friend with whom she'd once been inseparable but now felt universes apart from. It was like her brain was moving in slow motion, stuck in the shock.

"Wow, congrats, guys," Maggie finally managed. Her first words to Cam and Liz as basic as could be. She kicked the dormant screenwriter in her, but it didn't matter. Even poetry would have had no power in preventing how Liz's jaw dropped when she saw Maggie's face.

"Maggie," Liz said, voice tight. "I forgot you were back." It was subtle, but Maggie could tell that her words were strained, empty. She could barely look Maggie in the eyes for more than a few forced seconds.

She wasn't happy Maggie was here. She wasn't happy Maggie had moved home.

Maggie felt her cheeks turn bright red, but the awkwardness was suddenly eclipsed by Brenna and Quinn rushing to inspect Liz's ring up close. Maggie was grateful for the relief, as the boys took turns patting Cam on the back with sheepish grins, listening to him recount the story of his proposal by the park. Liz had been completely surprised, and Cam had been so completely overcome with emotion that he could barely string together any of the sentences he'd rehearsed without choking up. They ended the night with a dinner party in the private room at Pier A, surrounded by immediate family. Bottomless prosecco and a postcard view of the Statue of Liberty? Perfection.

Through the retelling and the awed reactions, Maggie watched the magic of an engagement spread like a luxury perfume. It reached everyone—the promise of a partnership, the hope of a happily ever after. The feeling that maybe your own future could be that bright, too.

That someone might know you enough, know your flaws and weaknesses, and still decide to never not know you again. To live with the good, the bad, and everything in between.

Despite Liz's initial curtness, Maggie was happy for her. Truly. This had been the theme of cafeteria daydreams throughout their senior spring. Marrying the Peters twins. Liz would marry Cam, of course, but they also always teased or hoped or simply assumed that Maggie would eventually marry his twin brother, Mac. They'd have one big wedding on the same day. They'd move into houses on the same block. They'd raise children in the same school system.

Best friends turned into sisters. *Real* sisters, finally.

Together.

Of course, only half of that fairy tale was now coming true.

Maggie looked around at all these once-familiar faces, backdropped by the beach's signature and dreamy early-evening lighting. Liz and Cam were engaged. Mac would join them in Ocean Beach soon, too.

But as she took in the feeling of her old friends, Maggie

couldn't help but notice that Liz's face was still frozen in a fake smile.

Something about her looked off, felt wrong.

Maggie wondered what it might be.

She wondered if maybe this, if Mac and Liz and Cam, held the real story she was meant to have returned for. The reason she had been wrapped up in so many surprises.

Welcome home.

Chapter 2

How romantic, Liz thought to herself at 5:27 A.M., when she was abruptly awoken by a jarring snore from Cam atop the pillow next to hers. "Is this what every morning of my life will sound like?" she whispered angrily, even though she knew Cam wouldn't respond. He was deep in a drunken, passed-out slumber.

Liz, on the other hand, had tossed and turned all night.

Cam had said he wouldn't drink that much. He was the one who'd made that promise. But then he was the one who'd poured rounds and rounds of shots the second the group had gotten back from their evening at the beach. When Liz had suggested slowing down, he said she didn't trust him.

"Sorry I want to *remember* our engagement weekend," she had warned.

"Well, sorry I want to celebrate. To have fun. It's like you refuse to be happy about this."

"I am happy," Liz said.

"So now I'm just another person you lie to?"

"What the hell is that supposed to mean?"

Liz didn't want to remember the rest. She massaged her forehead, where a tension headache had appeared. If falling in love was a fairy tale, why did the engagement suddenly feel like a trick, like being trapped in Rapunzel's tower?

Outside the sun was climbing, a blur of hazy pinks and bright orange hues. She scanned the view and picked a color, playing her favorite grounding tool, a therapist trick she'd picked up and tucked in her pocket like a lucky quarter.

Orange: the sky outside.

Orange: Liz's mother's hair. Curly and reckless, always twisted and perched on the tip-top of Nancy's head. Just like her own.

Liz fell into the memory. Would a sunrise ever not remind her of the way her mom used to knock on Liz's bedroom door each morning? A gentle maternal wake-up, no need for an alarm. By the time Liz moved into her NYU dorm on University Place, she'd bought herself a proper clock, but there were still some mornings when, before Liz even opened her eyes, she heard a phantom knock, and it sent her right back to her childhood bedroom. Purple curtains and princess costumes. Magic in the mornings with Mom.

Now her morning alarm was Cam's snoring.

Liz needed coffee. She got up and headed to the kitchen.

It felt strange but special to be back at the Serendipity

House, which was larger than Liz remembered. She'd forgotten how the ceiling in the living room was lined with wood beams that made the room feel enormous yet cozy. Or the way the dining table comfortably fit twelve chairs and still left room for twelve pairs of flip-flops by the door to the patio. The way the kitchen sink was deep enough to hide the towers of glasses and stacks of crusted pizza dishes leftover from last night's antics, all accented by a decorative canvas sign that read "Serendipity by the Sea."

The bedrooms were tucked upstairs, a series of rooms. Their sleeping arrangements were nearly identical to those of their senior year trip: Liz and Cam once again had the primary suite, and Mac would take the neighboring queen bedroom—but with Robyn this time—when they arrived later that morning. Georgie and PJ were in the "dorm room," where two sets of bunk beds anchored each wall. Brenna, Quinn, and Maggie occupied the final room, where Brenna and Quinn shared a queen mattress and Maggie had the pull-out trundle. Liz had been dating Cam for so long that she'd never been assigned to the "girls' room" on friend group overnight trips. She always shared a mattress with her high school sweetheart. Now she wondered what pre-sleep gossip she might have missed last night.

She wondered what Maggie might have told them.

Maggie. Liz couldn't believe that Maggie was here. That she'd moved home so suddenly. That she had the audacity to crash their trip after surgically removing herself from their friend group. Maggie always had a flair for the dramatic. Some people moved with a noticeable gravity, and Maggie was comfortable being at the center of any crowd. She was never short a story or a punch line or a new adventure to lead the group in search of. They'd all called it her "Hollywood quality," and yet somehow her departure for Los Angeles had still been shocking.

Maggie's announcement arrived at the end of their freshman year at NYU. She and Liz were roommates, which had always been their plan. Undergrads together, taking the city by storm. But as spring semester finals rolled around, Maggie sat Liz down and told her she was leaving. She'd given it a lot of thought, but she was struggling in New York, and she needed a change. California was calling, and Maggie was transferring to UCLA. Apologies fell from Maggie's tongue: *so, so, so sorry.* She promised to thank Liz and Nancy in her first acceptance speech, as if that would make the abandonment all better.

Liz had trouble listening to the rest of Maggie's explanation, her excuses. How could she not have told her sooner? Why hadn't she looped her in? It had been a stressful year for both of them, Liz knew. Maggie had seemed off since the day they moved in, but the majority of Liz's time was unexpectedly preoccupied by evenings and weekends spent back home on Long Island, with her mom. After that long stretch, things were finally looking better and Liz had started to feel settled, like she could return to campus with her full attention on school and friends. That she could end the year the way she wished she'd started.

Maggie's transfer news felt worse than pulling the carpet out from under her.

How was Liz supposed to respond?

A part of her wanted to be a loyal friend. Maggie must have had her reasons, and Liz couldn't hold it against her for pursuing her dreams. Maggie had always loved movies, dreamed of making her own, of interning at studios and talent agencies alike. Growing up, she made them watch reruns of *Entourage* just to study the assistant lingo, the maneuvering of a mail cart. They'd go to midnight premieres of blockbusters at the Cineplex in Bellmore and in a single viewing, Maggie would somehow memorize all the best lines. During the summer, she'd sneak into the city to look for film sets, to find any production that might be shooting. The buzz of the PAs running for coffee and keeping the streets locked down, the smell of the crafty snack van, the thrill of catching sight of the director or the actors making their way to set—Maggie so clearly adored it all.

Of course she wanted to give making a career out of it all a try. Liz had been surprised that Maggie ever agreed to be prelaw at NYU in the first place. And to be honest, after two semesters spent tiptoeing around the dirty clothes Maggie tended to leave anywhere *other* than in her hamper, Liz didn't totally hate the idea of living alone for sophomore year.

But the other part of her, the larger part of her, couldn't help but feel betrayed. Pushed aside when she needed help the most. And it wasn't solely Liz, left behind like outgrown clothing. No, she would never forget *Mac's* face that summer, when reality had sunk in that Maggie wasn't coming home.

Liz was struggling, missing her best friend. But her heart broke right open watching Mac's heart crumble. He didn't have to say it, but Liz and Cam still knew: Maggie had left him, too.

When Maggie and Mac started dating, Liz had tried to respect their relationship, to give them privacy as they went from friends to more. It wasn't like there was a rule book for how to behave when your best friend started dating your boyfriend's twin brother. But she didn't need Mac's inner monologue to interpret the utter sadness on his face when he realized she was really gone, that Maggie had ended things with him.

She'd left them all.

Liz wished she'd had the foresight to realize this would be the first of Maggie's many forsaken promises. So many unanswered calls.

Now she was sleeping upstairs in a trundle bed. It felt annoying. Ironic, though Liz couldn't quite articulate why. Words were never her forte. A fashion designer, she dreamed in colors, shapes, and sketches.

Well, she used to. Lately, everything had felt mostly gray.

Outside on the patio, Liz sipped her coffee and listened to the birds. The furniture was still slightly wet from last night's showers, but she never minded feeling close to nature. She kicked her feet up on the picnic table, settled back into an oversize chair. Her eyes fluttered; her mind slowed down. For a moment, peace.

Until a chirp came from her phone.

Liz's screen showed an email from Roseanne with a hyper-linked article: **10 Things to Do the Day After You Get Engaged! Trust me, it's true what they say about brides snoozing and consequently losing—let's get cooking! XOXO!** Cam's mom had typed out below.

Liz groaned. She loved Cam's mom. She really did. After all they'd been through the past year, Roseanne was there whenever Liz needed her. She was trustworthy and dependable. She was someone who cared. So much so that when Cam and Mac moved into their freshman dorms at UVA, Roseanne transformed her subsequent empty nest into a successful event-planning business, where she continued to fine-tune her caring skills by supervising the orchestration of neighbors' weddings and baby showers and fortieth birthday parties galore. Famous herself for the annual, all-out Peters Family Back to School parties she'd throw every first day from K–12, Roseanne had been not-so-secretly counting down until the crown jewel of her planning portfolio: her twin boys' wedding days. Now one was finally happening, and she was clearly excited.

It wasn't Roseanne's fault that Liz still felt like she couldn't be.

What Liz never expected about loss: the lows were painful, but the highs were worse.

She'd deal with Roseanne's email later. For now, she closed her eyes and counted to ten. When she opened them again, she picked the first color she saw and connected it with a memory.

Green: the leaves poking out above the house's roof.

Green: the color of Cam's eyes. Her favorite shade. She thought about how they'd shone with such surprise when she kissed him in the tenth grade. Liz couldn't help but laugh back then. How hadn't he seen that coming? It had been a decade of dropping hints, of smiling at all his jokes, of finding a reason to sit by his side. On the bus home, in study hall, in the stands at Mac's soccer games. Any excuse to brush her knee against his. To hope Cam might respond.

Some of the other girls would tease, saying that Liz had crushes on *both* Peters boys. That she just flipped a coin and decided which of the twins to "*like* like" any given year. Someone, usually Maggie, but sometimes also Quinn, would make a quick retort to shut them down, but Liz would just wordlessly blush. Yes, the boys were identical, but how could she explain to a bunch of middle schoolers that there was something *special* about Cam? He was quieter than Mac, sure, but his brain was so loud. He was brilliant and driven and while maybe objectively Mac was the better athlete and the better conversationalist and perhaps the "better catch" for other girls, for Liz, it had always been Cam.

She liked how Cam got caught in soccer practices staring at the sky. How he was quiet, but once he started talking, he couldn't stop. How he would spend his free periods drawing maps of fictional cities, just for fun. Liz liked so much about Cam; she was just always too afraid to use her words.

Until the first time they drank vodka—a marshmallow-flavored Smirnoff that still made her stomach swirl at the thought—and she used her lips instead. Liz felt bold and brave and grabbed his face and kissed him before she could chicken out. When Cam kissed her back, his face firm against her own, he tasted sweet, like the fluff sandwiches Liz's mom would make for dinner whenever she had to work late at the store. It was new yet familiar all at once.

Liz and Cam were inseparable from then on. Boyfriend and girlfriend, <3 hearts in BlackBerry address books, kisses at the locker before he'd walk her to class. Their circles merged. Their friends were furniture being pushed together, Maggie and Liz and Brenna and Quinn joined up with Mac and Cam and Georgie. Their East Meadow friend group officially born.

Green: the color of Cam's tuxedo jacket at senior prom two years later. Liz had sewn it for him herself. He said it was his favorite thing he'd ever worn. He even brought it to UVA with him, kept it hanging in his closet, assuring Liz that it still smelled like her. Whenever he missed her, he'd hold it close and remember that night. Remember all their dreams and promise to make them come true.

Recently, it seemed like Cam had forgotten everything. Even during their four years of collegiate long distance, New York to Charlottesville, Cam had somehow never felt farther away than he did right now. What had gotten into him? They'd been living together for three years. They were engaged. Now Cam was upstairs in their Serendipity House bedroom, but he may as well have been on Mars.

A noise snapped Liz back to earth. The sound of the screen door creaking open.

Maggie stepped out. Did she hear Liz's subtle groan?

"Ah, sorry, didn't realize anyone else was up." Maggie's apology cut through the patio, her voice flustered as she turned around to head back inside the house.

"No, no, don't be silly, I'm sorry," Liz said, because what else could she really say? She had no more claim to the outside space than Maggie did. "You can sit. I must look strange, staring into the void." Liz wiped her eyes under her sunglasses and was startled to find them wet.

"Not strange, just . . . focused," Maggie said with what sounded like a very forced chuckle. Liz wondered if Maggie was also realizing that this was the first time it had been just the two of them, alone, in years. Liz had purposefully avoided Maggie most of last night, not ready for this moment. Now she had to laugh. Why had she thought preparation would make it feel any more pleasant?

"You never used to be a morning person," Liz said, mostly to fill the air, but she tasted daggers, sharp on her tongue.

"To be honest, I haven't slept much this week. Drove as fast as I could from LA, I think my brain doesn't know what time zone it's in."

"Rough."

An awkward silence plastered the space between them. They never used to have awkward conversations as kids. If words had run empty, the air remained comfortable, pure.

Liz decided to be the bigger person, to keep things easy. She didn't need to be best friends with Maggie again, but she could try to be nice. For now. For the sake of the weekend. For the sake of her *actual* friends. The ones who wouldn't leave her.

"How was the rest of last night?" she asked.

"Fun," Maggie said. "We didn't make it to the bars, though. It was raining pretty hard."

"We'll make up for it tonight. Forecast looks like sun."

"Yeah, I'm sure everyone will want to head to the beach early."

Another pause. Maggie looked anxiously inside, toward the still-empty kitchen.

A light bulb clicked for Liz. "Just ask it," she said.

"Ask what?"

"You're wondering where Mac is. When he'll get here."

"No, I'm not." Maggie's face turned red. She'd always had trouble hiding her emotions.

Liz rolled her eyes. "Nine a.m. ferry. They should be here soon."

"They?" Maggie's eyebrows rose.

"Oh my god," Liz realized. "Did no one tell you?"

"Tell me what?"

"Mac's bringing Robyn. His girlfriend."

Maggie's jaw dropped. Liz watched her face change a hundred times—surprise, sadness, shock, sadness, followed by a fake laissez-faire coolness—and she immediately felt guilty for not being more delicate with her delivery.

"Wow, um, that's great. What's she like?" Maggie stammered at last.

Liz paused. Now it was her turn to get flustered. She knew better than to share her honest feelings about Mac's latest girlfriend, and she didn't feel exactly ready to reward Maggie with any Mac-related gossip either. "You'll see for yourself," she decided.

"Can't wait." Maggie sighed. "Cute cover-up, by the way."

Liz let out an actual laugh, catching herself by surprise. "Cute topic change. Thank you. I made it, actually."

"No way!" Maggie leaned in to admire Liz's creation more closely. It was a mix of different black-and-white printed fabrics in a top-and-miniskirt set. Liz didn't feel like adding that it was one of the last things she had made outside of work in years. How to explain everything that prevented her from picking up a pattern and slipping into the rhythm of a sewing machine again?

"Whoa, it's amazing." Maggie continued, "That reminds me, you still owe me a rainbow dress."

Liz cackled loudly then, her signature authentic laugh coursing through her body, as if struck by the cupid of comedy. Liz had been known for her laughter, voted Best Laugh of their senior class. Accolades like yearbook superlatives were brought up often when you stayed best friends with your high school cohort. Now Liz quickly covered her mouth with her hands, afraid she'd woken up the entire house, and lowered her voice. "I almost forgot about that!" she whispered.

"Well, I haven't," Maggie whispered back. "You made me

stand there for ten minutes while you practiced taking mea-
surements. It was exhausting."

"I'm the one whose fingers bled. Those early days of
pinning." Liz shuddered.

"Let me see your fingers now." Maggie grabbed her former
friend's hand, inspected her fingertips for signs of fashion-pin-
induced bruising. Liz's nails were always free from any colored
polish so that she wouldn't be distracted while she worked, but
her fingers looked free from injuries, too. "Not bad."

"I told you I've gotten better." Liz grinned, allowing herself
to feel the sense of pride. She'd watched her mom make dresses
for most of her childhood, but it wasn't until the tenth grade
that she decided to test out the family trade for herself. Like
most things, it was a decision she turned to with Maggie, after
they'd spied an insanely expensive yet adorable rainbow dress
while window-shopping at the Roosevelt Field mall.

Liz suggested she try making something similar herself.

Maggie offered to be her first customer.

Liz and Maggie had always cosigned each other's dreams.

Now Maggie was holding Liz's hand again, the way best
friends who felt more like family would. But she was staring at
Liz's ring, and her face was morphing into a frown.

"I'm so excited for you and Cam," Maggie started. "But
Liz—"

"Thanks, Mags." Liz pulled her hand back, fidgeting with
the diamond, the band still too loose. All the while, she refused
to meet Maggie's eyes. "Means a lot."

"Liz, if something's wrong, you know you can always come to me, right?"

"Nothing's wrong."

"I know."

"We're engaged."

"It's pretty amazing."

"I'm happy."

"I'm not saying that you aren't—"

"What would you even know about it?"

Maggie swallowed. "Fair enough. But if there's anything that's bothering you . . . anything at all . . . just know I'm here. I'm home now. I want to be here for you, for Cam, for everyone. I promise."

Maggie's words sounded pretty, but to Liz they felt sour. Instead of gratitude, annoyance rushed through her body. This was classic Maggie, she thought. Swooping in, trying to play the hero, the lead. The Hollywood dramatics. Trying to forget the hurt she'd caused to anyone not on the path of her dreams. This time, Liz had the foresight not to bother fighting.

She didn't feel the need to point out exactly all that Maggie had missed since she moved to California.

She didn't point out all the crucial moments when Maggie's support was nowhere in sight.

Instead, Liz stood up, smoothed her outfit, and smiled. "I'm glad you're home."

While Maggie had been chasing stardom in LA, Liz had gotten pretty good at lying.

Chapter 3

Maggie couldn't lie. She was grateful that she hadn't been holding a cup of coffee. No breakfast plate in her grip. If she had even been clutching a fork, she might have stabbed the table when she saw Mac and Robyn enter through the Serendipity House front door.

The house erupted in cheers when the latecomers arrived, but Maggie's world went silent the second she and Mac finally locked eyes. Sound dropped out, like in a Nicholas Sparks adaptation.

It was Mac.

Her Mac, exactly like a memory. His blond hair poking out from under a backward baseball cap. His signature navy sweatshirt, perfectly oversize.

The same sweatshirt Maggie had worn one entire summer.

She gave him a half wave, mouthed "Hello" from across the kitchen.

He smiled back, green eyes shining right at her soul.

"Hey, M," Mac said aloud. Their mutual nickname. "Welcome home."

Butterflies flew from Maggie's toes to her heart, rising with the picture of Mac, seven summers ago in this very beach house. The mattress upstairs, the view from the window a direct shot at the stars. How it had felt when Mac's tongue dipped past her teeth. Holding hands on the moonlit beach, sneaking out for a midnight adventure of jumping off the lifeguard chair. Falling onto each other, sand on their backs, in their hair. They didn't care.

Was he feeling the same rush now? His mind filling with the same flashbacks?

Did any of it even matter, considering the stranger who'd walked in beside him?

Poised, petite, with a Prada raffia tote bag at the crease of her elbow. Mac led the introductions. "Maggie, it's great to see you. This is my girlfriend, Robyn."

His *girlfriend*.

Maggie felt like she might be sick as she extended her hand to meet Robyn's. She looked like all the girls Maggie had worked with in LA. Designer labels even though they all made ten dollars per hour. Perfect shoes and suspiciously straight noses. Maggie hated how insecure this newcomer instantly made her feel.

"Nice to meet you," she said, relieved when her voice didn't shake.

"Pleasure's all mine," Robyn replied, voice as honeyed as

her hair was blond. She lifted her sunglasses from the bridge of her nose to her perfectly styled head. "This place is adorable! So sorry we're late, but I brought a case of Dom in apology. What do you say? Shall we start with a round of mimosas?"

"Perfect idea, babe," Mac said, putting his arm around Robyn, and Maggie tasted vomit in her throat.

She needed to get out of there, fast. She glanced at her phone's clock, remembering Brenna's chore chart for the day. "Bren, didn't you say something about the grocery order arriving at the dock?"

"I've trained you well!" Brenna said. "Let's get a move on, roomies."

Relief came in the form of a wagon and the ten-minute walk from the rental to the Ocean Beach dock. In the end, Maggie had been in the same air as Mac and his gorgeous new girlfriend for a mere two minutes, but it was more than enough.

What had she been thinking?

It wasn't so much that Maggie had been expecting Mac to be single just because she had deigned to move back home. He'd had other girlfriends earlier in high school, camp crushes or hookups from sports programs in the neighboring towns. From what she had deduced from his social media pages during college, after their breakup, Mac's romantic life at UVA continued in much the same fashion. Why would adulthood be any different? At some point he'd deactivated any social media account through which Maggie might have tracked his love life, but it didn't matter.

Logically, her history with Mac was exactly that: history.

They were a classic senior year coupling, best friends exploring boundaries like so many do by the end of their high school days. Emotions running rampant, hormones exploding, graduation around the corner. It's only natural that you start to make out with your friends.

After the Valentine's Day dance floor pushed their bodies together, Mac and Maggie's romance seemed inevitable. It felt easy: best friends turned into a second semester fling, followed by a summer of filling the space by each other's sides. Falling in what felt like an entry-level course on love. Mac and Maggie had always had similar personalities—both loved to laugh, to tell stories and compete for the punch line, to make plans. Double-header reservations were their date night trademark.

It was fun for a while, but of course it didn't last. After a strained two semesters of long distance between NYU and UVA, a fizzling due to geographical distance, Maggie called it off before she moved to California for good. It was cleaner this way. She'd start at a new school, with a new slate. Like a simple "Undo" function on Microsoft Word, she could revert Mac back to the friend category before any major disasters.

And yet.

What was it about being home that made thoughts of Mac so sweet? That made her crave to see how their relationship might have bloomed, if she hadn't plucked the bud by moving so soon?

Would they be sharing that queen bedroom upstairs?

Would a diamond ring be wrapped around *her* finger?

Could they have been so much more?

This Ocean Beach weekend was going to be a lot more complicated than she'd thought.

Now, walking down Surf Road with Brenna and Quinn by her side, Maggie inhaled deeply and tried again to pivot. She took in the sandy streets, the cloudless sky, the way the sun felt like a spotlight shining on her messy ponytail. The timing was ironic: she had pulled up these same Ocean Beach streets on Google Maps just months ago for a writing project, but she was reluctant, embarrassed a bit, to bring it up now. To tell her friends what her screenplay had been about, what had happened after.

Instead, Maggie traded smiles with strangers who were similarly assigned to the morning chores. Passersby with coffee travel trays and bags of bagels, or stacks of chairs headed to stake a claim on the shore. Prime beach real estate a coveted prize, worth the early wake-up. They spied a schoolyard, and then a small chapel as they made their way down Midway Walk. Ocean Beach was a tiny village with no cars, just bicyclists and beach lovers in lockstep with the beating heart of a town.

With each step of her own, Maggie took stock of her social standing. Liz was avoiding her like the plague, poorly concealed anger practically painted on her cheekbones. Brenna and Quinn had kept Robyn a secret, but Maggie didn't want to ask them why. Friday night had been a kickoff game of catch-up, and Maggie had done her best to remember the rules, but it was obvious that she didn't know the new jokes, the new stories and references. She laughed along when she could, trying not to curse her impulsive self, the past Maggie who had paved the way for her to be here in the first place. She wanted to get off on the right foot, but her shoes all seemed too small. Mac had always been a safe spot, her most recent home base, but now he had his arm around Robyn.

Where did Maggie belong?

Gossiping voices snapped her out of her spiral. Quinn and Brenna were moving at rapid fire, their words outpacing their footsteps as their trio inched toward the Ocean Beach town square. They were talking about Robyn.

"Can you believe she wore a white dress?"

"I don't think Mac told her it was an engagement. Just that it was a family dinner or something."

"That would be a weird detail to leave out."

"Because Mac is such a great communicator these days?"

"I just think it would have come up. Oh my god, do you think she'll have to be a bridesmaid?"

"Bridesmaids are antiquated."

"Do you think *we'll* get to be bridesmaids?"

"Bridesmaids are antiquated," Quinn simply repeated.

"I hope I'm a bridesmaid," Brenna said. "Maybe we should bring Liz back a little treat. A congratulatory signal. Some chocolate chip muffins or bagels or something. But what if she's on a wedding diet? And we're just throwing carbs in her face. Shoot, maybe an iced coffee, then? Nonfat milk? Black?"

"Brenna?"

"Yes?"

"Please?"

"Yes?"

"Stop."

Brenna and Quinn went back and forth and Maggie half listened, trying and failing not to focus on the fact that once upon a time, Liz had asked Maggie to someday be her maid of honor. Her "Mags of honor," they'd said. It had been a premature fantasy, a nice hypothetical. A cafeteria conversation between seventeen-year-old girls over harvest cheddar Sun Chips. But Maggie remembered it still.

She was home, but so much had changed in her wake.

She swallowed and opened her Notes app:

To be a Maid of Honor, one must be made of honor. Are you a bridesmaid or just a broken promise?

"Whatcha typing over there?" Brenna asked when she saw Maggie with her phone.

"Thought you said you were done with writing," Quinn piped in.

"It's nothing," Maggie said quickly, putting her phone away.

"Perhaps the smell of dried beer and salt water just screams 'inspiration,'" Quinn said with a laugh.

"Just feels good to write, I guess." Maggie shrugged, surprised by her own honesty.

Brenna softened. "Then that's probably a sign to keep writing."

"Maybe," Maggie said, though she wasn't so sure. She had spent the length of the road trip rationalizing her decision to quit. Not just her job, but the industry entirely. Movies, screenwriting, all of it. She was done, she had said. It was over.

Maggie had given it her best, but her best wasn't good enough.

It only took one morning with Kurt for her to realize that she had done her math all wrong. Two years as his assistant wasn't learning experience. Three years studying screenwriting at UCLA wasn't preparation. A lifetime of loving cinema wasn't career manifestation.

It was simply denial on a cosmic scale.

A sudden horn blare was a welcome distraction.

"Ferry's here!" Maggie called out, pointing toward the dock.

"About time, I'm famished." Quinn led the charge to where a small crowd had gathered to greet the arriving freight ferry, loaded with boxes of groceries and cases of alcohol. The Ocean Beach Trading market was notoriously overpriced, only good for emergency purchases like bags of ice or sliced American cheese or salsa. To bulk up affordably and properly to feed a group of oft-inebriated twenty-five-year-olds? A grocery order by ferry was all but mandatory.

Maggie always got a kick out of tradition, out of groups of people doing the same thing all together. Singing an alma mater at a football game, cheering at a big city marathon. It was no surprise that a simple morning task like collecting bags of burger buns and patty meats and liters of soda now sparked a smile on her face. There was beauty in routine, in an island's traditions.

So when Maggie caught that once-too-familiar whiff of cinnamon mixed with sunscreen, when she heard a familiar voice call her name, it was a good thing that a large smile was still plastered on her face.

Because if she hadn't been so caught up in the local charm, she might have screamed.

Ty was here.

Two bags of groceries in his arms. A dark blue wagon to transport them.

Maggie gulped. Ty Bandera was *here*?

Maybe it was a trick of the sunshine, the way the light danced along Ocean Beach's town square, the way the music from the Sandbar had started playing right as Maggie met Ty's eyes, but there was something about the moment that felt like a movie. The very thing she swore that she would quit.

Which is exactly why Maggie turned and ran.

"Who was that?" Brenna whisper-shouted, struggling to keep up with Maggie's new pace.

"Nobody," Maggie insisted, but even Quinn and Brenna weren't blind to the blush spreading from her ears.

"Well for a nobody, he looks pretty good."

"Yeah, can we get an introduction to this nobody? Maybe a phone number?"

"He just looked a lot like someone I knew back at my first job in LA."

"It sure seemed like he knew you," Brenna said. "Think he said your name."

"Why are we running?" Quinn huffed.

"It's a long story." Maggie grimaced. She had moved home to avoid LA, to erase the memories.

The last thing she needed was her former and annoyingly competitive colleague Ty showing up and reminding her of the past.

Or worse, threatening to expose the truth from which she was running.

When they'd made it safely out of town, Maggie let herself take a breath. Brenna and Quinn stared at her with wide eyes and open mouths. "Sorry, guys," Maggie said. "I'm not sure what just happened. Too much sun, I guess. Do we have all the bags?"

Brenna pulled the wagon to the side of the road, shifting her focus to their errand. The girls cross-referenced the boxes of snacks and supplies with the receipt and order inventory Brenna had preprinted and pulled from her purse.

Then a brown bag caught Maggie's attention.

"Who added M&M's to the list?" Maggie asked, hoping her voice sounded even, calm.

"A last-minute addition from our dear Mac, I believe," Brenna said. "Oh god, they're probably melting in the sun, though. Let's get a move on, ladies. I need a mimosa and a spot on the beach."

"Sounds good to me," Maggie said with a forced swallow. In reality, her feet felt like concrete.

Even a thousand miles away from this beach, M&M's had still tasted like senior year at East Meadow to Maggie. Ditching last period and driving in Mac's car, buying chocolate at the local 7-Eleven and listening to classic rock in the parking lot. Here? She was helpless against the onslaught of memories.

Fingers coated in candy, laughter on their tongues.

M&M's. A code word for Mac to cut class, to bring the car around.

M&M's.

Maggie and Mac.

Their nickname, their past.

Was Mac feeling as reminiscent as she was?

Chapter 4

L iz tossed another three pink lemonade bottles filled to the brim with illicit alcohol into the cooler and closed the top with a thump. It may have had her reminiscing about college again, sneaking around the town's "No Alcohol on the Beach" rule, but Liz surprisingly didn't mind the youthful aura those stealthy vodka plus Crystal Light Pink Lemonade bottles invoked.

She missed the days when the biggest concern was sneaking alcohol into a party. How easy, how naive Liz's youth now seemed in retrospect. She missed that energy; that flavor seemed out of reach.

"How are we looking on supplies over there?" Cam said, walking into the kitchen.

"Ready for takeoff," Liz said, accepting his kiss on her cheek.

Cam had apologized this morning. He had pulled Liz aside as the friends cleaned up after the scrambled egg breakfast Mac had cooked for the group. Cam told her that he didn't know what happened last night, but he went too hard and wished he hadn't. He promised to be better the rest of the weekend.

Liz accepted his apology; she always did. They had been together too long to be stingy with forgiveness. They'd also been together too long for her not to make a mental note of what had transpired, to pick up on the pattern: something was off with Cam.

The party-loving energy was nothing new. Cam was both a people pleaser and an extroverted introvert, adept at matching his energy to that of any given room. He loved a good book, but he also sparkled in any crowd. Especially if Mac was there, too, striking them both up like a box of matches. Now they were in Ocean Beach, a weekend trip with their best friends. It wasn't unusual that Cam would want to have some fun.

No, what bothered Liz was this subtle feeling, a peripheral sense of dread that he was keeping something from her. But what?

As if decoding her thoughts, Cam pressed his forehead against hers. "I love being back here with you, Lizard. Feels like old times."

"Me, too," Liz said. She meant it. Ocean Beach had been the source of some of their happiest moments. The final high school hurrah filled with friend group magic. Now Liz resolved to make sure their first postgrad weekend felt like magic, too.

She turned her face toward her fiancé's and kissed him square on the mouth.

"Get a room!" a voice cut in, startling Liz and Cam out of their PDA. Liz softened, though, when she turned and saw Mac's face. Her future brother-in-law had already changed into his bathing suit.

"Leave them alone! It's romantic!" a higher-pitched voice called out from the hallway, the walk-up song of high-heeled sandals announcing Robyn's arrival as she joined them standing by the couches. It had been five months, but Liz still felt slightly unsettled whenever their trio turned into a foursome with Robyn's addition. Sure, Robyn looked at Mac like he was the dreamiest man in the world, and always bought the first round when they went to a bar, but she also suggested that Mac avoid wearing the color yellow because it hurt her eyes. She was opinionated and whip-smart and certainly unique. But was she sister-in-law material? Was she Mac's future wife? Liz and Cam had no idea.

"The newly engaged lovebirds! Congratulations again," Robyn squealed, pulling them all into a suffocating hug. "See, Mac, there's nothing wrong with some extra hugging. *So* sorry we missed last night. We had to see my family Friday, since we were with you guys on Thursday night. Even an engagement can't override *the Rule*."

"Balance is key," Cam said. They had all heard this before.

"It *is* key," Robyn continued. "If we see Mac's family one night, then we must see my family the next. The secret to a healthy relationship. No exceptions. Balance makes all right. That's the first lesson I learned at Wharton, by the way. Besides Statistics and Managerial Econ, the first real *takeaway* that *transformed* my *soul* was the more metaphysical practices." Liz couldn't tell if her emphasis was genuine or if she knew the whole thing was a little ridiculous. "Mindfulness. Balance. Purpose. Passion. A good idea, a good product, well, it can just bleed into your *being*. But you must be open, anchored, *balanced*, to let it in, you know?" Nope. Definitely genuine.

Liz had heard this exact same manifesto a dozen times already. Robyn was an "intuitive entrepreneur." She lived in the "intersection between commerce and compassion," or "mindfulness and monetary success." All the buzzwords, all the half-baked business ideas. Eucalyptus-lined shower curtains meant to calm and center while you cleaned, but that accidentally sprouted weeds in the drain. Cocktail-flavored toothpastes that were designed to bring creativity and a "cool factor" to your health routine, but accidentally still had alcohol in them. Nothing like a morning buzz mid-brush.

Her latest, Mood Me, was a phone case that was also a mood ring. It was big and bulky and promised to transform in color to correlate with your mood. After days of badgering, Liz agreed to Robyn's relentless request that she test it out herself. One afternoon into her "volunteering," the rubbery texture had malfunctioned, overheating so that Liz dropped it with a yelp, shattering her iPhone screen. Robyn was regretful, but upon seeing the case was red, the color of stress, she suggested

Liz take the opportunity as a sign to recenter, to breathe more during the day, to stay calm. (Liz didn't need a phone case to tell her how *that* made her feel.) Mac made sure Robyn volunteered to pay for her screen replacement instead.

Liz tried to stay silent through all this. It wasn't her place to judge, and she knew she had no business interfering. Still, she bit hard on her tongue when she remembered that Robyn's pontifications and profit plans often left out the key principle: she was bankrolled by her grandfather, one in a line of oil tycoons. He funded her prototypes, leaving her with way more first attempts than an average MBA student was typically afforded or allowed. It seemed even a bottomless down payment couldn't guarantee the next big idea's success. At least, not yet.

"Grandfather sends his deepest congratulations, too, though. Right, Mac? Did you pass those along already?" Robyn asked. "Oh! We must email them Cam and Liz's address. My parents want to send an engagement gift. Text me your mailing address again, Liz? I know it's saved here somewhere but ever since the launch of Mood Me, my phone is just exploding with sales and updates and PR requests, I simply can't find anything. Oh! Last thing! Text me that photo with the boat behind your proposal, Liz? Maman thinks it might have been her tennis partner's boat. What a magical coincidence. Just gorgeous all around." Robyn looked up from her phone, and Liz was shocked to see that a semblance of tears had filled her eyes. Robyn reached out, eyes shining, and clasped her hand on Liz's shoulder. "Thank you so much for including me in such a special night. I'm so happy for you both."

"Of course," Liz stammered.

"We're so glad you could be there," Cam added.

Robyn's phone rang, interrupting the moment. "I have to take this. Macky, wait for me? Shouldn't be more than thirty. Love you guys!" In a flash, Robyn was out of the room, dashing up the stairs and out of sight.

Liz always felt a little winded after talking to Robyn, but if that was who Mac wanted to spend his time with, Liz would have to get comfortable with her. Just because she had never become best friends with any of Mac's girlfriends didn't mean that he shouldn't have dated them. What was Mac's alternative? Pining for Maggie, like those first years as college students? At least he was trying.

In Robyn's absence, Mac sat down on the couch and rested his left leg on a stack of pillows. "You guys go, head to the beach with the others. I'm good to wait here."

"Knee hurting again?" Liz asked.

"Nothing major. Just a little tight." He rubbed his kneecap.

"Did you go to PT yesterday?" Cam asked.

"Was too busy recovering from your guys' proposal party." Mac gave them a firm grin, but it was clear he wanted the conversation to be over. It had been five months since the accident, and the only direction he was running was *away* from his physical therapy appointments. No matter what Liz and Cam tried.

"Speaking of which, I'll give Robyn's parents your address, but can you send me that photo?" Mac asked now. "And maybe a few others? Those teasers came back incredible."

"Right?" Cam said, proud of the proposal.

"I want to print one out for myself."

"I'm sure Mom is already at Staples." Cam laughed. "I'll tell her to make you a copy."

"Do you remember when she printed those flyers for my soccer finals senior year?"

"And got in a fight with the manager because he wouldn't let her use the biggest size possible?"

"The image was so blurry! Dude was right."

"*Never* tell Mom that," Cam said, laughing again.

"It's still framed in the basement," Mac added.

Liz left Mac and Cam to their memories as she opened the camera roll on her phone and toggled through the dozen or so favorited photos from their engagement. Cam had booked a photographer to meet them by the esplanade in Battery Park City, near the Peters family's pied-à-terre. The Hudson River shone behind them, the sun danced off the ring in Cam's shaking fingers, as he bent down on one knee. His mother's ring, a family heirloom, sliding past Liz's knuckle.

Every emotion surfaced in Liz's bloodstream, overflowing so much that it almost felt like she was drowning. With love, but with that all-consuming feeling that she was at last doing something the way she ought. Checking off the boxes, she was walking that road she had been paving for a decade. Everything had been building toward this exact moment. Cam Peters, her childhood dream. Her destiny.

Her fiancé. Finally.

And yet.

There was something coating that moment in the slightest, subtlest sadness.

Now Liz opened the Gmail application on her phone, ready to send a collection of the day's happiest memories to Mac. Then, an unread subject line sandwiched between Blick Art sales and Madewell promotions sent a shock to her core.

"I'm just gonna run to the bathroom," she said. "Be back in a sec." She raced to the first-floor bathroom and closed the door behind her, before either Peters brother could get a word in edgewise.

Sitting on the tiled bathroom floor, head against the wooden pane, Liz allowed her fidgeting fingers to open the email.

Dear Elizabeth Grey,

Congratulations! You have been nominated to apply for the inaugural Domus Fellowship program. This program is designed for fashion industry creatives and entrepreneurs from all different walks of life, to gather for one year of integrated study. It is our mission statement to create a new generation of well-rounded industry executives with an emphasis on sustainability.

If accepted, all students will receive a full scholarship to obtain a master's degree in Sustainable Fashion Design and Technology. The

scholarship includes room, board, and travel
expenses necessary to relocate to Milan, Italy.
Application details are enclosed below.

The rest of the words cut in and out of Liz's focus. She remembered her favorite NYU professor reaching out the other
month, letting her know about a new international opportunity
that she would be perfect for. A chance for a scholarship that
could change everything.

Liz, in a career rut. Liz, in a design rut. Her job as a tech-
nical designer at her favorite high-end clothing line had been
more corporate, more cookie-cutter than she'd ever expected.
Even New York had somehow started to feel stale, the streets
like her once-favorite songs after a year on repeat, suddenly
overplayed. Maybe this opportunity was exactly what Liz
needed.

A year in Italy, soaking in all the colors and fabrics and
teachings a foreign city could offer.

A year abroad when she was supposed to be planning a
wedding.

Could she apply?

What would Cam say? His mom already had a list of
venues for them to tour next week. She wanted to get a date
booked for next spring.

Liz had checklists to follow. An event to plan. A husband to
marry. She had responsibilities. She had an apartment lease in
New York.

How could she not apply?

She looked around at the beach house's bathroom. The walls were covered in silly and clichéd decorations, and yet when Liz's eyes landed on a rainbow sign, she took its words as a personal instruction. *Life at the beach means painting the day with all the colors of the sun!*

She nearly laughed.

What harm was there in applying? She probably wouldn't even get in, Liz told herself. Admission rates were low, so she set her expectations even lower.

She'd just give it one shot. One honest shot.

She would apply.

She just wouldn't tell Cam yet, she reasoned. It wasn't a lie; she would tell him eventually, as soon as she had to.

But she couldn't kick the guilt entirely. Two days engaged and already the secrets were building.

Liz starred the email and promised herself that this secret would be her last.

Chapter 5

I t was no secret. Maggie was finally having some fun. "Aaaannnd, action!" she called out, as sand shot up into the sky and her stars began the scene as planned. Her heart sped up like it always did at the start of a shoot or a project or a dream. That the morning's drama was momentarily disguised by the all-consuming task at hand was icing on the cake.

It was the Ocean Beach Sandcastle Competition, and the Serendipity House didn't care if it felt juvenile or silly. The friends were determined to win.

Maggie oversaw production as the team's director/ producer, Liz was the production designer / set decorator, Cam and PJ the trusty construction crew. As the guys filled toy buckets with sand, a collection of shapes and cylinders they'd found in the shed outside the rental house, Liz walked the shoreline looking for seashells or seaweed worthy of their palatial design. Brenna called out words of encouragement from her beach chair, a *People* magazine open on her lap, while Quinn failed to nap through the ordeal despite her best efforts.

When Maggie first saw the flyer advertising the sandcastle competition, a faded piece of paper stapled to an announcement board at the entrance of the beach, she almost didn't draw attention to it. She wasn't sure how most of the group would want to spend their first eighty-five-degrees-and-clear-skies Saturday. Georgie was stuck at the house, laptop hooked up to a hot spot because the rental's internet wasn't high-speed enough for his law firm's urgent work.

Mac and Robyn, meanwhile, had disappeared into the bedroom. Liz claimed Robyn was finishing up some work, too, but the noises ricocheting from upstairs sounded definitively like pleasure.

So much for M&M's, Maggie thought.

Maybe Mac hadn't been sending any subliminal messages after all.

Maybe he was simply craving some candy.

That morning, Liz had been extra quiet, eyes practically glued to her phone, straggling behind with a frown as the group walked toward the beach. As kids, Maggie had been the frazzled one while Liz was always calm. Liz had even learned to meditate in the third grade, teaching it to their friends at recess. Now she looked like she didn't know the meaning of the word *nirvana*.

Maybe a sandcastle distraction would help Liz, too. And

sure enough, as soon as Maggie pointed out the contest, Liz wholeheartedly agreed: the Serendipity House would compete.

Maggie signed them up.

An hour later, the shoreline was well populated with those competing. The $150 gift certificate to the Sandbar enticed hungover weekenders, groups of grown twentysomethings, to spend their Saturday morning patting down sand and filling moats with ocean water as purpose brimmed in their eyes.

The teamwork of it all put Maggie at ease. A performance of its own. She felt like she was back in the director's chair of a UCLA film set. She loved the pandemonium of a group working to accomplish a single goal. That feeling of landing a plane while still building the runway. Of getting her hands dirty for a dream. Of trusting in the madness.

Until, of course, Kurt proved that when it came to hard work, there was no point in trusting at all.

"What do you think of these?" Liz asked now. A collection of misshapen shells and sea glass shone against her palm.

"Oh my god, they're perfect. How'd you even find them?"

"I saw a speck after the waves receded. Went with it." Liz beamed.

"You still have the best eye," Maggie said. "It's insane."

"Hell yeah she does," Cam called out from where he was crafting the base of the castle. "That's my girlfriend—"

"Fiancée!" Brenna reprimanded, eavesdropping from her chair.

"*Fiancée,*" Cam repeated. "Fiancée. I love hearing that word."

"Yeah, yeah, hand 'em over." PJ beckoned for Liz to drop her discoveries onto the pile of shells, waiting for the finished structure to be assembled before she would decorate it all.

"All right, what should I do next?" Liz asked Maggie.

"This is like senior fall all over again," Cam laughed. "Director Mags."

"Hopefully with fewer calluses this time," Quinn called out.

PJ groaned, out of the loop. "Okay, fill me in. What'd I miss?"

"Maggie's video production class required a short film as a final during our senior year," Brenna explained.

"You're looking at her star-studded cast and crew," Cam said.

"It was actually pretty fun," Liz offered.

"You're just saying that because you two got to be in front of the camera!" Quinn said.

The friends continued bickering, but Maggie revisited the memory. While Cam and Liz had been the only actors in her project (the script required a steamy kiss), the entire group had answered the call for production help that fall weekend. The shoot lasted for two exhausting twelve-hour days. Liz provided the costumes, Cam designed the props, and Brenna funded the snacks, her own version of craft services. Georgie was the sound operator, holding a boom until his right arm nearly fell off. Quinn acted as script coordinator, making sure each line was recited just so. Maggie directed them all.

Mac, too, Maggie remembered. He wasn't here now, but

he had been then, volunteering as her assistant director, ready to do anything she asked. Ready, always ready, to help with her big dreams.

"Everyone was perfect," Maggie said now. "It was perfect."

"That's amazing," PJ said, looking at her as his eyes glowed with sincerity. "So cool. I'd love to see it sometime."

Maggie felt her cheeks warm, though she wasn't quite sure why. Was it from the reminder of how wonderful it felt to be on set? The heat of wanting Mac again by her side?

Or was it a new, spreading intoxication that came with settling back among her group of friends? She soaked in the laughter of the group, grateful that it felt familiar again. Some friendships worked that way, Maggie reasoned, like tattoos. The shape, the texture surviving spans of silent years. This could be her story, too.

This afternoon was already off to a better start than Friday night had suggested. Maybe the rest of the weekend would follow in a similar fashion. She could think of more group-project activities, plan some grand gestures, find her way back into the fold.

"Anyone up for a walk?" Maggie called out, determined to keep up the pace.

Soon, she was leading PJ, Georgie, Cam, and Liz westward down the shoreline, weaving around pairs of Frisbee players and dogs chasing waves, evaluating each sandcastle they passed. Most were admirable, some creative in shape and design (a mermaid and a flip-flop, for instance), but none as lofty in stature as their own. They would win the contest, she dared to hope.

She pulled out her phone, typing and smiling as she walked:

Feet in the sand feels like stepping in a time machine. Youth and happiness as effervescent as the coast. The waves rock in and warn us that the world spins and spins. That we are small, and life goes on. But the sand reminds us that we've already been here. We've built castles once before; we drank the magic of the sun. Isn't that refreshing? Even though we've grown, we can always find a way back home.

"Watch out!" A voice called, but it was too late.

A Frisbee thwacked against Maggie's shin. Her balance thrown off, her phone toppled out of her hands, the screen face-planting in the sand. She quickly rushed to pick it up, to save it from the oncoming waves, moving so fast that she forgot to look up and see where the disc had flown from in the first place.

Ty stood there, holding her phone in one hand and a bright green Frisbee in the other.

"Maggie May Monroe. I knew that was you. You always had your head stuck in your notebook. E-notebook, in this case, but still." Ty grinned. His hair was jet-black, his face tanned.

Meanwhile, Maggie's face flushed. Thoughts she'd locked away came racing back. "Well, I'll be taking that." She grabbed the phone from Ty's clutches, abandoning any attempt at daintiness or charm. Charm didn't matter, considering where her brain had started steering.

"I didn't read anything, I promise," Ty said with a genuine smile. "I'm sure it's genius, though. Not as good as my stuff, of course, but you always had promise."

"Thanks, I guess," Maggie said. She knew he was teasing, but she had no patience for it then.

"Are you out here all weekend? We should get a drink, catch up on work—"

"Actually, I gotta go." Maggie quickly pivoted and started briskly walking back toward the direction of Quinn and Brenna until she felt someone grab her arm.

It was Liz, following her, with a concerned look on her face.

"What was that about?" she asked, panting slightly from running to catch up to Maggie. "Who was that?"

Maggie didn't want to get into it all. "Don't worry about it. It's nothing."

Liz's face remained fixed, unimpressed by Maggie's obvious lie.

"Fine, just some boy I knew in LA. We worked at the talent agency together, my first job out of college."

"Oooh. Romantic?"

"He was an assistant already, a few years older than us. I was in the mailroom."

"I repeat. Romantic?"

"It's not like that. We were coworkers. He's fine, he just . . . reminds me of someone. Something. I don't want to think about it."

Liz's face softened instantly. "Well, let's not think about it then."

Growing up, Maggie had always been grateful for the way that Liz seemed to understand a problem despite hearing the bare minimum of words. She had the ability to call her friends on their bullshit, to make them address problems head-on. But she always did so while standing right by their side, sharing a smile and a shoulder, despite the sadness. Maggie's heart pulled as she realized Liz was doing the same now. How had she ever let a friend as tough yet special as Liz just fall through her fingers?

By the time Maggie and Liz returned to their sandcastle, she was reminded of her answer.

Mac.

In the distance, Mac and Robyn were walking away.

"Sorry guys, you just missed them," Brenna said, tracking Maggie's and Liz's eyelines.

"Robyn sat down for maybe three minutes before saying her 'relaxation window' had ended and it was time to go back to work," Quinn said.

"Did they say where they were going?" Liz asked.

"To the bay, I think? Some photo shoot for Mood-y or Mood Ring or Ring My Mood, or whatever she calls it," Brenna said.

"Wait. Do you think the *ring* is a play on, like, how phones ring? I didn't know she appreciated puns," Quinn said.

"And Mac went with her?" Liz asked, ignoring Quinn's question.

"Robyn said he had to model. Or take photos. Or both," Brenna said.

"Robyn is intense," Quinn said.

"Agreed," Brenna said.

"She's just entrepreneurial," Liz said. "Can't sit still. Some people are like that."

"But is *Mac* like that?" Maggie asked. "I've never seen him leave the beach so early. It feels wrong."

Then she instantly regretted it.

Liz turned to her, her lips tight, her face suddenly cold. Any rekindled kindness drained away. "You haven't seen Mac in years. How would you have the slightest idea of what's right or wrong for him?"

Maggie had struck a nerve. "I'm just saying he never used to—" she started, trying to backtrack, but it was too late. She had overstepped.

"Leave Mac alone, okay? He's over you. *Finally.* Just let him be," Liz snapped. She grabbed her beach bag and started walking back to the house before anyone could stop her.

With Liz gone, Maggie fell into her chair, head in her hands. Brenna and Quinn resumed their reading and nap, respectively, giving Maggie an awkward privacy.

Maggie knew her place. Mac and Cam were the friend group's lifeblood, but Liz was the real leader. And Liz was loyal. How could Maggie have forgotten that? Ever since Maggie had picked LA over all of them, Liz had drawn a line. Maggie was foolish for thinking that she would forgive and forget.

Now she remembered what Liz had said, when she came back home from UCLA for the first time. After their freshman year ended, Maggie dove headfirst into the film industry, moving to LA for a summer internship at Paramount.

As such, it was winter break of their sophomore year before she returned home to East Meadow. Even ahead of her plane touching down at JFK, Maggie knew she was in fragile friend territory. All semester long, she'd barely answered the East Meadow group chats, she'd missed all the Skype calls. She'd wanted to participate, but she was drowning. The three-hour time difference between LA and New York was just enough to make it feel like Maggie was always ever so slightly behind. She'd wake up when her old friends were already in their classes, or get home from a long day right as her East Coast–based loved ones were about to fall asleep. As a transfer student, it felt even harder to catch up with new campus maps and assignments amid classmates who'd already found their footing. She loved her new film curriculum and the California air, but she hated to admit that she was struggling.

That winter, that rush of returning to her roots after her first semester spent so far away, left Maggie homesick and hungry at the same time. So when she was invited to Mac and Cam's holiday basement party, she went.

And even though everything was different, just for one night, she let herself pretend nothing had changed. Like life was still easy and simple, known. She sang along to Taylor Swift with Brenna and Quinn, quoted all the best parts of the latest season of *Brooklyn Nine-Nine* with Georgie. But the easiest, most natural part was finding her way back to Mac.

It didn't take long. Seeing him again felt like pressing play on a movie she'd seen one hundred times.

They stayed close all night, teaming up as beer pong partners, like they always had in high school. Mac could make anyone feel welcome, his smile was easy, and he was quick to laugh at any joke. He loved to make others comfortable. With Maggie, he displayed no drama, no awkwardness, despite the fact they hadn't seen each other since she'd moved away. He was welcoming, which was classic Mac.

Then his arm kept accidentally grazing hers. Shoulders touching, fingers overlapping as they restacked cups. Maggie felt herself lean into it, like muscle memory. It was as if their bodies were magnets, an electric pulse keeping them near. It felt like old times.

Flirty and easy and fun.

Right?

An hour into the party, after refusing to make eye contact with Maggie all night, Liz pulled her upstairs.

"I know what you're doing," Liz said, once they'd gotten to the quiet, darkened living room. "And it's low, even for you."

Maggie bristled. "What's that supposed to mean?"

"You don't think we can all tell that you're leading him on? After ignoring him since summer? After breaking his heart?" Liz's voice cracked.

"You don't know what you're talking about. You don't know what it's like—"

"How could I? You've barely answered any of my calls, and now you're just showing up, pretending like everything is fine again?"

"We're just catching up, hanging out. Look, Liz, I'm sorry about NYU, really, but it wasn't about you—"

"Save it, Maggie. Honestly. Forget about me. You clearly already have." Liz's chin crumpled. "But unless you're coming home anytime soon, or unless you've suddenly changed your mind about long distance, about breaking up with him? Do me one last favor and leave Mac out of your identity crisis."

There are only a few moments in life that sear into your soul, that leave an imprint you can remember verbatim simply by closing your eyes.

This was one of those moments for Maggie.

She had been left stunned. Liz had read her like a textbook, and Maggie felt mortified. She did already have spring and summer internships lined up in LA. There was no intention of coming back to New York, other than the occasional academic calendar break. She didn't have proper prospects of her and Mac getting back together. Not in a real way.

Not in a relationship way.

Not in anything more than a hometown hookup.

Suddenly, she felt like the worst person in the world for thinking this was okay. Mac was more than a rebound. He had been her best friend. He was the twin brother of her other best friend's boyfriend. It was messy, and Maggie was only making it worse.

She went home that night in tears. Chastised, and rightfully so. But beginning that next morning, she had accepted that Liz was right.

They were better off without her. By that sophomore spring, Maggie's parents moved to a new house, on the waterfront in Oyster Bay, a different town on Long Island. If and when Maggie did fly east—and that count only declined year by year—it was easy to avoid East Meadow entirely.

She gave them all their space, as promised. Eventually, there was enough space to fill six years.

Maggie had hoped that after all that time, she could come home to a fresh start, a blank slate. That they could act like adults about it. That she could try to fit in again. But it seemed her former best friends' walls were still built high against her. She had well-deserved grudges to undo.

That's okay, Maggie resolved. She could pivot. She was flexible. She could rewrite this, too. Her specialty. She'd just have to work harder than ever if she wanted to manifest what her New York life might have been. The path not taken that she felt desperate to carry through. A summer-long experiment to prove that LA hadn't been a colossal waste of time, a massive mistake. That she could pick up the pieces, retry it all.

Even if she'd chosen the wrong route once, maybe she could still find her way back on course.

Where else did she have left to go?

Three Ocean Beach weekends. Three months in New York.

Maggie was older now; she would be wiser.

She had to prove that this time, their stories could all end differently.

Chapter 6

All afternoon, Liz felt guilty for snapping at Maggie. She hadn't even wanted to follow Maggie down the beach, chasing after her like she was some damsel in distress from a storybook, Liz the requisite rescuer, but Cam and PJ had looked at Liz with such guilt-tripping eyes, she knew she had to be the person to make sure Maggie was okay.

Liz had overreacted. Again. *Ugh*, she groaned. It felt so high school. So immature. Nothing like the Liz in the years since their East Meadow graduation, the Liz who had worked at keeping her every emotion in check, even when she wanted to weep and scream and run away. At first it was to keep the negative away from her mom, in those early semesters at NYU. And then it was to process everything that came after. This past year, especially, when everything changed for good. By the time she turned twenty-four, Liz was practically professional at not burdening strangers with the truth. At preventing her own heart from breaking daily.

But she also had spent this past year painstakingly coming to terms with the family she had left. She would always defend them. She would always protect them, and if that meant snapping at Maggie Monroe, then so be it.

Liz didn't know how to feel around Maggie anymore. Their friendship was buried under so much bitterness. So much silence. She felt like the past had slapped her in the face. A rushed reminder of the Before. Liz felt her blood racing again, so she took a deep breath in and looked down.

White: the onion dip she was violently mixing to transfer her frustration.

White: the Domus Academy logo shining bright at the top of the application invitation, the email that she'd been reading and rereading all day.

The Milan scholarship had so many requirements just to apply. A portfolio of a new collection, a sample of a design. Not to mention a personal statement about why she deserved this chance over the tens of thousands of other hopefuls.

She was desperate to talk to Cam about it. She knew she should. She just wasn't quite ready for his opinion. Cam had always hated change, big or small. Moving to a new apartment took months of convincing, and he spent hours reading every review on any new product—from their in-window air-conditioning unit to a forty-three-dollar Mets short-sleeve button-down—until he officially added it to the digital shopping cart (where it would sit for a one-week "trial thought process" before actual purchase). If Cam thought the Domus program was a bad idea, or even suggested Liz defer it for a few years, well, it would break her. She wanted this chance, she wanted his support, but she had a bad feeling about what he'd say.

Because her mind was filled with worry, she nearly jumped when Cam tapped her on the shoulder.

"Babe? I think you're going to break that bowl if you keep whisking at that pace." Cam smiled, but his eyes hinted at his concern.

"Sorry, you startled me. I guess I was in the zone," she said with a forced laugh, hoping to clear the expression on her face. She picked up the onion dip and delivered it to the living room coffee table, which already boasted a large helping of buffalo chicken dip and a platter of cheese and crackers. Cam headed outside, but Liz plopped onto the couch, needing a minute to herself.

Shortly after her fight (Could she call it a fight? Strong words?) with Maggie, the group had staggered back from the beach to change and get ready for the night. As soon as enough towels were located (the stash was kept under the sink, Mac remembered after eight minutes of searching), a shower schedule was created: Quinn called dibs on the outdoor one, whereas Robyn said she'd only ever shower inside—"One word: bugs." Georgie sheepishly admitted he'd forgotten to pack a toothbrush, but luckily Brenna never traveled without a brand-new spare.

PJ was the first one ready, so he heated up the grill and flipped hamburger patties and hot dogs. He had worked in his family's restaurant growing up, so he felt most comfortable in the role of Serendipity chef. The smell from the grill worked its way through the house and soon everyone transformed into evening clothes, adorned with wet hair and pink noses daring toward a burn. Liz had combed through her own red hair, detangler aiding her fingers as she tied her locks into careful braids.

Anything to keep her mind off not only Maggie, but even more critically, her own phone.

The group text thread with Cam and his mom had been pinging ever since his mother, Roseanne, sent a message with a "spectacular, lightbulb of an idea" earlier that afternoon.

Roseanne Peters: Hi lovebugs! Sorry to bother you when you are surely out soaking up the sun! Just had a spectacular, lightbulb of an idea I wanted to share. Two words: Engagement Party. Saturday, August 12th? When Grandma Peach is up from Florida? She'd love to celebrate you two with the whole extended family. You can invite as many friends as you'd like! Our treat, of course!

Cam had still been on the beach, so Liz had texted him on the side, in a private thread.

Liz: C, re: your mom's text. Aug 12 is the same weekend we have the house in OB.

Cam: Crap, you're right. I'll tell her.

Cam: Also, miss you on the beach. ☺ All good at the house? Be back soon.

Liz hadn't realized how much of their adult relationship would be spent covertly side-texting messages regarding different family group chats. Cam responded back on the larger chain:

Cam: Thanks, Mom! Love this idea. Only thing—August 12th is when we have the Ocean Beach rental with our East Meadow friends . . . ☹

Liz: Such a fun idea though!

Roseanne Peters: Hmmm. Maybe this is silly. And feel free to say no. But what if we hosted it *in* Ocean Beach? Georgie's parents had an anniversary party at Maguire's a few summers ago and it was just GORGEOUS. All your friends can come, too! Think about it and let me know?!

Roseanne Peters: Just called Maguire's and they're available for a party but we'd have to let them know ASAP Rocky!

Roseanne Peters: Just ASAP Rocky. Not sure what ASAP Rocky is.

Roseanne Peters: ASAP Rocky

Roseanne Peters: ASAP Rocky!!!!!

Roseanne Peters: Grr! I give up!

Roseanne Peters: Think about it and let me know! Soon, please! Xo

Roseanne Peters: *every wedding emoji under the sun*

Liz had groaned and closed out of her Messages app. So much could be different by August 12. According to the Domus

Academy invitation, the rolling admissions began mid-July. She'd most likely know her application status shortly after. By the time August rolled around, would Liz be celebrating an acceptance? Would Cam be supportive? If she spent the next year abroad, when would they even get married? Would they need to postpone the engagement? And then what good would a party do?

"Liz, are you okay? Your face is, like, not looking great," Mac said, walking into the living room, startling her slightly.

"Are you calling me ugly?" Liz teased, but she could feel the tension of her frown loosen as she massaged her forehead. "I'm fine, just a headache. You good? Where's Robyn?"

"She went out to explore the restaurant happy hours. I wanted to eat with the crew, but she doesn't like burgers. Or hot dogs. Or onion dip. Even when it's clearly been pulverized by you." He laughed.

"Very funny. You could've gone with her. We'd have saved you some leftovers," Liz said.

"It's fine. Space sometimes counts as 'balance' in her books." Mac grinned a bit devilishly. "Keeps things fun."

"How's your knee feeling?"

"Better. Took some Advil when we got back from the beach," he said, but Liz could sense him eager to avoid the topic of his injury. "Awesome about the engagement party, by the way. I've always wanted to go to a big party on Fire Island. Robyn and I are already securing the perfect gift."

If Liz had taken a bite of onion dip, she would've spit it out. "What did you say?"

"Robyn and I are getting you a gift? She has a connection to an oil painter who can do live portraits—"

"No, before that."

"The engagement party? That my parents are throwing?"

Liz's stomach flipped. "I need to talk to your brother."

She sped outside to where Cam was playing cards with Quinn and Brenna. Georgie was sitting at the patio table, still glued to his work laptop, but at least this time he had a frozen margarita in his hand.

"Liz!" Georgie called out. "Can't wait for the party!" His margarita glass was now raised as if in a toast. "My parents gave Mrs. Peters all their catering contact info. It's such a killer space. You'll love it."

Liz couldn't believe her ears. She looked at her fiancé.

"Cam? Did you tell your mom we were in for the engagement party?"

"Yes, shoot, sorry, I wanted to tell you—she called me when I was walking back from the beach," Cam said. "The restaurant apparently got another offer for the same date, so we had to commit right then if we wanted to book. Which we did, right? She's really excited."

"So, this is you telling me?"

"Yes?" Cam's face was sheepish.

"And not asking if it's something I want to do?"

"You said it was a fun idea!"

"I was just being polite!"

"Well, I didn't know that—"

"So, you just unilaterally made a decision with your mom about something that affects us both? I'm the one you're engaged to!"

"I know!"

"You really should have talked to me first."

"Liz, it's not that big of a deal. We'll be in Ocean Beach already. It's just a party."

"Party!" Georgie cut in with another cheers. "Yeah!"

"My mom will plan the whole thing. We don't have to do anything but show up," Cam added.

"It's not about the amount of work or having to do something—" Liz started.

"Then what's the problem?" Cam pulled her aside, held her hand. He lowered his voice. "I'm sorry. I should have talked to you before agreeing. That was stupid. So stupid. I just got excited by how excited she was. I really want to celebrate us. To do something fun. I'm so sorry."

He pulled her into him and Liz let her head rest against his shoulder. What good would it do to stay mad? "I know," she said.

Did she really want to ruin the whole evening by clinging to her anger?

"I'm sorry about the party. Really," Cam whispered. "It won't happen again. I'm just too damn excited to celebrate my bride." He kissed the top of her head, and despite it all, she melted.

"Okay," Liz relented. "Party it is."

"I promise it'll be amazing." Cam smiled his most convincing smile, which always made her smile back.

"Next round of burgers coming up!" PJ called out from the grill.

"Want to eat, babe?" Cam asked Liz, squeezing each individual finger on her left hand, stopping only to thumb over her engagement ring. She nodded in reply.

As Cam and Liz approached the grill, they saw Maggie standing next to PJ, receiving a hot dog on a paper plate. "Did you guys say you're having an engagement party?" she asked, timidly.

"Apparently." Liz frowned, her earlier annoyance toward Maggie bubbling back to the surface.

"Well, if you guys need any help with planning, let me know. I can even film some of it if you'd like. I can bring my camera," Maggie offered. "I did videography at a few weddings during college, to make some extra cash. Obviously I wouldn't charge you guys, though."

Liz paused while Maggie rambled. She wasn't sure why Maggie was extending an olive branch so soon. The Maggie in her memory would have never made the first move to apologize. But she didn't feel ready to take it just yet. In fact, Maggie's face was starting to make her feel nervous. Anxious with reminders of the many things Liz preferred to keep closed off in her mind, shut away with everything else that had since been buried.

Cam, on the other hand, had no hesitation. He was back to

the warm, bubbly, life-of-the-party Cam. The Cam she'd fallen in love with. Always putting everyone else at ease, the Peters twins' best party trick. "That would be awesome. Thank you," he said. "Such a genius idea. There will be dancing, and hopefully some of those cheesy engagement party games, too. And my grandma will be there. Video footage of everything would be great, thank you."

Maggie's face lit up. "You got it. No problem. My pleasure."

Liz wasn't convinced. What was Maggie's endgame? Get close to Cam, to Liz, and then sneak back in to break Mac's heart? Once again leaving Cam (and consequently Liz) to pick up his brother's broken pieces? Heartbreak management didn't fit into Liz's strained bandwidth.

Maybe Maggie was just genuinely hungry for friendship? Maybe she really was as lost and lonely as her eyes seemed to cry?

Or was Liz maybe turning toward paranoia as a way of coping with her anxiety and her sadness and, let's face it, her trust issues? Maybe she was just looking for a person to blame. She could hear the words of her therapist coursing through her brain. She took a deep breath and looked around.

Red: the plastic cup Cam just handed her, filled with vodka and soda.

Red: the lipstick her mom always wore to parties and nights out, to special occasions where dresses were long and fancy. Where makeup was a mandate, not an afternoon playtime routine. Now: the lipstick sat in Liz's nightstand drawer back home, one full year spent unopened.

She turned around and saw Maggie's cheeks reddening, too, brightening with shock as the backyard fence's gate swung open with a creak.

Robyn stepped in, perched tall on strappy high heels with black leather shorts, despite Ocean Beach's near-universal uniform of flip-flops and denim. Her face was dolled up, bright lipstick coating her slightly tipsy smile.

"Macky!" she purred. "Let's go. It's time to hit the town."

Chapter 7

Ocean Beach on a Saturday night was a beer-soaked Atlantis. The heart of town packed with restaurants, bars teeming with beautiful faces as music from live bands' performances poured from cracked windows. All against the backdrop of the bay, the mainland a ferry ride away.

The Serendipity House had scored second place in the sandcastle contest. At first, the results were met with a chorus of boos, complaints that the first-place champion was in fact shaped like a *mermaid*, and therefore not a *sandcastle* at all. Yet when the jurors announced that the second-place prize was a hundred-dollar gift certificate to the Sandbar, PJ accepted the honors with a salute and a smile.

It was a given that the Sandbar would be the first stop of the night. Located right at the center of town, the crowded bar boasted a ceiling that was covered with colorful, glued-on

flip-flops, signatures scrawled on the soles with names of patrons past. As the band onstage played "Jessie's Girl," the
friends squeezed their way toward the bar. Robyn had already
charmed the bartender during her happy hour excursion, so
one signature smile was all it took to get his immediate attention. "Nine Rocket Fuels, please," she said, as PJ exchanged
the gift card. Their hands were soon filled with the free round
of Fire Island's drink of choice: rum, amaretto, pineapple juice,
and coconut cream, blended and topped with Bacardi 151.

For now, it didn't matter that Robyn was dancing with
Mac, their hips pressed together, her lips on his neck, making
their way up toward his ear.

It didn't matter that Liz was still avoiding eye contact with
Maggie.

It didn't even matter when someone stepped on Maggie's
flip-flop-exposed big toe, and barely grumbled an apology as
they shoved right on by toward the bar.

Maggie was singing along to her favorite songs, dancing,
and yes, maybe she was also a bit more than tipsy, but it meant
that her mind's hamster wheel of worries had slowed at last.

For perhaps the first time since she'd arrived back in New
York, Maggie felt free.

The friends formed a circle on the dance floor, singing at
the top of their lungs. She blinked and saw that familiar memory
reel from high school, a collection of Peters basement parties
projected like a film. Nights would often end like this, with Mr.
Peters's karaoke machine plugged into the television set.

After Maggie moved to California, she searched and searched, but nothing compared to what she'd had with her East Meadow friends. The people who'd first drawn up their dreams together, who'd recorded custom music videos to catchy pop songs in the basement or played kickball for entire afternoons in backyards. The friends who'd learned to drive together, that special brand of trust to let teenagers take the wheel. The people who'd learned their powers together, but also their limits, like when they first held back each other's hair after filling their stomachs with too much gin.

She looked around their circle, taking in their smiles with that sheen of Saturday night splendor. So maybe it was the Rocket Fuel, or the tequila shots back at the house, or the vodka water bottles on the beach, but when Maggie realized a face was missing, she felt an ache.

Mac.

She missed him. Even if they'd both moved on, she would never stop missing their friendship.

Tracking a gaze through the bar, Maggie's eyes landed on Mac outside, smoking a joint. Alone. She glanced back toward the stage, where Robyn was now dancing solo, arms raised over her head, apparently clueless about her boyfriend's whereabouts.

Maggie bit her cuticle. Closure with Mac was important if she was going to be living in the same city as him again, with Brenna and Quinn. If she was going to fix things with Liz, his sister-in-law to be. If she wanted to reside in the East Meadow circle. This weekend was an opportunity to move forward, even if he had found a new partner in Robyn. Conversation didn't count as a crime. Right?

"I need to get some air," Maggie shouted above the music. "Be right back."

She left the dance floor and walked outside, but not directly toward Mac.

First, she popped into the neighboring Town Pizza and ordered two "cold cheese" slices, to go. During after-prom weekend, Maggie and Mac had ended each night with at least two of these slices, a Fire Island tradition. The pizza itself was a classic cheese, fresh from the oven, but coated in a layer of shredded cold mozzarella. She hoped a piece of it now might earn her some goodwill.

Pizza in hand, she crossed her fingers and found Mac. He'd settled onto the dock, looking out at the bay.

"Look what the tide brought in." He greeted her with an easy smile, the kind that always gave her goose bumps when they were kids. Even when things were purely platonic, she wasn't blind.

"Call me paranoid, but dare I say that you've been avoiding me?" Mac teased.

"Once a diva, always a diva." Maggie laughed, snatching the joint from between his fingertips. "I could say the same thing about you," she said, as she let her legs dangle above the bay.

"All right, Hollywood." Mac smirked. "Easy now."

"I brought pizza." Maggie presented the box.

Mac whistled forlornly. "I wish. That's the best slice in all the tristate. But Robyn's off dairy this month, so I said I'd join in solidarity."

"What?" Maggie could feel her eyebrows lifting to the sky. "Oh, I get it, you're joking."

"Don't tempt me. I'm not allowed to touch the stuff." Mac laughed as he pushed the box away, filling Maggie with a flash of regret. Now she felt like an idiot holding two slices of cheese pizza no one wanted. Would it be worse to take a bite or to leave them in the box?

"How's Eastern Standard Time treating you so far?" Mac asked.

"Honestly, it's changing by the hour."

"Is that the truth, or just a really bad time pun?"

"Ha ha." She dared herself to knock her knee briefly against his. "Brenna told me about your knee, by the way. Those where the stitches are?"

"I prefer the term 'battle scars.'"

"Valiant. Nice." Mac had torn up his knee in January, or so Brenna and Quinn had told Maggie on the train ride over. He hated talking about it, and hated when his friends talked about it, but she had pieced together certain details: an indoor soccer game, torn cartilage, and a warning to never play competitively again. She wanted to take his mind off it, the way she would have in high school, when they were still close.

"Well, injury or otherwise, the water looks amazing right

now. In fact, I just might have to dare you to stick your foot in, see what the temperature feels like." She elbowed him teasingly in the ribs.

It was dark outside, but Maggie swore she saw Mac's eyes light up, exactly as she'd hoped.

"Do my ears deceive me, or is this the makings of an M-and-M dare?" he asked.

"Figured we were overdue." She grinned.

The summer going into their senior year of high school, Maggie and Mac had worked together at the Bellmore Playhouse movie theater. They called it their M&M shift, because of their initials, but also because of their dares.

It all started with M&M's. The first dare was to steal a pack of the candy when their supervisors weren't looking (they'd always put a few dollars in the register beforehand). Then, it was eating an entire pack of M&M's as fast as possible. Then it was tossing said M&M's into the garbage can three feet away, the goal to score more hoops than the other. No matter how quiet the midday shifts could be, Mac and Maggie would end up laughing until their abs were sore. When they returned to East Meadow for their final year of high school, *M&M* became their dare to cut class.

To escape for a moment, together.

Now in Ocean Beach, they were sitting next to each other again, a dare on their lips, smiles again on their faces. Maggie bumped her shoulder against his. "If you're going to use stall tactics to get out of this, just admit it."

"No delay, no delay." Mac laughed. "It's just been a while. I have to pump myself up."

"I'll mark that down as a forfeit, then."

Mac smirked, and in one swift motion, slid off his sneaker and plunged his foot directly in the bay's water.

"Christ, that's cold." His voice was loud, but it was happy, too.

"Aren't you an athlete? I thought ice baths were, like, a customary ritual."

"I see you haven't learned a thing about sports since you left." Mac kicked water in Maggie's direction. "All right, M, up to your shin. Dare you."

"Easy," she teased, removing both her flip-flops before she dipped her legs firmly into the water. She went past her shins, up to her knees, so the water was almost at the hem of her white denim shorts. The water was freezing, but that wouldn't stop her competitive nature from kicking firmly into overdrive. "I could do this all day," Maggie said, hoping Mac couldn't tell that her teeth were threatening to chatter.

But all she heard was the sound of his laughter. "All right, all right, you win."

"Like always." She smiled, pulling herself back up and next to him on the dock.

"Though I feel like we both pulled the short straw with this one," Mac said, motioning toward his sopping wet foot.

Maggie clucked her tongue as she tugged off her cropped cardigan, revealing a black camisole underneath. She used the sweater to wipe the droplets off her legs before offering it to Mac for him to dry off. He smiled as he did so, though Maggie could have sworn she felt him sneaking glances at her calves, her legs, as she slid her flip-flops on. It felt like they'd traveled back in time.

"I've missed this," he said, having tied his laces. Reading her mind.

"Me, too," she said. There was an easy silence, a blissful beat.

Was this her chance to apologize for her recent distance, to explain herself, to restart with Mac on the right page? "Listen—"

But Mac had the same idea. He started first: "I don't know what made you decide to move back home. And you don't have to tell me. But I'm really glad you did."

Her heartbeat picked up. "Yeah?"

"Of course." He smiled. "The crew is back together."

"I don't think everyone would agree."

"Is it Liz you're worried about? She's just protective, you know that," Mac said.

"From where I'm sitting, you've never needed protecting."

He cocked his head and squinted his eyes and suddenly Maggie felt a shiver explode through her spine. She thought about the M&M's in the grocery order. The way Mac had always felt like an extension of herself. He was part of her story, her history. Was this Maggie and Mac's second chance?

"I mean it, Mags," he said, his voice low. Electric. "I'm glad you're back."

Was this a move? Was he leaning in? Was she?

Maggie didn't have time to consider the answer.

"Macky!"

Robyn's voice filled the air, drowning out the waves themselves. Music poured from where she stood at the Sandbar's exit, door propped open with her high heel behind her.

For a moment, Maggie had completely forgotten about Robyn.

"They're playing our song! Come dance!"

Maggie tried not to let her heart break into a million pieces. This was what she deserved.

What had she been thinking?

Mac was dating Robyn. Mac had a song with *Robyn*.

"That's my cue," he said with the slightest, subtlest wince. "See you on the dance floor, M?"

"Sure thing."

He patted her on the shoulder twice, before pushing himself up and off the dock's edge and back into Robyn's orbit. The door slammed shut, muffling the music, cutting off the sounds of glee and leaving Maggie in silence.

It was better this way, Maggie thought. This wasn't her.

This wasn't who she wanted to be.

She pulled out her phone.

I didn't move home to be a homewrecker. No matter how home sweet home he feels. Maybe it's time for a demolition. To start with new framework. To build something with new bones?

"Where'd he go?" a voice said from behind Maggie.

She looked up over her shoulder and saw PJ, silhouetted by the sky.

"Back inside, dancing to his and Robyn's song," Maggie replied.

PJ rolled his eyes and sat down in the space left vacant by Mac, started to rummage in his pocket. "I'm always getting ditched in pursuit of a woman."

"Tale as old as time," Maggie said. In the company of someone else, she wanted to recalibrate to a better version of herself. Not the heartsick Maggie, but the genial one. "Can I offer you a slice as a consolation prize, at least?" She remembered the pizza, handed the box to PJ. "It would be a crime to eat this all alone."

"Twist my arm," he said. He raised a slice in one hand, a freshly lit joint in the other. "To new pizzas, and new friends."

Maggie took a bite of hers and moaned. "My god. How can something so simple be so delicious?"

"The best things in life are simple," PJ answered between bites. "Especially on vacation."

Simple. Maybe PJ was right.

Maybe Maggie didn't need to make everything so complicated.

She was home to unwind. To find herself, to start from scratch. Why not let herself go with the flow? She looked at PJ, who was smiling into the bay. Content from pizza and good weed and a Saturday night. His cheeks were rosy, his hair long and brown and effortlessly cool. Maggie blinked and saw his biceps from earlier on the beach.

PJ. Interesting.

Was *this* her new story?

"To new adventures, too," she said, voice daring.

PJ turned and looked at Maggie with a glint in his eyes. She felt her heart skip.

What would Mac say?

What *could* Mac say?

She didn't know what Mac would say, because Maggie wasn't Mac's girlfriend.

Maggie was lonely and tired, and tired of feeling alone.

So when PJ leaned in to kiss her, she let him.

She didn't care if it might end in a mistake.

Chapter 8

PJ was used to being a mistake.

Well, maybe not always an on-the-surface mistake, but at least a less-preferred choice. A last resort. A decision that lingered with the sweet scent of missed opportunity, of regret.

PJ knew he was attractive. He had the long hair, the muscular arms. His mom had made sure he knew how to act like a gentleman, to ask about a woman's day, to listen to her answers. His dad had made sure he knew how to cover the bill, to open the door, to take proper care of a date. PJ read the news, he mastered the drinking games, he watched all the latest television shows (even the ones with roses and contestants all living in one mansion). He was primed and prepped and prolific with conversation. PJ was, by all textbook definitions, a catch.

But even PJ knew that he'd always pale in comparison to the Peters twins.

His curse was that he genuinely *loved* hanging out with them.

Who didn't? Mac and Cam had a spark to them that couldn't be taught by caring parents or studied on the web. It was inherent, genetic. And both twins had it in spades— allegedly since birth. Mrs. Peters would fill Parents' Weekend conversations with tales of how, since infancy, her twin boys had been telling jokes. Giggling at punch lines that the other told in their secret twin language. Natural-born centers of any given crowd.

PJ wasn't immune to their pull. He'd met Mac and Cam during freshman orientation and was ecstatic when all three of them had been admitted into the same fraternity that next semester. They had a gregarious generosity to them, always making plans but making sure everyone was included. Their years at UVA were spent with PJ, Cam, and Mac sharing dorm rooms and homework assignments, whiskey handles and bow ties for football tailgates—a UVA tradition—and leftover Marco & Luca dumplings, a UVA specialty.

And for PJ, they were also spent with Mac's and Cam's leftover romantic pursuers.

Each weekend brought a new cycle of women who'd arrive at their house parties, eyes always eager with the same budding look as they'd scan the room for a Peters face. Cam was loyal, always, to the illustrious Liz at NYU. She was the envy and the scorn of many UVA coeds doomed to be selfishly disappointed in Cam's fidelity. Mac had started the term with claims of a long-distance girlfriend, but by the end of the year, it seemed the high school sweetheart he'd left at home had ended things for good. But even if and when one fortuitous prospect managed to connect with Mac, that always left at least a handful of partygoers hoping for a Peters romance and now looking for a consolation prize.

PJ could do the math.

The women who shrugged and made their way to him were perhaps inherently disappointed, but he always tried to treat them the very best he could. He was gentle and generous, refilling drinks and heating up pizza bagels and spinning them to any song choice, singing along. Sometimes they'd briefly fall for something in PJ, date him for a few weeks. But usually, they would stop the dance early or wake up the next morning with apologies and rushed goodbyes. A number saved but never called again.

Maggie let PJ kiss her, but then she pushed him away. He felt slightly embarrassed for an instant, but then it was over. Because he was used to it. By now, PJ was immune to the pain of rejection.

There was a sliver of surprise, though, for PJ hadn't pegged Maggie as a current Peters hopeful. Cam was newly engaged and permanently off the market, and PJ had barely seen Mac and Maggie in overlapping moments this weekend.

He'd only just met Maggie, but she seemed so independent, so tough. PJ had moved to Charlottesville from Columbus, Ohio, to pursue business at UVA, and now he was working in consulting at Deloitte, one of the Big Four. He knew what it felt like to walk away, to have to build a new ground control, far away, from scratch.

Maggie's skin had to be so thick, PJ knew. Not just from working in the entertainment industry and taking orders from hotheads, but more so from having to tell your loved ones that you needed something bigger, something they couldn't give you. That their proximity wasn't going to be enough. It hadn't been enough for PJ or Maggie, for anyone who transplanted for a dream.

PJ had been thinking about this as he kissed her. How hard it must have been for her to walk away from her high school friend group all those years ago. He had spent so much time with them since he moved to the city after college, Mac and Cam taking him under their wing, introducing him to their eccentric and bighearted East Meadow circle.

Introducing him to Maggie, their old friend, now home.

It was silly, but he'd wanted to kiss her from the moment he saw her at Penn Station. She was so effortless, so different. There was an electricity to her, and PJ liked it immediately.

Yet when he did kiss her, on that Ocean Beach dock, he knew something was off. Maggie pulled away and glanced back toward the bar almost immediately, disappointed and frowning, toward their friends dancing inside.

Toward Mac.

If life were a cartoon, PJ would have had a light bulb above his head. How could he have missed this? It was so obvious.

This was *Maggie*. Mac's Maggie. Of course. Cam and Liz were gentler, the sensitive pairing, but Maggie and Mac were bold. They were force fields. No wonder they circled each other even still. Two stars in orbit.

"I'm so sorry," Maggie said, wincing. "You're a really great guy."

"Don't be sorry," PJ said with practiced nonchalance. He was used to not taking this part personally. "Pretend it never happened. Let's go back to the party." He was used to it all.

As they tossed the pizza box in the trash can and opened the Sandbar's doors, PJ knew he'd be okay. After all, he had thick skin, too.

Chapter 9

I f only all of life's mistakes could be washed away with a thick stack of Clorox wipes and a spritz of Windex, Liz thought as she wiped crumbs off the kitchen counter and started scrubbing the pile of dishes that had accumulated in the sink. If that were the case, she'd have been spared the morning's headaches after last night's messes. Instead, as she loaded up the dishwasher and rinsed out the coffeepot, replacing the beans with a fresh brew, she tried to think about anything other than the disaster that last night became. Anything other than her fiancé.

She thought about all the work she had to do on her application when she got back into town.

She thought about the comforting shelves at Elegant Fabrics, the store she'd visit in the Garment District during lunch.

She thought about a new pear-and-ravioli recipe she'd try for dinner this week. A taste of Italy. Was that jinxing it? Or manifesting? (Was there a difference?)

Mostly, Liz thought about how she couldn't wait to get off Fire Island.

She'd assumed she was the first of the group awake that morning, so she was pleasantly surprised to see a bag of fresh bagels on the counter and two pitchers of iced coffee already stored away in the fridge by the time she got downstairs. Was this an apology from Cam? A belated gesture of goodwill from Maggie?

Liz was less pleasantly surprised when she read the accompanying note in Robyn's handwriting:

> *We had to head back super early for an unexpected appointment! Please accept these bagels (gluten free) and coffees (black or oat milk only—almond is killing the planet, people!) as a token of our gratitude for a fun weekend, and an apology for not sticking around to clean.*
> *XO Robyn and Mac*

They'd snuck out early without so much as a goodbye. Liz wished this wasn't recent par for the course with Robyn, but she seemed to be the queen of Irish exits. She silenced the tiny Maggie in her ear broadcasting the ways Robyn brought out an un-Mac-like side of Mac. He had always loved a long goodbye. He hated leaving any party early, especially a weekend getaway. They were usually the ones dragging Mac out by his heels.

Robyn was bringing out a different side of him, but Liz reasoned that different wasn't necessarily bad.

It was just new.

She put that out of her mind as she picked up around the share house. She was an anxious cleaner.

Last night had started out wonderful, which is what made Liz feel even worse. The air had been perfect, crisp and light. The sunset had exploded in shades of orange and pink. She and Cam had watched the sky from the bay before heading into the bar. He took a photo of her standing in front of the water, a candid smile on her lips. His sunset, his sun, he had said.

It was the type of June night that could make even cynics fall in love.

She and Cam had walked into the Sandbar hand in hand. They danced and sang, vocal cords straining in their necks, sore throats a souvenir. Cam knew every word to every song that had ever existed. It didn't even feel hyperbolic. He would change the lyrics to add their friends' names. "*Brenna* and Eddie were still going steady." "All I do is *Quinn, Quinn, Quinn* no matter what." He called himself the "Piano *Cam*" whenever the Billy Joel closer played.

Other patrons would look across the dance floor at Cam, obvious attraction in their eyes. Liz was used to it, but he never even noticed. He'd sing right at her, or keep a free arm planted around her waist. She didn't pay mind to the jealous stares. She didn't need to. It wasn't that she was proud to be with him, which of course she always was. She was simply proud *of* him. He was magic when he wanted to be.

Liz loved re-falling in love with Cam whenever she could.

She had found herself doing it again last night. That jolt of attraction, of appreciation. An out-of-body experience of looking at your partner and counting your lucky stars. He was the best decision Liz had ever made; she realized it again in that moment, watching him laugh and dance and sing. She loved Cam in a crowd, but mostly because it reminded her of the other sides of Cam, the juxtaposition of it; the Sandbar customers glimpsed the Saturday-night Cam, but she had so much more all to herself. She had the Cam who spent Monday nights watching *Jeopardy*, calling out every answer like a wizard in disguise (while both admitted to secret crushes on the game show villain, James). The Cam who would spend what felt like hours pouring, failing, and re-pouring batter just to get that perfect pancake flip. The Cam who could get so quiet, so pensive, so serious, it was like he was on the brink of discovering a new world.

The Cam who only Liz got to see and know and love.

No matter what else had happened, she had Cam. She had his entire spectrum, his shyness and his magnetism. She had his every part.

Now she was going to marry him. She was never going to be alone again.

In that moment, Liz decided that she needed to tell him the truth. She hated smiling at him while keeping the fellowship a secret. She resolved to bring it up soon, maybe during the band's next break. She'd be honest and ask not necessarily for his blessing (though she'd gladly accept that), but for his advice.

But then Cam did that thing that he'd started doing recently.

Scaring her.

It started when PJ joked that Cam and Liz should book the Sandbar's band, Tradewinds, for their wedding. Cam answered that his mom had already reached out to the Hank Lane band company, right at the same time that Liz said she'd actually prefer a DJ. It was awkward, sure, but it shouldn't have been that big a deal.

But after that, Cam's mood turned sour. He kept drinking, and the destruction followed. The yelling came later, as it too often did these days. It was so unlike him, all the screams, the anger. The arguments were nonsensical—that he didn't want to go home yet, that the band wouldn't play his song, though they never took requests, that Liz was being mean because she wasn't smiling as he made a scene.

Blue: the breakfast plate Liz was clearing the morning after in the kitchen.

Blue: Liz's pajama shirt last night, soaked with tears.

Crash.

The plate dropped to the floor. Pieces scattered across the tile.

"Shit." Liz kneeled to the ground to pick up the shards, willing herself not to cry again.

"Lizard, wait, I got it," Cam said. He'd appeared in the kitchen with a broom in one hand, a Ziploc bag in the other. He'd heard the crash and come running. Liz let him pick up the pieces. She was tired of being the one to play that part.

Once the plate was carefully discarded, Cam helped Liz finish with the rest of the cleaning, even as the remaining friends headed to the beach. Liz never minded cleaning, one of life's only sure successes. Easy wins. Together, they stripped the beds, started the laundry, emptied the trash. They were silent but their rhythm was natural.

They'd spent many nights like this after her mom was gone, wordlessly cleaning out casserole containers, emptying closets, getting the house and the store both ready to sell. Even when they were working in different rooms, they were somehow always aware of where the other stood. When Liz sold her mother's house, her store, when she packed up all those memories, she had never felt more alone. It was Liz's decision, but Cam held her hand every step of the way.

Cam was who she leaned on. Cam was who had saved her.

That's what hurt Liz the most. They were a good team. The best team. They had been for a decade. They had been through hell and back this year.

Why was Cam now risking everything? A quieter voice asked, why was she?

Liz was back at the kitchen sink again, handwashing the slew of water glasses and coffee mugs she'd found in the bedrooms. She used her elbow grease, pushing and scrubbing through her pain.

What if all of this was the wrong path? What if Cam was changing his mind, about Liz, about their life together? What if this was Cam repelling, regretting? What if she had put all her eggs in a trick basket?

Liz gasped slightly as arms found their way around her stomach.

Cam was hugging her from behind, his chin on top of her head. He pulled her in tight. She'd always loved when he held her that way.

"I love you," he said.

"I know," Liz said.

"I'm sorry."

She looked down at her ring, reflecting the window's light. She would need to get it tightened when they got back to Manhattan, the band was a size too large. Now the diamond was covered in dish detergent suds, the soap making it shimmer even brighter. It felt like a dagger. A reminder of all that could go wrong. By marrying Cam, was Liz making a terrible mistake?

She wished she could talk to someone. Sure, she had some college mentors, a few friendly coworkers, a distant cousin in Seattle who always liked her Instagram posts. But when it came down to it, Liz's support circle was, well, gone. Quinn and Brenna were too close to them all, too excited about the wedding, their friend group, to see the forest for the trees.

After Maggie left, and then her mom, Liz never let anyone in that close again. Anyone who wasn't Cam. She'd thrown herself into him. She'd lost herself in him alone.

Liz's heart broke open. She wished she could talk to her mom.

"I know I don't deserve you," Cam said. "Please trust me. I'm so sorry. Last night won't happen again."

Liz swallowed.

"I'm so, so sorry."

"Okay," she said, and Cam exhaled in relief. He kissed her cheek, and then her mouth, and then her ear and her hair and her nose.

"Okay," Liz said, despite all the apologies that were building. Each incoming sorry undercutting the worth of the last. For wouldn't "sorry" lose its magic if it happened all the time?

Chapter 10

rust me. This honestly happens all the time."

PJ's voice was earnest. She'd believed his every word.

As soon as Maggie woke up, she wanted to talk to PJ. To apologize for the mixed signals, to hope they could go back to becoming friends. And considering how this weekend had unfolded so far with Liz and Mac, Maggie knew she needed all the friends she could get.

It was early afternoon when she finally had a moment alone with him. Georgie was set up, once again working downstairs while the rest of the group finished packing after the morning's beach trip.

Maggie knocked on the bedroom door. "Can we talk?"

PJ took off his headphones when he saw her. "Sure, come in."

"Listen, about last night—"

"We really don't have to do this," he interrupted. "All's good."

"You're such a great guy, and it's been so great getting to know you—"

PJ groaned, but he was laughing through it, too. "You don't know how many times I've been told this. I really don't want to be told this."

"Cuz it's true."

"Yeah, yeah."

"Really. I'm just . . . I'm adjusting to being back home. It's all a bit more complicated than I thought it would be. I'm sorry."

"Trust me. I get it," PJ said.

"You do?"

"It's Mac, isn't it?"

Maggie's stomach did a jumping jack. She rested her head against the bunk bed's post. "No? Maybe? I don't even know anymore. He's with Robyn now, though, so it doesn't really matter."

Mac had spent the rest of the night ignoring her, pretending she didn't even exist. And then he'd left this morning without so much as a goodbye. Not just to her but to anyone. If she needed a signal that Mac had moved on, she'd gotten it in the form of an empty rental bedroom. Luggage gone, a discarded M&M's wrapper in the garbage.

"Maybe you can help me with something, then," PJ said. "While you figure things out."

"Yeah?" Maggie asked. "What's up?"

"Can you keep an eye on Cam and Mac with me? In the city when we get back, and the next beach weekends, too?"

Maggie's brow creased. "Why, what's wrong?"

"It's hard to explain," PJ said, "but I've spent so much time with these guys. I used to see Mac at Deloitte more, but we've been on separate cases so we're not even in the same building. But I can tell there's just something off these days, and I'd feel better knowing someone else was looking out. Especially if you still care about him, too."

Maggie couldn't deny a kernel of truth in PJ's words. She had noticed it with Liz and Cam on Friday. And while Maggie clearly had her opinions about Robyn's influence on Mac, she had never spent time with any of his previous girlfriends. Mac could have changed a hundred ways since the last time they'd spent uninterrupted time together. Yet if PJ, their most recent addition, sensed that something was wrong, then maybe Maggie should be worried.

She didn't need to be dating Mac to look out for him, to have his best interests at heart. She didn't need to be best friends with Liz and Cam to want them to have a perfect engagement, a happily ever after, a fairy-tale life. Maggie could repay them for the friendship they gave her in high school, reconcile the years she knew she could have, should have been better at staying in touch. She was back in New York for some reason.

Romance or not, she wanted to help.

"Will do," she said, nodding. PJ smiled in relief. "So, we're cool?"

"As a cucumber." He grinned.

Maggie rolled her eyes. "Jeez, no wonder you're not getting girls, with those lines."

PJ burst out laughing. "Tough, but fair."

"Twenty minutes till the ferry!" Brenna's voice rang through the house. Moments later, the friends loaded their duffels and suitcases back onto the rickety red wagon and headed to the Ocean Beach dock.

⁂

The town was crowded with reluctant travelers. No one enjoyed leaving the beach on a Sunday afternoon. Georgie handed out ferry tickets as Cam loaded the bulkier bags into the suitcase-check section on the ferry's lower level. By the time the friends weaved their way onto the boat and upstairs to the open-air deck, most of the aqua-blue rows were occupied by families and pets who'd arrived early enough to secure seats together.

Somehow, Liz found a row that fit almost their entire group. Space for almost everyone.

Everyone except for Maggie, who had been standing at the back of their line.

"You guys take this row, no problem," Maggie said, swallowing the burn. "I think I see a free seat in the back." She ignored Brenna's pout and scanned the crowd, looking for a patch of blue to call her own. The majority of seats had been taken already. When the singular space revealed itself at last, she sashayed down the aisle like in a round of musical chairs, pushing away the embarrassment of Liz's slight. Maggie exhaled onto the bench, ready to settle into the ride. Alone. She opened her phone.

A weekend wrapping up means reality crashes back tomorrow. The procrastination of the beach no more. I'm nervous, I'll admit it, to go back to a city where I'll build routine anew. To look for a new job, a new purpose, a new plan. But a part of me can't deny I'm excited, too.

Then Maggie's typing was suddenly interrupted by a finger, tap-tapping her shoulder.

She turned around to see Ty, in sunglasses and a Yankees hat, sitting in the row right behind her. Maggie immediately wished she had paid closer attention to the faces surrounding the spare seat before making her frazzled selection, but Ty must have been facing the back of the ferry, talking to one of his friends. Maggie hadn't had the opportunity to recognize his face and run.

"How was your weekend?" he asked.

"Fine," Maggie said, still facing forward. She couldn't believe she'd moved all the way to New York and still ended up next to Ty. It had been a few years since they'd connected, but Maggie had spent the majority of those first months of her career training to be an assistant under his tutelage.

He continued, "I always hate the ferry home. Wish we could stay forever."

"Reality calls," she said.

"Are you headed straight to the airport?"

Maggie paused here, raising her brows. She finally turned around to look at him. "What for?"

"To fly back to LA?"

"Oh." Her heart dropped a little. "No, I'm living here now."

"Wow." Ty faltered. "I hadn't pegged you as the type to leave so soon."

"Well, this is my first weekend back." She coughed, deflecting the feeling that she'd made some colossal mistake.

"You'll like it here, don't worry. I've been back for about two years myself. Got a job in documentaries, must've been shortly after you left the agency, now that I think about it," Ty said. "My coproducer and I have made a ton of great stuff since. One's even premiering at Tribeca next week. You know, the very prestigious film festival." He cocked his head.

"I'm familiar with it," Maggie said, rolling her eyes at his joke. He must have remembered how she could detail all the major film festivals and their recent winners before she'd even graduated. Still, when they first met, Ty would rib Maggie for her more commercial taste in film compared to his preferred highbrow documentary scene. "What's your latest project about anyway? How all humans are inherently awful?"

Despite having asked about his doc's content, Maggie really wanted to know if Ty had felt any embarrassment when he eventually moved home. If he'd felt like he'd fallen short on a prize, failed a test for which his friends all knew he'd spent years studying. Yet she anticipated what his answer would be. Ty was confident, convinced of his own actions, his surefire success. She was sure he regretted nothing.

Maggie tried to act like that, too. She wanted to be easy, to be extraordinary. To extrapolate the torpedo of impulsive energy often permeating her body and orchestrate it all with grace. If anyone called her effortless, she'd be honored. But she always feared she'd be humiliated, too, if they knew how much work went into acting like she had some sort of master plan. She loved feeling put together, but she hated how often that felt like a foolish version of pretending.

Regardless, Maggie knew that Ty definitely wouldn't understand how it felt like the air was whooshing out of her now, like she was suddenly deflating. She listened as he rattled on about his slate, his projects, his collaborators, his dreams. It was all working out for him, a picture-perfect plan. Her heart seized with something that felt like a useless mixture of envy and regret.

And then Ty said something that made Maggie feel much, much worse.

"So, did Robinson move out here, too? I'm sure you guys are constantly on the go with his production schedule. What's next on the slate? I assume you're shooting something in New York, right? That's why you're here?"

Maggie tried to respond, to correct his conjecture, but words wouldn't form in her throat.

"Fine, fine, I know he's so strict about that NDA," Ty continued, oblivious. Only worsening Maggie's nausea. "But when you're rich and famous, too, don't forget I helped get you that job in the first place."

She gave a winded, half-hearted laugh in reply. In truth, her tongue was stunned by the reminder. Ty *had* gotten her the Kurt job.

He had handed Maggie her misfortune on a silver platter.

Hindsight is twenty-twenty, of course; it wasn't so obvious at the time. Not when Ty was on a desk in the motion picture literary department, working as an assistant to the department head, film agent Ava Hollander. Ava's client list boasted some of the very best screenwriters and filmmakers the business offered. And when those masterminds needed new, tailor-made, agency-trained assistants, Ava Hollander was their first call.

That's exactly the call that Kurt had made.

Maggie remembered how it had felt like the opportunity she had been waiting for her entire life. To go from the mailroom straight to assisting the wunderkind Kurt Robinson, "cinema's next best filmmaker." His directorial debut had smashed its opening weekend at the box office, won prizes at festivals. A dazzling romantic comedy with speculative fiction elements, based on his own original idea. It was like *Her, Arrival,* and *Ordinary People* had somehow had a baby with *Forgetting Sarah Marshall.* It was incredible. Maggie had been in her senior year at UCLA when it premiered, and she watched it six times in the following month, loving every frame.

She immediately knew that she wanted to make movies like Kurt's. If she could learn from him, study his process, it would make everything—the move, the cross-country goodbyes, the heartbreak on her parents' faces—worth it and more. She needed to work for him.

Maggie pinched herself and crossed her fingers and applied. Then she begged Ty to put in a good word for her with Ava. In the mailroom, she had jumped at the chance to cover Ty's work whenever he needed help, whether he was renewing his license at the DMV or running late from a dentist appointment, or even interviewing for a new job, which was customary for agency assistants. Other times, Maggie would print Ava's scripts, organize her mail, pick up her afternoon pistachio croissant when Ty couldn't leave his desk.

At first, Maggie was hoping to put herself in the best position to take over his tenure on Ava's desk, if and when Ty secured said new job. Ava was one of the most powerful agents in the business, always nominated for *The Hollywood Reporter*'s "movers and shakers" index. And somehow, mind-blowingly, she'd taken a liking to Maggie.

So when Ty agreed and told Ava how Maggie had put her horse in the race for the Kurt assistant job, Ava called the filmmaker herself with a glowing recommendation. Ty had grinned at Maggie as they heard Ava make the call, whispering, "You're welcome." They both couldn't help but be in awe of how convincingly Ava could sell.

It had felt like all the pieces were falling into place at last.

Maggie's career finally getting started. An unprecedented rise, from mailroom to director's assistant. She could skip years, get closer to on-set experience, to real writing experience. To making her own work, next.

She had no idea her professional life had been peaking just so that it could all come crumbling down.

"Well, I've got a decent group of entertainment friends out here," Ty said now, pulling Maggie back to the ferry, where his voice was picking up volume to compete against the wind. "Non-scripted mostly, but some film folks, too. Give me your info, I'll add you to our Slack group."

Ty was naturally competitive, but he was often generous, too. He'd patiently taught her how to roll calls, even when the phone lines were blaring. He'd said he recognized a kindred spirit in Maggie, a skill, and he might as well use it to his advantage.

Was he doing that again now?

Maggie didn't have time to decide. She'd do anything to prevent the conversation from lingering on the topic of her old boss. Grabbing Ty's phone from his outstretched hand, she entered her details into his address book.

"So, more Ocean Beach weekends in your future?" he asked as she typed in her phone number.

"Yup. We have a share the weekend after July Fourth, I believe." Maggie handed his phone back, their fingertips grazing ever so slightly.

"Us, too," Ty said. "Perfect." His smile was so genuine it almost caught Maggie off guard. A part of her pushed to confess the truth about Kurt. About what he'd put her through. About her failure. She didn't feel right leaving the conversation with Ty thinking she still was on Kurt's payroll.

Yet the other, smaller but more selfish part of her enjoyed being thought of as a success, still. In the grind. On a path. She looked at the spark Ty had in his eyes. Would he be acting so kind if he knew how badly Maggie had botched her shot?

How she'd fallen off her career ladder and broken every bone on her way to rock bottom?

She didn't want to find out.

The ferry pulled into the Bay Shore dock just in time.

"Well, see you around," Maggie said, grabbing her bags and bolting down the stairs. She didn't look back to see if Ty even matched her exit with a wave. She couldn't risk it. She didn't exhale until she was safely on the David Bros. shuttle bus, the private transfer her friends had booked to drive the group back to the city. A one-way trip from Fire Island to Murray Hill.

Maggie rested her forehead against the window as the air filled with chatter, exchanges of "roses and thorns," high and low memories from the trip. The radio played "Mr. Brightside" and she heard Brenna and Quinn start to sing.

Maggie tried to control her breathing, to drift off to a *Pop Culture Happy Hour* podcast as the shuttle picked up speed on the highway, but her phone soon pinged with incoming texts:

Ty: See you next month, Maggie Monroe. (PS—This is Ty.)

(PPS—Join the Slack.)

Maggie felt her cheeks warm as the "Ocean Beach Buds" group thread chimed next, Mac's name sliding onto her screen:

Mac: Hey guys sorry we had to dip out early, but this weekend was a blast. Robyn and I can't wait for July.

Maggie groaned at the mention of Robyn. Reality crashing back, indeed. Mac last night, punctured by his rushed morning exit. What did all that mean for Maggie?

Then she saw a text that had arrived earlier, when she was on the ferry, distracted by Ty.

The most unexpected one yet.

KR: Maggie. Call me.

Maggie's eyes blurred. Not him. No.

Kurt was in the past. Locked away, forgotten. New York was her future.

New York was the only path that mattered.

She felt the PTSD crawling up her throat and instantly deleted the text message, heart moving before her brain could stop her.

There would be none of that now.

Maggie opened her Notes app. It was time to rewire, to rewrite:

Goodbye, for now, Ocean Beach. Thank you for your sun-soaked distractions, even if they left a bit of a burn. I guess it's time at last, for this next strange chapter of my reality to resume. New York, here we come. Settling into a new apartment, searching for a new job. Time to figure out how and where to fit in. I promise to tell you all about it when we're back here in July. Try not to miss us too much.

Already, Maggie felt a little better. Life was all in the word choice, right?

Wedding Bells are soon to be Ringing!

Please join us in celebrating the engagement of
Cameron Peters and Elizabeth Grey
As we toast to the beginning of their happily ever after.

Saturday, August 12th

6:00 pm at Maguire's Bayfront Restaurant
1 Bungalow Lane, Ocean Beach, NY 11770

Please see enclosure for ferry schedules and travel details

~~~~~~~

KR: Maggie, check your email.

KR: NDA. Remember that, from your very first day?

KR: You probably didn't read it. (Maybe you should've gone to law school, like your parents said. Ha.)

KR: Pay close attention to Section 14.

KR: This is your last warning.

~~~~~~~

WEEKEND TWO

July

Chapter 11

M aggie read the words and instantly wished she hadn't. Minutes ago, she'd promised to give anything a fair try. Where would she draw the line?

The past month in New York had been filled with the fast and furious settling of a new routine. The job search had been surprisingly fortuitous, the first of the ups in her first week back. A listing for a temporary bookseller position in Brooklyn quickly turned into a five-day-a-week commute to Cobble Hill, where she opened the indie store and spent the shift shelving books, or her favorite, chatting with customers and making recommendations. It was quieter than her previous jobs had been, and a part of her already was beginning to miss the chaos of the film industry. But for now, it was peaceful. She could write on the subway, essays or journal entries, the occasional poem. No screenwriting or prose; she wasn't ready for that yet. But still.

Maggie would ride the F train from Bryant Park to Bergen Street station eager for the bookstore's magic.

Sometimes after a shift, she would wander up and down Smith Street and listen to the way strangers' laughter danced off the concrete. It reminded her of Los Feliz, her home in LA, where the streets held mostly two- or three-story buildings, coffee shops, and family-owned restaurants. Nights in South Brooklyn had a similar ease.

But soon the lows of this new life followed. Maggie tried her best. She attended the Monday night trivia games, participated in the group chat's "selfie Friday" tradition, where everybody texted a photo at some point during their Friday with plans for the upcoming days off.

Just this past Tuesday, Maggie had spent the Fourth of July listening to the East River fireworks from her apartment's balcony (if one could call a fire escape a balcony; outdoor space was an area where LA certainly had NY beat). She'd started the night with the East Meadow friends, celebrating on Robyn's parents' penthouse roof, but Liz wouldn't look Maggie in the eyes, and Mac strangely left any room or conversation she entered, their June reunion on the Ocean Beach dock clearly forgotten. It was getting to feel a bit masochistic, putting herself directly in the path of pain. By the time the sky darkened, she took herself home.

She tried to stay true to her pledge to PJ. She wanted to keep an eye on Mac and Cam, she wanted to repair things with Liz, but it was all much easier said than done. Alone on the F train, though, Maggie found her peace. She didn't have to confront her confusing feelings for Mac, or her twisting guilt over her past mistakes with Liz.

Alone on the F train, she didn't have to rehearse all those procrastinated phone calls to her parents, who she still hadn't seen since moving home. They'd been on back-to-back business trips and were now in Italy with friends. Reuniting with their daughter was a low bullet point on their to-do list, it seemed. Maggie had only been back to her parents' house in order to drop off the Ford Escape, unable to afford Manhattan's parking fees. With an emptiness, she emailed her parents that the keys were back in the old hiding spot and called a taxi to the train station.

Alone on the F train, she didn't have to read the texts from Kurt, or the emails ominously forwarding her a copy of her signed NDA, all of which she'd routinely delete and ignore. She didn't address the sinking feeling that something bad was around the corner. Instead, she pushed it away, to the side, any direction that wasn't front and center.

Alone on the F train, she didn't even have to keep her focus on the road or reroute for LA traffic. Instead, she could close her eyes. Let the subway rock her worries. Let her brain dig deep, really dream, about where and who she wanted to be. She was beginning to feel comfortable charting new plans. Less on edge. Less raw. The need to run had left her pores; promise lay waiting in its wake.

One month home and she was ready to begin.

Now, as the Fire Island ferry pulled into port on a hot and humid Friday afternoon, Maggie decided to make the most of the weekend. She would smile her way through the inevitable interactions with Mac and Liz once they were all stuck in the same rental house. She'd be there for her friends, whether they wanted her or not. Maggie wrote a quick message of hope on her phone.

The air smells fresh. A sea-salt-covered chance. July in Ocean Beach: I promise, anything you throw at me, I'll give a fair and honest try. Let's see what stories you have in store.

Yet when Brenna and Quinn called Maggie's name from over where they'd raced ahead off the dock and toward the town square's bulletin board, she cursed her earlier promise.

Chance, as fate would have it, came in the form of a flyer.

THE FIRE ISLAND FILM FESTIVAL IS BACK!

Submit your short films by July 30th for consideration to compete. Finalists will be announced August 3rd. All accepted films will be screened at the Ocean Beach Village Community House on Sunday, August 13th. We hope to see you there!

It felt like a trap. Maggie's stomach flipped. Brenna and Quinn, however, were ecstatic.

"Maggie! How perfect is this?" Brenna said.

"What are the chances it's the same weekend as our August rental?" Quinn marveled.

"And the day after Liz and Cam's party."

"It's a sign. Your moon is in rising this month, yeah?"

Brenna nodded vehemently. "You have to enter. I bet you'll blow the competition out of the water. The *salt water*, that is! Get it?" She laughed at her own dad joke.

Of all the ups and downs the past month had brought, the hardest low had come in the form of movies. Glancing at the marquee for the Cobble Hill Cinemas still filled her with a sense of shame, and she feigned headaches during Brenna and Quinn's weekly movie nights. Movies, television, they mocked her in a foreign, uncomfortable way.

A reminder of a career she'd never have. A talent she'd miscalculated.

Competing in a short film festival, making another project? It felt like one part hope, nine parts chaos. She wanted to say yes, to try this out, too, but whenever she thought about opening the Final Draft screenwriting tool on her computer, she froze.

She'd close her eyes and see Kurt's face. She'd be consumed by the fear, the disgrace.

The Fire Island Film Festival was tempting, but her wounds were still too fresh.

She couldn't open herself to that chance of failure again.

"Sorry, guys, I don't think I'm up for it," she began, but she quickly realized Brenna and Quinn were no longer looking at her.

Instead, they were looking to the right of her ear, above her shoulder.

Maggie was hit by that familiar scent.

"Maggie Monroe. Was hoping I'd run into you today."

She turned to face Ty. "Lucky you, we're trapped on an island." He was grinning.

Ty had texted her a few times in the past month. Links to movie reviews or funny tweets comparing New York and LA. Still, she never joined that Slack group. One had to still *work* in the industry in order to join the industry Slack, she reasoned. Regardless, if Maggie was going to chart a new course, she didn't want any unnecessary reminders of the past.

Even if those reminders did look undeniably good in a Yankees hat.

He gestured toward the flyer. "You're signing up, aren't you?"

"I'm not so sure—" Maggie started with a sigh, only to be cut off by Brenna's voice.

"We're in the process of convincing her to do exactly that," Brenna said, her hand outstretched. "Brenna, Maggie's friend from high school."

"Ty, Maggie's friend from LA." Ty's introduction followed. "And future winner of the Fire Island Film Festival."

"Friend is a stretch," Maggie said with a smirk. Of course Ty was entering. Of course Ty had something prepared to submit. It was probably moving and beautifully shot and gut-punching with a message about saving the elephants or ending human trafficking. Something important. If Maggie could scrounge together a short film with such short notice and a non-existent budget, she'd be lucky if there was one good line of dialogue. One laugh.

She was rusty, but even when she'd been in her so-called prime, her projects were popcorn compared to the stories Ty produced. She tried not to feel insecure about the subject matter of her scripts and shorts, but they always lived in the realm of romance. Of happily ever afters. Of falling and flying in the least expected situations for love. Meet-cutes and getaways, set in a place exactly like this. Maggie swallowed the irony. These second chances, these handsome men, frustratingly reappearing at every turn. It was something she would write.

She needed to snap out of it. To tell Ty the truth about Kurt, which she had still (reluctantly) evaded. To remind Brenna and Quinn that her moviemaking days were over.

Yet before Maggie could find her voice, she saw Quinn extending her hand to shake Ty's. This time, it wasn't for an introduction.

It was accepting a dare.

"You're on," Quinn said.

"We're going to win this thing," Brenna followed.

"Challenge accepted," Ty said.

Maggie rolled her eyes. They couldn't be serious. "Wow, can't wait to see what you put together, Quinn."

"Well, if you guys want any pointers, we're staying at the Bamboo House. Happy to help out an old friend." Ty smiled his signature smile, knocked his shoulder against Maggie's. Goose bumps ran down her back as she watched him rejoin his group of friends, who had arranged their luggage onto wagons by the dock and were headed in the direction of their rental.

Once he'd rounded the corner and disappeared down the street, Brenna and Quinn erupted in giggles. "Please tell me you two hooked up in LA," Quinn said.

"Just colleagues. Barely even work friends. But no, I'm not making a short. Sorry to disappoint you on two counts," Maggie said. "Time for food. My stomach is growling so loud, it might just learn how to talk." She hoisted her tote bag onto her shoulder and led the charge down Bay Walk.

Well, it was more of a stroll than a charge. Everything seemed to take on more of a relaxed quality once on the island. Collars loosened, sleeves rolled up, hair free to blow in the wind. They passed the Scoops ice-cream store, Kline's gift shop with colorful Fire Island T-shirts in the window, the Ocean Beach Village Community House.

It felt warm, walking with Brenna and Quinn again, even though it also made Maggie deeply aware of what was missing: Liz, the fourth puzzle piece to complete their girl group of yore. The friends passed a boutique called A Summer Place and wandered inside. It was a store Liz would have insisted on venturing into. "This looks like something Liz would make," Brenna said, holding up a dress and reading Maggie's mind.

"Nah, too basic," Quinn said. "Liz's designs all have a certain spark."

"Or sparkle." Maggie laughed. "Remember in gym class in sixth grade, when she made us those uniforms for the badminton championship?"

"I'm not sure if you can count diamond-studded headbands as a uniform," Brenna said.

This was one of their friend group's favorite stories, the tale of how Liz and Maggie brought their team to badminton victory. All friend groups had their calling cards, stories told and retold so often that everyone had identical phrases memorized. *When Liz tightened her headband, it was all over from there!* Liz and Maggie had joined forces with Quinn and Brenna by the end of the fifth grade, paving the way for allyship through middle school and beyond. A true love match of its own kind, the way young girls cling to the people who make them feel protected even when their bodies are in the hellfire pit of pubescent change. Awkward noses and ears and haircuts, Abercrombie clothes they were constantly getting too tall for—Maggie's memories of those days glowed with nostalgia.

She missed it. She missed Liz, the simplicity of their friendship. Now everything felt convoluted, like whatever was going on with Liz and Cam. She wished she could get through to Liz long enough to help broach it.

But first, lunch.

Maggie, Quinn, and Brenna wound back toward the ferry dock to eat on Island Mermaid's outdoor deck, their favorite lunch spot, which was decorated with blue and red umbrellas. They ordered a round of seafood appetizers to share—steamers, crab cakes, mussels, clams on the half shell, fried calamari. When on Fire Island, Maggie thought, lean in. And thank god for summer Fridays, which had allowed them all to get here so early.

The sun shone down as a couple at the next table over couldn't keep their hands off each other, an empty rosé bottle next to their finished plates. Maggie couldn't exactly blame them. Ocean Beach was a romantic setting. There was something sentimental about it, something that made your heart overpower your brain, leaning toward love over logic. She had been feeling it since they'd stepped off the ferry. An appreciation, an urge, for the lovelier things.

As Brenna and Quinn fell into a mussels-versus-clams debate, Maggie pulled out her phone.

Is it just the way the sun shines down on these sandy streets . . . or is a part of me hoping, dare I type this, to fall face-first in love? My soul is itching. It wants something more. I never intended to be the girl next door on the movie screen. No, I wanted to be The Girl. The star, the lead. But then plans changed and life got busy, and my heart took second string. We're reshuffling priorities this summer though, it seems. Might it be time to let my heart soar?

She rolled her eyes. What prospect of love was there, anyway? Mac was taken, not to mention uninterested. Did dating apps work on Fire Island? All of this felt out of sync for Maggie, like riding a very old, should-have-been-recycled-a-decade-ago bicycle. She hadn't had a serious boyfriend since Mac. There had been suitors, surely. The drunken make-out sessions at UCLA. Crowded dance floors with strobe lights, hands on her hips and Avicii in her ears. Casual ways to blow off steam.

There hadn't been much room in her calendar for anything more serious than that.

In LA, Maggie was focused. She hadn't moved cross-country for the wellness shots or vegan options or to hike Runyon on Sunday mornings or to date a future movie star (though she wouldn't have complained if the latter fell in her lap). That's why long distance was never a possibility.

Maggie had moved to LA to work.

She had spent her teenage years feeling like she needed to prove herself. Like she needed to shine as brightly, scream as loudly as humanly possible to get an iota of attention. She'd ace her report cards and her parents would barely register the success. So she'd fail a test just to compare their reaction. She didn't know whether to be angry or relieved when the response was the same as it was for her wins: silence. Maggie kept pushing; she'd follow the rules one night, break curfew the next, just to see if anyone was paying attention. Nobody ever was.

When she got to NYU, she still felt restless, like she was following the path her parents had forced her on. They'd pay for NYU, but only if Maggie was prelaw. That was always the catch. They never understood her love of writing or her interest in film. They thought she was being reckless, childish. What were the job prospects? Making ten dollars per hour as a production assistant on set or pushing a literal mail cart at a talent agency upon graduation? Getting lunches and coffees for bosses for the next ten years? Why not just work as an usher at the theater in town forever, if she was going to throw away any real hope of career longevity? Of homeownership? Didn't Maggie want what they had?

By the end of that first semester at NYU, Maggie knew her answer. It was scary, but no. She needed more, something different. A change. Was that so selfish? Was she so ungrateful to follow this new rhythm that had started to soundtrack her heart? Maggie wasn't sure.

All she knew was that once she had the idea of transferring to UCLA, it was as if there was no other option.

She had to move. For an intoxicating career. For work that pushed her. To grow.

But also, to prove to her parents, to prove to everyone that she had something special in her. She had a spark. She was going to Make It Big. She loved her high school friends, but deep down, she also needed to see if there was something out there for her beyond the borders of their youth. A new story, an unexpected plotline, meant only for her. *Was* that selfish? To want to see what else life had to offer?

Maggie didn't wait around for an answer.

Even when she was a film student in LA, studying the canon and learning how to Save the Cat, writing screenplays for final projects and pulling all-nighters editing short films,

Maggie was always committed to her task. Days and nights, weekends and holidays, she was studying. She was writing. She was working.

She knew it was ironic, considering that love stories were the sorts of projects that had called her out to LA in the first place. Those were the scripts she'd work on in her free time. Nora Ephron and Rob Reiner movies kept her up late into the night. She would fall in love right alongside Sally and Annie and Kathleen whenever she could. In Maggie's postcollege world, she wasn't blind to the swath of new cute coworkers—like Ty, for instance, who she now remembered all the mailroom girls having crushes on—but her evenings were exclusively for networking. For meeting and dreaming with fellow industry hopefuls over dollar oysters, all they could afford.

For a long while, Maggie loved it. The focus, the adrenaline, the scrappiness. She was talented, but she was also driven, and she loved how satisfying it felt to work this hard and be this disciplined. It was no different, she assumed, than those early grinding years of medical or law school, any commitment where hustle was a symptom, a sacrifice. It was worth it for the finish line.

But now that was gone. And it was like her brain was still trying to compensate for a vacuum of energy, of attention and desire. Seven years later, and what did she have to show for it? All those sacrifices, all those blinders, all those missed plans and ignored relationships.

For what?

When the friends had finished eating, they heard the next ferry's engine as it floated into the dock. Maggie walked with Brenna and Quinn to the terminal, watching as the next batch of weekenders descended, including the rest of the Serendipity House.

Georgie and PJ were the first ones off, a case of Bud Light in each hand. Maggie's heart involuntarily jumped at the sight that followed: Mac and Robyn and Robyn's comically oversize sun hat drooping across her head. Mac's hair shone and a part of Maggie couldn't help but wonder if she was staring at yet another regret. Was the best happy ending something she'd already passed on?

"You made it!" Brenna waved.

"Where are Liz and Cam?" Quinn asked, the first to notice their absence.

"They're going to come tomorrow morning," Mac said with a shrug. "Cam said something came up."

"I bet wedding dress shopping ran late. It's so beautiful, being a bride." Robyn beamed, and Maggie's mind annoyingly imagined what Robyn and Mac would look like at an altar, hand in hand. Would things with Mac always have to feel this hard?

"I'm surprised to see you ladies here already," Robyn continued. "I would have thought you'd be out dress hunting with Liz. I guess she's more of a solo shopper, though."

Her words cut through Maggie. It was surreal that Liz was planning something as monumental as her wedding and Maggie had nothing to do with it.

Was she really dress shopping alone?

Maggie hated that she didn't know the answer.

"I've always wondered about the practicality of wedding dress shopping," Georgie said as the friends started walking toward the Serendipity House, dragging the wagon filled with their weekend luggage behind them. "It makes for great sequences in movies, but can it be that simple in real life? Or even that enjoyable? Take *Wedding Singer*, for instance."

"Or *27 Dresses*," Maggie added, determined to focus on the conversation, and not on how Mac and Robyn had somehow already splintered from the group so Robyn could take a call.

"And don't forget the Carrie closet scene in the *Sex and the City* movie," Brenna piped in.

"Objection," Quinn said. "That's just a regular fashion montage. Not wedding specific."

"Overruled," Maggie teased. "Same energy applies."

"Is it as fun in real life, do you think?" Brenna asked.

Maggie paused. "We wouldn't know, I guess. Never been before." The ache of Liz's absence started to rise through her again.

Luckily, her phone pinged with a distraction.

Ty: Hey hey. If we hypothetically had a party tonight, would you hypothetically want to come over? Your whole house is welcome.

Ty: But no taking video footage for your short. I know, you'll think all my friends look like movie stars. (Myself included, naturally.)

Maggie's heart sped up ever so slightly. Wasn't this what she'd been waiting for? A dare, a diversion. A new plotline for the evening. A way to keep her mind off everything else.

"What do you guys say about mixing up the locale tonight?" she asked her friends. "We just got invited to a pregame at the Bamboo House."

Georgie's eyes instantly lit up at the prospect and Maggie knew how to reply.

Chapter 12

Georgie was having the time of his life at the Bamboo House party until he started bleeding. The injury was extra painful because it was the first time all summer that he felt like he might have found his shot at love.

Growing up, Georgie had always believed in love. Happy endings were never just a hypothetical. He knew every word to *Notting Hill* and had practically memorized *Pride and Prejudice* by the age of twelve. He was a sucker for romance films, for kissing in the rain, for tear-soaked apologies and the sweeping reconciliations that always seemed to follow them.

It wasn't Georgie's fault. He'd been raised by a relationship straight from the storybooks. His parents, George Sr. and Georgine, had grown up in the same town but were sent to different private high schools. They went to the same university, but never crossed paths. Later, they'd piece together that they'd even attended many of the same Rolling Stones concerts and Giants games. Star-crossed strangers. Even their names were matches. But it wasn't until a share house on Fire Island that they'd finally met and fallen instantly, madly in love.

Georgie was ready for his own story to begin. He wanted a romance like his mother and father's. A love that felt happenstance but was always meant to be. Something predestined, something revelatory, something fortune had planned. That was why he'd enthusiastically supported Mac's pitch for a return to Ocean Beach this summer. Why he'd spent weeks helping him research rentals until an occupancy at Serendipity House popped up like fate.

Fire Island had worked for his parents. Was his romance waiting on deck?

Yet when Georgie was presented with the first moment all year that felt like it could have been love, or at least a step toward it, he was tragically disappointed to realize he was bleeding all over the Bamboo House kitchen counter.

Profusely bleeding.

And while Ocean Beach may have had romantic origins in spades, it was certainly lacking in its emergency room capacity.

Georgie's Friday night plan was simple, he had decided on the ferry ride over. It was time to take back his life. Earlier in the day, he'd called in sick to work. He hadn't slept in three weeks, and the case didn't even go to trial. He was desperate for a break.

When Maggie shared the invitation to a party at her

friend's house, Georgie took it as Sign One. He insisted they attend. True love didn't live for Georgie in the Serendipity House. Brenna and Quinn were like his sisters, and since everyone suspected that Mac was still nursing a lifelong crush on Maggie, even though it had been years since she'd broken up with him, she was off-limits.

No, if Georgie was going to find love in Ocean Beach, he needed to look beyond East Meadow's borders.

The party at the Bamboo House seemed like the perfect place. Georgie could hear the music before he even walked up the porch steps. Inside, two dozen or so beautiful faces were a billboard for youth. It was a house member's birthday, Georgie realized, so there were banners and balloons, and something called birthday cake shots being handed to anyone who walked in. Georgie downed the sugary drink gladly. He loved every second of it.

He loved every second of dancing to a catchy song in the kitchen, of making small talk by the spinach-and-artichoke dip, of commenting on the Mets game on the TV in the living room corner. They were winning, somehow. Thank you, Conforto. Sign Two for a magical evening.

He loved every second of not looking at his work phone, of not mistaking random sounds for phantom rings, of not worrying about doing anything so enchanting that he might forget to refresh his email, to answer a late-night demand from his boss.

He loved every second of meeting the brunette goddess

Charlotte. She was petite and smiley and wearing a sequin tank top with high-waisted denim shorts. It was her birthday, she told him, and he was cute. Did he want to make her a margarita?

Georgie nodded. Absolutely. She guided him by the hand toward the kitchen. She pulled ingredients out of the cabinets and fridge—chilled tequila and orange liqueur, coarse kosher salt, and a handful of limes. Something sweet, agave, to add at the end.

She asked about his family and his childhood dog and his favorite place to eat in the city. She didn't once ask him about his job, and Georgie thought he might have fallen just a little bit in love right then and there. Was this Sign Three?

Who needs law firms? Georgie thought as he pulled a paring knife from the wooden block on the counter.

Who needs corporate jobs and billable hours and partner tracks? Georgie thought as he put the limes on the cutting board.

"Who needs any of it?" Georgie realized he was speaking the words aloud now, waving the knife in the air.

"Who needs the law? All I need is love," Georgie said, knife still outstretched, prepared to slice open the lime placed squarely in front of him, which he held steady with his other thumb and forefinger. "Hey! Like the Beatles, baby! *All I need is love!*"

He sang and he swung the knife down, missing the lime completely. Hitting only his thumb. Charlotte fainted at the sight.

Love wasn't Georgie's fate. Not tonight.

"He's bleeding!" someone called out.

"Where are the Band-Aids?" another voice cried.

Georgie just stared at Charlotte's perfectly symmetrical face, passed out on the floor. Her friends were patting her forehead with a wet towel as she slowly came to. Her eyes fluttered and her brows were damp, and Georgie still thought she looked perfect.

"Happy birthday," was all he could manage, as Mac and Maggie pulled him aside and tried not to panic about the state of their friend's bloody thumb.

"I can't find any Band-Aids here," Maggie said.

"I have some back at the house. Never travel without them," Mac said. Georgie was grateful his friend was an athlete. Athletes were more prepared for injuries than sleep-deprived paralegals.

"I'm so sorry, guys," Georgie said, the pain starting to announce itself. The alcohol had delayed it, but not enough. "This fucking hurts."

"Let's get out of here. Do you think he needs a doctor?"

"Are there even doctors on Fire Island?" Georgie said, trying to stay calm.

"I think he'll be okay. Cam cut himself like this once when we were kids. Just need to compress and to ice," Mac said. He had his superhero voice on, but Georgie wouldn't make fun of him for it this time.

"You guys are seriously leaving already?" Robyn's lower lip was pouted out, her hand on her hip. "That's so lame."

"He's bleeding. What do you want me to do?" Mac asked.

"Have someone else help him!"

"He's my friend."

"It's okay," Maggie cut in. "We're just getting some Band-Aids. We'll be right back."

"Whatever." Robyn turned and left.

"I'm sorry, man, you don't have to come," Georgie said, but Mac just shook his head.

"Are you kidding? Of course I'm coming with you."

"Let's get a move on, boys. He's still bleeding." Maggie steered them in the direction of the front door, where a tall guy with black hair stood. "Thanks for having us. Sorry for the mess," she said. Her voice was lighter than normal, her cheeks a little rosy. This must be Ty, the one who had invited them in the first place. The one who, in doing so, had dangled the opportunity for love in Georgie's face.

Walking back, Georgie wondered if maybe he wasn't meant for a happy ending. All his life, he'd been told to work hard. To succeed. Then he'd be happy. He had worked tirelessly for years. He'd gotten the best grades, the best test scores. He'd given up nights and weekends and free time. Adulthood was one long stretch with no summer breaks in between. July was the same corporate mundanity, only the commute was hotter.

When was it going to be the good part?

Were happy endings a scam? Georgie wondered morosely, as Maggie tightened a Band-Aid around his thumb. The bleeding had started up again when they'd gotten back to their share house.

Georgie couldn't stop worrying as he lay down on the couch, resting his head on a throw pillow. Were his parents the exception, and not the norm?

His eyelids fought to stay open, flickering against themselves like a camera's quick lens.

He ignored the snapshots of Mac and Maggie staring over him.

And then the snapshots of them staring at each other.

He didn't need to see how Mac still looked at Maggie with that sparkle in his eye. The same sparkle his parents shared. His grandparents. Everyone else so happy.

Georgie let his own eyes close, his vision fade to black. He'd drift to sleep. If he couldn't find love in Ocean Beach tonight, maybe he could find love in his dreams.

He wasn't ready to give up entirely.

He'd find his happy ending one day.

Just not today.

Chapter 13

Wedding planning should come with a hazard warning, Liz thought to herself as the wind whipped her hair. Wedding planning was nothing like the dream that all those movies made it out to be.

She and Cam were seated on the upper deck of the ferry, where a blond goldendoodle with big brown eyes grinned goofily at her from across the aisle. His mouth was wide open, a pink tongue slipping out with each pant. The red bandanna tied around his neck read "Meet Me on Fire Island." His owner held the leash like a clamp, the dog practically buzzing, as eager to jump off the ferry and leap toward a beach weekend as the humans on board.

"What's his name?" Liz asked the dog's owner.

"Sunny," she replied with a smile.

Liz gestured to the gorgeous day, the gorgeous bay. "Fitting," she said.

She wished she could appreciate the simple joy of this moment, but she was still a hundred miles away, back in New York.

Yesterday had started out fine enough. After weeks of dodging to-do lists and half-heartedly participating in the daily "Peters Plan" Wedding Summit calls, where Roseanne and her assistant, Meghan, debated the merits of low-rise floral centerpieces versus tall ones, with fancy verbiage Liz was sure they used but was never inclined to remember, she finally made the only appointment to which she was genuinely looking forward:

Dress shopping.

She called the boutique and scheduled the appointment for only one. No guests, no bridesmaids, no friends, no parents. Only Liz.

The one person whose taste Liz had ever trusted was her mom. She'd never had any sisters to shop with, to share hand-me-downs. Liz's dad had picked up and left, ditching their family and any responsibilities of fatherhood before she could walk, but it didn't matter. Loneliness had been a rarity in the Grey household. Nancy had made even an empty room feel full with her loud Brooklyn accent and infectious, generous laughter. Mother and daughter alike had earth-shattering bellows that charmed any who passed. Nancy would sneak the "Closed" sign on Grey's Garments, her alterations and custom gowns studio, pick up Liz early from school, and the two would spend the late afternoons spinning around any vintage rack they could find. They'd take the train to the city and run their hands along the bolts of fabric at S&J Garments. They'd envision their next designs as they walked down Eighth Avenue, a street hot dog in one hand, a bag with their successful finds in the other. Mother and daughter both dreaming of fabrics and dresses, the clothes they would make.

Maggie used to join, Liz hated to remember now. Their next-door neighbor never missed an excuse to grab her camera and a notebook and explore beyond their Long Island enclave. Maggie's parents were hardly around, always working late evenings at their law firm downtown. They never encouraged Maggie's filmmaking itch. Instead, Maggie and Liz often spent their after-school time together. They both sought inspiration, creativity. It was probably why the two of them got along. Well, why they used to get along.

Before it all.

Her nerves danced again, so she looked for a color.

White: the foam hugging the bay waves as the ferry cut through the water, propelling toward the Ocean Beach dock.

White: the dress Liz never thought she'd have to try on by herself.

"You should have asked my mom," Cam had said Friday morning, over coffees in their dollhouse-size kitchen. "Or Brenna or Quinn or Maggie, even."

"Maggie would never come," Liz said.

"Hell, Robyn would probably go with you! It's not too late." Cam was smiling, but the concern was clear as day.

"The appointment is in a few hours. It's too late," Liz had said, shrugging between sips. "Plus, I want to do this myself. Unless you want to come?"

Cam shook his head fervently. "Do you want bad luck? I'm not seeing you in that dress until you're walking down the aisle."

Tradition didn't mean as much to Liz. Sure, she had day-dreamed about marrying Cam, about a house and a family and a marriage license, even, but she didn't care about escort cards or guest lists or venue uplighting or entrée selections. She just wanted to marry Cam. What did the other elements matter?

Cam disagreed, though. So far, he'd thrown himself head-first into every wedding task at hand. He loved the planning summits and had even downloaded Pinterest to make mood boards for his tuxedo and his groomsmen's shoes, at his mom's behest.

Liz wished she could match his excitement level, but there was something when it came to wedding planning, something that she couldn't or didn't want to articulate. When she found herself thinking about it, she pushed the words down and away into the darkest corners of her mind.

She wouldn't let herself go there.

Until she tried on the first dress at Amsale Bridal. She'd selected a beautiful princess dress, a classic ball gown. It was strapless with a full flouncy skirt.

It was also suddenly wrinkled. And slightly wet.

Because Liz was sitting on the dressing room's three-inch pedestal, her knees pressed against her chest, dress pooled around her. And she was crying.

It had hit her like a ton of bricks.

She couldn't do this without her mom. She didn't want to do this without her mom.

Why had she thought she'd be able to do any of this without her mom?

The selection was overwhelming. So many styles and shapes and silhouettes. Liz trusted her own taste, but it wavered amid the hundreds of dresses, crowded on dozens of racks.

The store owner had raised his eyebrows when Liz confirmed she'd be shopping alone today. She accepted the single free glass of prosecco he poured—"Just one? Really?"—with a judgmental stare, but Liz had felt independent and strong.

Now, as she wiped her face and dried off her cheeks, she took a sip. Still on the floor. She tasted the bubbles and tried not to harp on how everything felt broken. Empty.

She hiccupped and heard a voice.

"Liz? Are you back here?"

Liz gasped. Was it the store owner checking on her already? Were her silent sobs audible from the store's sitting room?

No, Liz reasoned. The owner was a man, and the voice piercing through the dressing room wings sounded feminine. It couldn't be her mom, so maybe . . .

Was it Maggie?

Liz couldn't believe that was her next thought. Did she *want* it to be Maggie? She closed her eyes and saw a flash of what the day would have looked like if she'd fulfilled her high school promise of Maggie as her "Mags of honor." If the two hadn't fallen out and drifted apart, but instead had stayed best friends. Like sisters. Would Maggie have selected gowns that matched

Liz's style? Would she have taken photos of Liz twirling, posing with those "I Said Yes to the Dress" signs? Would Maggie have held her hand while Liz cried?

It didn't matter.

Because a whoosh of the curtain slamming into the cubby's wall revealed the voice's source to be Roseanne Peters.

It was Cam's mom.

"Mrs. Peters?" Liz stammered at the sight of her future mother-in-law, designer sunglasses on her face, straight blond hair blown out, intimidatingly attractive even in athleisure.

Roseanne's jaw dropped at the sight of Liz, balled up in the corner, eyeliner running and nose red from crying.

"Oh, honey," she said, pulling Liz up into a hug.

Liz didn't know what was happening. Was this some sort of fairy godmother of wedding dress shopping? A maternal force when she unexpectedly needed it most?

"I know this is a lot. This is hard," Roseanne murmured, and Liz let herself be held a little tighter. She let herself whimper a tear-soaked exhale onto Roseanne's shoulder. "We'll find your perfect dress," Roseanne continued. "There's nothing to worry about."

It was like the record had been scratched mid-symphony.

"What?" Liz mumbled.

"No more tears over dresses, young lady. Unless they're happy tears, of course!" Roseanne didn't even notice Liz's face grow paler as she took in the ball gown Liz was still wearing, looking her up and down. "Let me go talk to the owner, I'll grab some options that feel a bit more . . . you. We can do better than this!"

Alone again in the dressing room, Liz felt like she'd had the wind knocked out of her.

She didn't take a deep breath and count to ten. She didn't scan for a color and remember a memory, the way her therapist had taught her. She didn't stretch her face into a smile and brace for the pretend.

Instead, she shimmied out of the gown and threw on her jean shorts and old Jones Beach concert tee faster than she'd ever gotten dressed in her life. She raced down the hallway, into the store, and out the door, leaving behind a frazzled Roseanne shouting "*Liz!*" while the disgruntled owner rolled his eyes. Liz knew she had made a scene, but she didn't care. She had to get out of there.

She sprinted the twenty blocks back to her and Cam's apartment and swung their door open with a shout. "Why was your mom at my fitting? Was she just standing on the street, waiting for me to mess up or something?"

"She asked me when you'd scheduled it for, and I guess, yeah, she texted me this afternoon confirming. I figured it was just part of her job. But wait—did you say she showed up at your fitting?" Cam's voice trailed from behind the bedroom door. He sometimes worked from home on Fridays and had made a makeshift desk out of the radiator next to the bed. Liz felt her heart speeding up, her breath shallow from the race home. She knew that Roseanne Peters prided herself on being a supportive, detail-oriented mom. And she was grateful, truly, that Roseanne was offering her expert planning skills on their behalf. But this was all starting to feel like too much. It hadn't been this intense, this exhausting, before the engagement. Liz wasn't sure how to reconcile this behavior now with the before.

"Yes, Cam," she called out, between pants, as she walked down the hallway to their bedroom. "It was humiliating. I wasn't ready for that—"

She opened the door, but the sight was so startling that she couldn't finish her sentence.

Cam was in sweatpants, under the blankets. Hair misaligned. Eyes empty.

In the middle of the afternoon.

"What's wrong, do you have a fever?" Liz rushed to the side of the bed to feel his forehead, but other than a little moisture from presumably an afternoon nap, Cam's head felt normal.

It was everything else that was far from it.

"Just feeling a little tired," was all he could manage back. "I didn't think you'd be home for another half hour at least."

"Sorry," Liz said, though she wasn't sure what for. How could she transfer her anger onto Cam when he looked so helpless, so hopeless? "What happened? Do you want to talk about it?"

"No, no. It's fine. Everything's fine," he said. "I guess we should pack if we're going to make the five p.m. ferry?" he continued, changing the subject, but his voice was drained.

"I'm exhausted, honestly," Liz said, still frozen at the doorway. "Can we just go tomorrow?"

"I guess so," Cam said. "Yeah, sure thing."

"Okay."

"Okay."

She turned and left him like that. Later, they ordered Chinese takeout, silently slurping noodles while watching reruns of *Seinfeld* on the couch. Cam fell asleep by nine p.m. and Liz hated that she let him sleep out there all night.

Now they were on the Saturday ten-thirty-a.m. ferry to Ocean Beach, and Liz had to remind herself to reapply her fake smile every few hours as if it were sunscreen. She ignored the incoming voicemails and texts from Mrs. Peters. She ignored the "weekend agenda" planning e-mail from Roseanne's assistant, Meghan. Instead, she looked right at Sunny the goldendoodle, who seemed to mock her with his unfailingly happy gaze. Never had Liz envied the life of a dog more.

Cam sat next to her, and he looked like a different person entirely from yesterday's fog. Whatever it had been, he was back. His easy smile, his charismatic grace. Liz couldn't help but wonder if she was marrying a professional pretender.

"He's adorable," Cam said to the owner, who grinned with puppy-parent pride.

He leaned closer still to Liz, lowered his voice to a whisper. "Liz, I'm so sorry. My mom is so sorry. She's calling and texting nonstop. She feels like an idiot, for not realizing what you really were—"

"It's fine," she said, cutting him off. She couldn't get into any of that again.

She had something else to focus on.

When Cam wasn't looking, she slipped out her phone and angled the screen out of his view. A few touches with her fingertips and her inbox refreshed. She bit her lip when she realized there were no new emails.

It had been a week since Liz had applied for the Domus Fellowship, having been encouraged by her professor and the program website's FAQ to apply early, to take advantage of the rolling admissions cycle. She'd seen a Reddit forum of candidates celebrating their acceptances over the past few days. It reminded her of her college-prep era, when Liz would scan message boards for commiserating posts about SAT questions, debating answer choices. A perfectionist through and through, Liz would crave her results immediately after any standardized test.

The Domus process was no different. Now that some contenders had received hopeful welcomes, Liz wanted hers, too. Would she find out this weekend? Could her acceptance come next?

How would she tell Cam?

Despite the sinking feeling in her stomach, Liz had decided that she wouldn't worry Cam with the program information unless it was serious. Unless she was admitted. It was a secret, but it wasn't selfish, she told herself. Their schedule was hectic enough already, with summer travel and work and the incessant wedding planning. Through it all, her fiancé still didn't seem himself, hadn't shaken off whatever funk had clouded his mind so far this summer. For all Liz knew, he was keeping secrets from her, too.

Why stir the pot if the water wasn't boiling?

A warm lick on Liz's ankle pulled her mind back to the ferry. Sunny had taken advantage of a momentary lapse in his owner's leash stance and bolted across the aisle, directly to Liz. Enamored, she reached down to scratch behind the dog's ears, allowing him to lick her calf.

Cam leaned over, too, smiling as he gave the dog some rubs. "You're the cutest thing, aren't you?"

There was an ease to this. A ferry ride with her fiancé, a dog by their side.

Life could be sunny.

Yet somehow Liz couldn't shake the restlessness that had taken residence in her body. Nothing felt right anymore. Nothing as sunny as it should have been.

She wished she'd hear back about the Domus program soon. Was Milan her destiny? Liz didn't know how else she would satisfy this newfound yet undeniable craving.

An itch to escape.

Chapter 14

Ever since escaping LA, Maggie had stopped expecting things to make sense. So when Mac texted the Ocean Beach chat weeks earlier suggesting a "Christmas in July" group theme for the Saturday beach day, she knew better than to question the instructions. Instead, she ordered a Christmas-themed bikini online, paying extra for two-day shipping. Maggie always loved a costume moment.

She hadn't expected, however, that Mac had learned of the themed celebration from an Instagram post, encouraging holiday gear for *all* Ocean Beach residents and tourists alike.

"This is great footage for Maggie's short," Brenna said.

"I'm not making a short." Maggie's reminder fell on empty ears. The group's focus consumed instead by the festive sight across the sand. Bathing suits were paired with red-and-white hats or reindeer antlers, and some even had stockings hung on the backs of beach chaises. Mac blended right in, his Christmas-tree-print tank top sharing in all the festive spirit—but none of the heatstroke potential—of the handful of (very) committed participants in full-fledged Santa Claus outfits. Beards and all. Maggie typed as their group planted chairs in a semicircle, facing the incoming waves:

Christmas in July gives holiday magic to the hot summer sun. Beach umbrellas double as mistletoe, white sand the first fall of snow. What gifts will these Santa Clauses leave below my beach chair? Beards optional, of course—tan line at your own risk.

Maggie chuckled to herself, before Quinn sent an elbow to her rib.

"See, look, she's writing our script already," Quinn teased. "I'm going to be a *star*."

"Leave me alone," Maggie groaned, plopping into her beach chair. "You guys make your own short film if you care so much."

"We just want you to be happy," Brenna said, softening. "And we know how much it always used to make you happy." She squeezed Maggie's hand from across the chair.

"And think of how happy *we'd* be, watching you win that thing," Quinn said.

Maggie sighed. "You're right. Maybe. I'll think about it."

As her friends scattered to dip their feet in the water or walk the shoreline, Maggie tried not to eavesdrop on Robyn and Mac, bickering back by the entrance steps. Were they still arguing about last night?

The Bamboo House party had been surprisingly fun. Through the night, she was grateful that conversation with Ty never steered back toward Kurt, that she never had to dance around the truth about her job's crash ending. Instead, she let herself be charmed by his friends' jokes and cocktail recipes, by Ty's uncanny ability to quote verbatim lines from her favorite shows. It was easy. It was fun.

Yet all the while, Maggie couldn't help but notice how Mac kept an eye on her throughout the room. It was so unexpected, she assumed she was fabricating it all in her head. She would look up and catch Mac staring, eyes drawn to hers across the kitchen like magnets.

So when Georgie's injury sent them walking back down the road to the Serendipity House, Maggie strangely didn't mind. She felt a bit guilty for cutting her conversation with Ty short, but she couldn't pretend it wasn't nice to stand so close to Mac again, even if it had taken their friend nearly chopping off his thumb to make it happen. Once Georgie had fallen asleep, Maggie suggested they head back to the party, back to Robyn, but Mac said he wasn't ready yet. He didn't want Georgie to wake up alone. Instead, they settled on the couch and turned on the TV. Fortuitously, the cable channel was playing a rerun of their beloved *Cash Cab*. The screen glowed like it had senior year.

A few hours later, Maggie woke up and realized she'd fallen asleep with her head resting easy and gently on his shoulder.

Mac's knee pressed, hard and warm, against her own.

She tiptoed upstairs, all too aware of the goose bumps that had spread over her body.

His skin on hers again, in all the familiar places.

Now, under the rays of sun on the beach, Maggie remembered last night, and it made her flush. But Mac was with Robyn. She had to move on.

This was all too much. She needed an escape.

Rummaging in her beach bag, Maggie pulled out a worn paperback. Jane Austen's *Emma*. Her favorite. It used to be her mother's favorite, too, back when they shared favorite things.

When Maggie showed the first inkling of creative interest as a child, her parents were surprisingly supportive. They gave Barnes & Noble gift cards and notebooks for birthdays. In fact, this *Emma* copy was once a Christmas present, taken on a family trip back when holidays were happy. Back when they still believed their daughter would follow their path down the road of corporate law and take over the family practice.

When Maggie dashed their NYU dreams and took out her own loans to transfer to the UCLA screenwriting program, the writing-themed gifts officially stopped coming. By the time she graduated and got a job in LA, most calls had stopped, too. They didn't understand her, that much was clear. They couldn't relate.

Through it all, Maggie dove deeper into her work, doing the best she could to prove her choice was worth it. But her parents had given up, they'd changed the channel.

They had stopped watching a long time ago.

How could they possibly have seen her shriveling away?

Thinking about her old job still made Maggie compulsively check her phone. Even though she hadn't worked for Kurt in over a month, she was finding it hard to shake that feeling of always being on the clock, of making sure she hadn't missed a call or text with some new urgent assignment. It was trickier than she'd expected to detach from all of his strings. Especially when she blinked and considered those most recent texts from him that she had deleted. When would he finally leave her alone?

So, when Maggie heard Liz's sudden shouts from down by the water, she was washed with relief. Liz sounded panicked, but at least it was something else to think about.

She found Liz at the edge of the ocean, soaking wet, tears streaming down her cheeks.

Maggie hadn't even realized that Liz had made it to the beach. She'd been quiet since her and Cam's ferry arrived, mentioned staying back at the house to finish some work. Something must have happened since. "What's wrong?" Maggie asked.

"My—My—ring," Liz stammered, between suffocating sobs.

Maggie's stomach sank. "It's not on your finger?"

Liz just shook her head back and forth, eyes pooling.

"When did you see it last? Retrace your steps."

"I just wanted some air. I went for a swim. I wasn't thinking."

She started pulling her fingers through the sand, looking wherever she could. "I knew I should have gotten it resized."

"When do you remember wearing it last? Is there any chance it's back at the house?" Maggie asked, while getting on her hands and knees to scour the sand, scavenging through the shells and seaweed.

"Do you think Cam will call off the engagement?" Liz's voice was low, filled with fear.

"What? Never. Never," Maggie said, looking right at her. "We'll find it."

"This is impossible," Liz said, her lip quivering.

Maggie wanted to help, but finding a lost ring at the beach was like finding a needle in a haystack. If this were happening in one of Maggie's screenplays, she'd write in one of those metal detector enthusiasts, a beachgoer with a comically large sun hat and a penchant for lost and shiny things. He'd find the ring in record time and offer cryptic yet heartwarming advice about love being found in the least expected places.

Yet after forty-five minutes of digging through the sand, checking the seaweed deposits with each wave, all underscored by Liz's staccato sobs, Maggie knew this wasn't anything like the movies. This was real life, and there were no quick fixes, no easy solves.

Liz must have arrived at the same conclusion, because she suddenly stopped her futile searching and hung her head in her hands. Soaking wet from vain attempts to search the waves. Shoulders heaving.

She'd given up.

There'd be no finding the ring now.

Maggie approached, tentatively placed a palm on her heart-broken friend's shoulder, not knowing what else to do. "Want to go back to the house, maybe? Get out of the sun for a bit?"

Liz nodded, wordlessly agreeing.

The girls walked back to the house in slow steps, as Maggie remembered how it felt to be in lockstep with their past: playing dress-up after school in Liz's basement when Maggie's parents had to work late. Pulling all-nighters to finish AP US History essays after spending an entire weekend rewatching old movies, re-creating costumes from their favorite scenes. Writing and re-writing text messages to Cam when he and Liz had just started dating. Maggie held her BlackBerry when Liz was too nervous to type. They'd celebrate with Friday night milkshakes and Buffalo Blasts in the Colony Diner's parking lot, counting sub-urban stars. High schoolers who felt like their friendships, their love, their adventures were the only true things in the world.

She wanted to be there to solve Liz's problems now.

At the Serendipity House, Liz practically collapsed onto the couch. But when Maggie moved to head upstairs, thinking Liz wouldn't want her company any longer, her friend perked up.

"Stay for a bit?" Liz asked.

Maggie sat back down, but not before grabbing two beers for them.

"Cam is going to hate me," Liz said after a sip.

"That's impossible and you know it."

"It's his mom's old ring—"

"Even better. There's no world where Roseanne Peters doesn't have insurance on her jewelry."

"Maybe you're right." Liz sighed, falling even farther onto the couch's cushion, head on a pillow. "It's like . . . it feels like my heart is collapsing in on itself or something. It's hard to breathe."

Maggie wanted to comfort her. Like in the before times. She inhaled and hoped for the best.

"Sometimes when I get upset, I think about this time from sixth grade," she said. "You probably don't even remember it. It was that day over the summer, I think it was June, when I decided it was a bright idea to cut my own bangs."

Liz groaned. "How could I ever forget?"

"I remember realizing how dumb I looked with bangs pretty instantly, and I just couldn't stop crying. Like full body, wretched, soap-opera-actress sobs."

"I remember that, too."

"So, you probably remember what happened next," Maggie said, giving Liz a gentle nudge.

Liz smiled, ever so slightly. "I cut my bangs, too."

"Your mom couldn't believe it when she came home that night, but she made us a batch of her famous chocolate chip cookies and told us to stay calm. And then the next morning, she went to the store and bought us those matching headbands."

"We wore them all year," Liz remembered. "God, I haven't thought about that in forever."

"Whenever I start to panic-sob like that again, I think about our bangs. And how it was awful, but it was also sort of funny, in retrospect. But most importantly, it didn't last forever. Those bangs grew out." Maggie took Liz's hand and squeezed. "I know it feels awful now. But Cam loves you more than any ring. More than every ring combined. He'll forgive you."

Liz squeezed back. "I really hope so."

Then the coffee table buzzed, an alert from Liz's phone. One glance at the screen caused her frown to resurface in full force.

"You know Cam will understand," Maggie said, gently. "But is there maybe something else going on? If there's something I can help with, anything at all, Liz, just say the word."

Liz chewed the inside of her cheek, deliberating for a moment before exhaling. "Promise you won't tell anyone?"

"I promise."

"Because I haven't even told Cam yet."

Maggie's temperature climbed. She wanted to be someone Liz could count on again. Desperately. "Cross my heart and hope to die. You can trust me."

Liz took a deep breath in. "I applied for this international fashion program. God, it feels good to say that aloud."

"Liz! That's amazing," Maggie said.

"But I heard that some people have started to hear back already. Now I can't stop refreshing my inbox, hoping it's an update. But I haven't gotten anything yet."

"I'm sure your acceptance is coming next. They'd be absurd not to take you."

"It would be amazing," Liz said quietly.

"So why haven't you told Cam?"

"Well, the program would start in the fall," Liz said. "And it's all the way in Italy. Milan."

It was like Maggie could physically watch as the other shoe crash-landed before her. The burden of secrets, of massive potential change. She was surprised that losing the engagement ring hadn't sent Liz into a full-fledged panic attack. Maggie would probably still be crying, but Liz had always been the tougher of the two of them.

"I'm trying to stay calm," Liz continued now, her voice speeding up. "It was easier when I could focus on my application, throw myself into the work, but now I'm sick with guilt over not telling Cam, and the anxiety of waiting for my results, and the fear of how much I really want it, and what it means that I haven't told Cam in the first place, and what we'd do about the wedding planning, and my chin keeps breaking out, and the program is super competitive—"

"Which is why you'll get in. And when you do, you'll figure everything out after that. I'm so excited for you, Liz."

Liz let herself exhale for a moment. "You think it's okay that I applied?"

"I'd be upset if you hadn't. And I think Cam would be, too."

"But what if I don't get in?"

"You will. Just promise you'll bring me home some dried pasta. Or at the very least, send a postcard."

Liz closed her eyes. She spoke with her eyelashes still pressed tight to her skin. "It's scary, to think about leaving. Leaving Cam, all this. Even just for a year," she said. "How did you do it? When you moved to LA?"

Maggie paused for a moment before answering. "I just knew it was something I'd never forgive myself for if I didn't at least try. Some dreams are worth the risk."

"Were yours?" Liz asked, opening her eyes, her voice free of judgment. There was only curiosity.

"I think so," Maggie said, because now she wasn't so sure.

Liz shifted so she was looking squarely at Maggie. "What happened out there, Mags? Why are you really back home?"

"I just changed my mind about it all," Maggie said, a half-truth.

Liz stared at her, her brow raised. That was the wrong answer. "Bullshit."

"It's not," Maggie said, feeling her cheeks growing red. "I got tired of the low pay and living so far away—"

"You've always been a terrible liar—"

"I'm not lying."

"Fine, then hiding something real. God, I should have known. You're just as selfish as you've always been."

"I just spent the afternoon helping you!"

"And I just told you my biggest secret and you're still lying to my face! Trying to make it seem like everything is perfect instead of just being honest. Being real." Liz's voice was high, words spinning fast. "And now you're back like nothing ever happened, no apologies, flirting with Mac—"

"Oh my god, everything always comes back to Mac with you. Come on, Liz, what about *us*? Our friendship?"

"You really want to go there? Friendship works two ways, Maggie. Especially after a funeral. Thanks for your condolences, by the way. I've been doing fine." She stood to go upstairs, to retreat to her room, wiping the tears that had formed in her eyes.

Maggie felt the world fall out from under her. "Liz, please, stay, I can explain. Let me start over—"

"You know, she may have been proud of you for following your dreams, but she sure was disappointed by how you treated us to get there."

Liz stormed up the stairs, slamming her and Cam's bedroom door behind her.

Maggie sat still, stung senseless.

In her mind, she remembered all the drafted messages she'd written and then deleted when she'd heard the news. All the times she went to call but choked, phone heavy in her numb hands. She'd even booked a flight from LAX to JFK, a red-eye landing the morning of the funeral.

But Kurt had needed her to work that Sunday. Like every Sunday back then. Every Saturday, too. They were in prep on his next movie and needed to redo the budget if they got a green light. His agent had sent in a new book for his consideration to adapt that was "going to territories," which meant moving fast, and she needed to speed-read and write up coverage for him by that night if he wanted to attach. Plus, his mother's birthday was coming up—where was the list of present ideas? The dinner reservations she'd made in advance? Didn't Maggie want this? Didn't Maggie care? Couldn't he trust her to deliver? It didn't matter. There were no days off, not even for a bereavement.

Maggie canceled her flights like a coward. She went to send flowers, but then Kurt filled up her schedule, screamed if she'd delay, and by the time Maggie remembered, it felt like it was too late.

Everything was too late.

There were too many things to say, too much to apologize for, too much distance to repair. In the end, she had decided on a text message, but the gesture was so insignificant that she might as well have sent nothing.

How could she have done that? Why had she thought that was okay?

Maggie had thought a lot of terrible things were okay when she worked for Kurt.

He'd had a way of sending her moral code through a funhouse mirror.

She'd just smile, desperate. Scared and submissive.

Now she let out a sob, opened her phone.

Woe is the writer who cannot use her words. Here's a suggested phrase to get you started. Repeat after me: I'mSorryI'mSorryI'm SorryI'mSorryI'mSorryI'mSorry

Suddenly, another set of footsteps ran down the stairs.

It was Robyn, giant pink suitcase in hand.

"What's going on? Is everything okay?" Maggie asked, wiping her cheeks quickly, so as not to expose how recently they'd been covered in tears.

Robyn turned to look at her. "Nothing is okay here."

"But where are you going?"

Robyn's mascara was running, her eyes empty. Maggie hadn't thought it was possible for her to look so weak, so vulnerable. So heartbroken. "To be with people who actually think I matter," she said with a sniffle so pitiful it made Maggie want to split in two.

With that, Robyn stormed away.

Chapter 15

According to Robyn's grandfather, there were only two things in life that truly mattered.

1. A paycheck
2. A partner to spend it on

He'd told her that in kindergarten, and Robyn had memorized it, lived by it, like a code of honor, ever since. She probably shouldn't have touted it in class the very next day (she'll always remember her teacher's snicker), but Robyn couldn't help it. Even as a precocious blonde and brilliant schoolgirl, she'd loved the picture that her grandfather's words painted.

A paycheck and a partner became her goalposts.

Robyn had always had an entrepreneurial bent. In the seventh grade, she rebranded the middle school store with a line of custom candies. Sure, all she did was unwrap the traditional boxes of candy, stir them up in a cellophane bag, and tie them with pink and purple strings, but she sold them at an upcharge and turned a profit in a blink. She transformed the store into Robyn's Candy Bar and proudly told her parents to put her allowance on pause.

The partner element was harder. Finding someone to love and trust wasn't as easy as building out a healthy bottom line. Robyn was turned on by profit sheets and marketing briefs. She woke up in the middle of the night with ideas, cartoon dollar signs spinning in her eyeballs. She worked hard and wore her wealth proudly. And why shouldn't she indulge in the Cartier bracelets, the Chanel purses, the Gucci sneakers when she wanted to? Robyn knew she could be beautiful and passionate about business at the same time. Sure, her nose was purchased, but the rest of her was as authentic as it came. Her grandpa had encouraged her to take the world by storm. To stop at nothing. To conquer her dreams!

Unfortunately, a Barbie doll blonde at Wharton touting an idea for a vibrator that doubled as a dust buster didn't do much to endear professors or peers to her mission statement. She was their Elle Woods nightmare. The secret scoffs, the pompous glares. The girls who got close just to stab her in the back. The men who gleaned the value of her bank accounts and dated her for the jets and the trips.

As a result, Robyn was constantly breaking up with people. Friends, boyfriends, employees. Call it trust issues, call it the curse of a vulnerable heart. The more success she saw, the more she craved a partner, a family, to spend it on.

By the time Robyn graduated, she knew she had to double down. If no one else would take her seriously, then at least *she* always would. She made rules and she stuck to them. Balance. Wellness. Health. She put her family above all else. Her parents were supportive, no matter what she did. Her grandfather a never-ending source of wisdom. Despite (or perhaps because of) their financial security, Robyn always knew her family's love came with no ties. It was unconditional. Even if she never found a partner, even if she never made 30 Under 30 (but thank God, she did), her parents would be proud. Boyfriend or not.

Dating in the city was even more challenging. Each new prospect came with all new friends, new experiences, new tests and hurdles. Some were enticing, like job interviews she knew she'd ace. Some were horrifying, like the sixth-floor walk-up where all the drinkware consisted of cups that were stolen from local bars and still smelled like stale beer. (That was the first and last time she'd sip pinot out of a pint glass.)

Then Robyn met Mac.

He was different. He was kind. He laughed at her jokes, encouraged her ideas. He even bought her a pair of fluffy slippers just to keep at his apartment, because her feet got so cold.

On their fourth date, before he introduced her to his brother and his brother's girlfriend, Mac had warned Robyn: Cam and Liz were annoyingly perfect, and his parents were annoyingly obsessed with them. Mac never seemed to realize that his parents were annoyingly obsessed with him, too. Cam and Liz were warm and welcoming. Their love was so glowing, Robyn felt like she could rub it on her own skin like lipstick or glitter.

Was Mac her partner? Was this her forever home?

By the time summer came, though, Robyn knew something had turned sour. Mac was different, stressed and tired. Cam was different, too. Dinners with Mrs. Peters weren't anything like mealtime with her parents, her grandfather. At the Peters home, there were strict questions and clear answers. Expectations and rules. Mac lied about his PT appointments, for instance, which Robyn had never seen him attend. And if he didn't check in with his mother daily, he'd get a disappointed text. Robyn loved Mac's puppy-dog eyes, but she knew that he wasn't a pet. She had been on enough private flights to recognize the sound of a helicopter.

And it was starting to seem like Mac was right under its blades.

Robyn tried to encourage him to stand up for himself, but his mother never took her seriously, and slowly, Mac stopped taking her seriously, too. She wasn't impressed by Robyn's family or fortune. She wasn't moved by their shared entrepreneurial energy. Instead, she hinted that Robyn shouldn't have come to Liz and Cam's proposal party, that everyone knew she wasn't long-term.

Robyn felt angry, hurt. She started nagging—ugh, she

could hear it in her voice. It was so unlike her, but she wanted him to stick up for himself. For her. To stop feeling like he had to play some civic part, fulfill some familial duty. Who did he owe but himself? Why wasn't he allowed to fall and fail just like everyone else?

She begrudgingly agreed to the Fire Island trips, even though she found the ferry schedule constricting and she detested the LIRR. She'd do it for Mac. Her Mac. She'd do it for that second ideal, that partner, that chance.

Then Mac asked for a break.

They'd fought last night, after he'd abandoned her at that disgusting Bamboo House. With strangers, drunk and shouting. Talking about a high school she didn't care about, references she would never understand.

Why couldn't Mac have stayed by her side? Why did he have to follow that Maggie girl she'd caught him staring at too many times when he thought no one was looking? Robyn knew they'd been best friends in high school, dated senior year. She'd heard the whispers in the group, about whether Mac and Maggie would get back together now that she'd moved home. As if Mac didn't have a girlfriend already? As if Robyn wasn't even an obstacle worth noting. Mac promised it was over, but she wasn't blind.

He said they had been fighting all summer. They didn't fit like they used to. She had seen it coming, but still, she was a bit surprised. She was typically the one initiating the breakups.

Strangely, in the end, Robyn didn't mind. It felt like the

leveling of some scale. Balance was good, she reminded herself on the ferry home. Breakups could have balance, too.

Robyn lifted her face to the sun as the Ocean Beach shoreline shrank from her vantage. She wanted to find her partner, someone to spend her paycheck on. She wanted someone to look at her the way Cam looked at Liz. The kind of look where you forgot to breathe. Romance more essential than oxygen.

Maybe it wouldn't be Mac after all.

Maybe Robyn would just have to think of some new ideas.

Chapter 16

iz and Cam had no idea, which meant the surprise was a success. Sure, it was a cheesy display of bachelor and bachelorette party decorations along the house's walls, but the East Meadow friends had insisted on throwing a "stag and hen" party for Cam and Liz. A celebratory night on Fire Island before Roseanne's party next month.

Who could say no to that?

After her fight with Maggie, her *most recent* fight, Liz spent the afternoon locked in her bedroom, regretting everything. What had she been thinking, trusting Maggie with the truth about Domus? Had she been so hoodwinked by the brief return of a friend that her lips had broken open so easily, secrets spilled like candy flung from a piñata?

Then Cam opened the door and Liz remembered what had happened earlier.

Her heart caught in her throat. "I-I-I went swimming," she

stammered, tears immediately pooling. She usually tried to keep her emotions more in check, but she couldn't shake this untethered feeling, this sense that she was totally losing control. All she could manage to do was lift her left hand, ringless finger evidence of her crime. What kind of fiancée loses her engagement ring so quickly? Did this mean their marriage was doomed?

What other mistakes would she make before they even arrived at the altar?

Liz's worries were silenced by the smell of oak and ocean. Cam's arms protectively wrapped around her, his lips kissing her hair. "It's okay," he whispered. "It'll all be okay."

"I'm so sorry," Liz said, words pressing into his shoulder, feeling how his T-shirt was dampening from her sobs. "I didn't realize it had slipped off until it was too late. I searched the beach, but I couldn't find it anywhere. I feel like such an idiot."

"You aren't an idiot." Cam rubbed her back and Liz felt her breath catch up to her. "I'm sorry for not getting it sized before proposing. I had a feeling it was too big. I was supposed to take it into the jeweler, and I was running behind—"

"No, it's my fault, babe," she said. "I shouldn't have worn it in the ocean. I don't know what I was thinking. Well, I wasn't thinking. That's why, I guess."

"Well, don't think about it anymore. Not one more thought," Cam said, tucking his chin over her head the way she loved. Enveloping her in his complete warmth, his safety. "We'll deal with it all when we get back home. Okay?"

"Okay," Liz said.

"Okay." Cam kissed her, deeply.

She wiped her eyes, managing to chuckle a bit. "I need to go wash my face before tonight. I can taste my tears."

"I wasn't going to say anything, but I could, too." Cam smiled. "We'll be okay, Lizard. I'm sorry you got so worked up about this, babe. You and me? You know we're way more than a piece of jewelry."

Liz did know that. She let herself remember what she loved about him. His tolerance, his resolve. Her commitment to Cam washed over her as she showered in the upstairs bathroom, did her five-minute makeup routine in record time. She painted her cheeks with pink blush, covered her eyelids with a subtle sparkly shadow. Her face would be the first sign of shifting her energy, her spirit for the night. Of leaning into the summer.

Cam handled the ring news with expert fortitude, she thought as she drew liquid liner on her lash line, followed by a perfectly shaped cat eye. Maybe when she came clean about the Domus program, if and when she was accepted, Cam's reaction would be the same.

How did she get so lucky to have found such a patient man?

Liz found Cam dressed back in their bedroom, donning a short-sleeve button-down shirt with a pattern of tiny hot dogs, hamburgers, and ketchup containers. He was perfect.

This night was going to be perfect, too.

So when Liz grabbed Cam's hand and led him downstairs to join the group for happy hour, she was shocked to walk into the living room and see Maggie inflating a pastel pink "Bride" balloon. So shocked that she nearly screamed.

"Surprise!" Mac said, popping a bottle of champagne. "Happy early bach weekends."

"We tried to be as quiet as we could," Brenna said, gesturing to their work.

"My fingers hurt. You're welcome," Quinn said.

"But it was all worth it," Brenna quickly added, pointing to a custom letter banner that they must have had to string by hand, punching the thin white rope through all the perforated holes to spell out *FIRE ISLAND FIANCES*. "We love you guys."

"Where did you even get all these?" Liz asked, laughing through her initial nerves. "Cam, you definitely knew about this."

"He didn't," Mac cut in. "I can attest. Quinn swore us all to secrecy. But Mom wanted to help, too, so I even had to pack a secret bag with all this crap—I mean, cute stuff."

Sure, bachelorette decorations were sort of tacky, but these had clearly been hung with care. Liz smiled. A part of her still wished that Maggie wasn't there, a reminder of all that had gone wrong, but Liz put that out of her mind. Maybe this was the opportunity they needed to finally celebrate the good. To remember that this was supposed to be a happy time.

That they were supposed to be a *happy* couple.

Cam put his arm around her shoulders, and she decided once again to lean in. To his warmth, to their engagement, to it all. It was a sweet, casual surprise, just her friends, all here together. Later they'd go to a beach town bar. Nothing stuffy, everything earnest. Just like Liz and Cam.

"The group wanted to officially celebrate you two," Mac said, handing a glass of champagne to Cam and then to Liz.

"We're all so happy for you," Maggie said. "Really." Liz didn't meet her gaze.

"To love," Brenna said, raising her glass.

"And an excuse for a party," Quinn added.

"Shoot, I didn't pack any white," Cam teased.

"Why don't you check outside?" Mac said with an air of campy mystery. He led the way out to the patio, which had been transformed with twinkle lights and streamers. The beer pong table was set up with wedding-themed cups, and from the outdoor shower's ledge, two costume sashes hung. "Bride to Be," in white. "Groom to Be," in black. Georgie put them on Cam and Liz as if he were knighting them after battle. Mac turned up the speaker and the party began.

It was silly, Liz knew. Totally against the traditional bachelorette and bachelor party rules dictating separate weekends split by gender.

But for that, Liz liked it all so much better. It was honestly exactly how she would have planned it. Soon, she felt like a teenager again, playing drinking games with Cam as her partner, or catching his eye from across the room and flashing a funny face to make him laugh. She felt young and free and daring, like she'd just left a note in his locker or sent a flirty

BBM. Liz scanned the party, happy and having fun, until she realized someone was missing.

Robyn.

What had happened to Robyn?

She pulled Mac off to the side. Cam saw and followed. "Where's Robyn?"

"Don't worry about it," Mac said.

"Did she leave?" Cam asked.

Mac groaned. "I don't want to talk about it right now."

"Talk about what?" Liz asked.

"She went home."

"*Home* home? Like left-Fire-Island home? Why?"

"Just enjoy your party," Mac begged.

"We are, we're just concerned—" Cam started.

"You guys are so annoying sometimes. There's nothing to be *concerned* about."

"We're just curious, then," Cam amended.

"And we just want to help," Liz said. "But fine, if you don't want to tell us about your girlfriend—"

"Oh my god, fine. Robyn and I are taking a break," Mac shouted just as the music faded between songs.

Liz's eyebrows narrowed as she heard Maggie gasp, jaw hanging open. Eyes wide.

"Thanks for the announcement, man," PJ called out with a laugh, cutting the tension. "Anyone else have anything they want to say?"

"You guys all hate her anyway."

"That's not true," Liz said firmly.

"She's interesting!" Georgie called over. "Keeps things fresh."

"We like whoever you want to be with," Cam agreed.

"Whatever, I don't want to think about her right now." Mac chugged the remainder of his beer and threw the empty can toward the garbage, and of course it went straight in. He stared at his hands. Liz felt guilty for prying, but before she could apologize to Mac for making a scene, she saw Maggie walk over to him.

"I'm so sorry, M. Are you okay?" Maggie asked, voice low.

"Is anyone okay?" Mac tried with unconvincing bravado. "I'm kidding. I'm fine, all's good," he said, and Liz noticed how his fingers lingered on Maggie's shoulder. "Hey." He turned toward the group, a painted-on sparkle in his eyes. "Is this a party or what? Aren't we supposed to play bridal games or something?"

"Excellent point," PJ said.

"Yeah, let's get this party started. We've got a bride and groom to game with," Mac said.

"I've never been to one of these things before," Brenna said. "What do we do?"

"I have a game, actually," Maggie said, rummaging through her tote bag, which was hooked on an outdoor chair. "I printed out some questions. I saw it in a movie once, thought I'd be ready if the moment came up."

"Knew we could count on you, M," Mac said, patting her shoulder again.

"Games are cheesy," Quinn groaned.

"Cheesy can be fun," Cam said. "I'm down for a wedding-themed game. Thanks, Maggie. Liz? You cool for a game?"

"Um, yeah, er . . . whatever you want to do," she stammered, when she noticed the group looking at her expectantly.

The rules were simple. Or so Liz hoped; she had a hard time tracking the words that spilled from Maggie's mouth. She was trying to ignore how Mac and Maggie had arranged themselves next to each other, how he stared intently into her eyes. Mac hated when Liz stressed about him, but sometimes she couldn't help it. He'd always felt like her only brother.

Mac, suddenly single, and they'd already returned to old routines.

Had he paused things with Robyn to explore a reunion with Maggie instead?

Liz didn't care who Mac dated. She really didn't. She just wanted him to be happy. Truthfully. More than anything, to find someone who made him feel the way that Cam had made her feel since they were teenagers.

She'd once hoped that person for Mac was Maggie. Cam had hoped it, too. They'd been best friends, all of them, the easiest, most natural grouping. And by senior spring, it had finally happened. Her best friend dating her boyfriend's brother? It felt like her future family had been guaranteed.

But then Maggie had left, and Mac was devastated. Even though he tried to hide it, he'd admitted to Cam one night that he wished he'd asked Maggie out sooner. Wished he could have had more time with her in East Meadow, when the days dripped with potential, and every young crush felt like a firework.

Liz felt guilty for not predicting how it would crash in the end. From their dorm room, perched on twin beds no more than three feet apart, she alone saw how Maggie never quite felt lonely without Mac by her side. She didn't pine for him the way Liz ached for Cam. She didn't send him BBM messages or keep him in the corner of her laptop screen on Google Hangouts, beginning episodes of *Always Sunny* at the exact same time stamp, anything that let them pretend to be together.

Sometimes, it felt like Liz was sharing a room with a Maggie-shaped ghost. Her best friend was distracted, off, oblivious to how desperately Liz needed her. How they all did.

Then she was gone, breaking Mac's heart. Breaking Liz's, too.

"Liz? You ready?" Maggie asked, snapping her back to the present. Ready for what?

"This is going to be easy," Cam said, nudging Liz's shoulder with his. "Maggie, kick us off?"

Maggie passed out sheets of paper lined with custom questions. The answers could only be Liz or Cam. The friends were to write down their individual guesses, and once everyone was ready, the couple of honor would reveal the truth. It started off simple enough.

"Who was the best student?" Maggie asked.

"Cam," Liz said, when it was time. Liz remembered his National Honor Society cords, his valedictorian speech at their graduation ceremony, out on the football field. It had been ninety degrees and sweltering but Cam never lost his cool. She'd watched him from across the field with such admiration, such pride. Her brilliant boyfriend.

The game continued back and forth:

"Best driver?" Liz. She could parallel park like no one's business.

"Date night planner?" Cam. He always had the best surprises.

"Cleanest?" Cam. A germophobe since his first science class.

"Best in bed?" A protest from Mac—"Come on, ew, that's my brother!" A tie, instead.

"First to say I love you?" Cam. He was always doting.

"First to suggest moving in together?" Liz. She had always dared.

It was fun, Liz admitted, a trip down memory lane. Reminders of how easy life had been when they were younger. How they'd effortlessly fit, balanced each other out.

It also hurt a little. Where had those two perfect matches gone? Why was it so much harder now?

"Most excited about wedding planning?" Cam. Liz groaned when everyone got that right. Was her heel-dragging so obvious?

"Most excited for the honeymoon?"

Liz and Cam paused before answering that one. The honeymoon? They hadn't gotten that far yet into their wedding-planning checklist.

"I guess a tie," Cam said after a beat. "But while we're on the subject, what do you think, babe? Rome? Paris? Maybe Japan?"

Liz was too tongue-tied to respond. A honeymoon meant a real wedding. What if she was abroad? Rome—what about Milan? She still hadn't told him. She needed to. She just couldn't. Maggie, maybe noticing Liz's discomfort, read the next question.

"Best cook?" Cam. His fancy mac and cheese was a weeknight staple.

"Best gift giver?" Liz. Cam pointed to his calf socks, sticking out of his sneakers as proof.

She gasped. She hadn't even realized that Cam still had those socks, let alone had packed them and put them on. (Cam had handled laundry ever since they'd moved in together.) There, sewn above the outside of Cam's ankle, was the Mille Grazi logo, the pizza place in town where Cam and Liz had their first date. The socks were a first anniversary present. Mac had wanted a pair, too—*They have the best slice in town!*—but Liz had made only one, custom for Cam. On the insides of the socks, Liz had ironed on the exact meal they'd ordered: cartoon garlic knots and pepperoni pinwheels. He'd kept them all these years.

This memory kick-started a round of stories as everyone shared their favorite Cam-and-Liz moment. The homecoming court parade when they'd been crowned class king and queen and escorted around town on a motorcycle. How Liz and Cam frequently showed up late to band class, but appeased Mr.

Fletcher with iced coffee from Starbucks so that he could never get too mad.

Liz smiled. She tried to let herself lean all the way back into the highlight reel of their relationship. Their romance "best-of" show. She wanted to remember it, re-create it.

She tried not to notice how close Mac and Maggie were sitting together. They'd answered all the questions correctly. Of course they had. Even with Maggie's distance, she had known Liz better than anyone for most of their lives. With each correct answer, Mac and Maggie drank. Now they were tipsy, shoulders touching. Flirty. By the time the game ended, they had tied for first place, and it only brought them closer.

Liz's stomach was in knots. Brenna and Quinn pulled her into a new drinking game, something about guessing the number of fingertips placed along a red cup's rim, finishing the beer inside if you lost.

Liz tried to have fun. Really, she did.

She tried to ignore the small, inner voice telling her to brace herself. To not get too comfortable.

After all, like the heroes in their memories, the night was still young.

Chapter 17

W as this what it meant to be young? The night was warm, but Maggie's arms were covered in goose bumps. The summer evening was making her every pore open up, alive. The air was sweet, the sky shining with stars. Maggie walking next to Mac, in the easy rhythm of a nursery rhyme.

Robyn was gone. For now, at least. Maggie tried to separate her current pace with Mac from whatever breakup battle had sent Robyn packing. She felt bad, of course, if Mac was hurting, but she knew Robyn was the wrong fit for him. Did that mean Maggie was right? Did this change everything? Or was this simply Mac in rebound mode?

Still, there was a familiarity to the electricity that pulsed in the space between their shoulders, the energy hinting at something more. They had been here before. Mac's car, the prom dance floor. The Serendipity House as teenagers, a weekend in Ocean Beach. The buzz of seeing a friend look at you like something more for the first time.

There was hunger in the space between them, and suddenly Maggie was starving.

As the group walked to town, she and Mac fell to the back. Their arms loose and swaying, fingertips grazing, out of the sight of curious friends. This, with Mac. Again. It was everything she had hoped might happen when she returned to New York.

Ty's face from last night blipped like a flashback in Maggie's brain, but *Mac* was who she'd been desperate to test out those first days home. To see what might have happened if she'd never left. To see if he was the happy ending to her love story.

Liz's warning followed, her words echoing through Maggie's ears. Liz's hurt-stricken face. *Did* it always come back to Mac?

Was that such a bad thing? It had worked out for Liz and Cam.

Should it work out for Maggie and Mac, too?

The hum from Matthew's Seafood House called to Maggie. The waterfront bar had been a favorite of their after-prom weekend, and day trips to Fire Island later that summer. Before college move-ins closed in on them, Maggie and their friends would spend full Saturdays in Ocean Beach. They'd grab sandwiches from the My Hero shop in town, throw them into travel coolers, and take the earliest morning ferry. They'd spend hours tanning on beach towels or swimming in the sea. When the sky turned pink, they'd stealthily sip cocktails at Matthew's, after the bouncer barely blinked at their fake IDs. They'd take the last ferry home with fresh sunburns and sweet memories. Maggie would fall asleep on the ride home, her head on Mac's shoulder.

It felt like a spell, a friend-group potion, to be back there with all of them again. This time, Quinn and PJ beelined for the bar, while Brenna, Liz, and Cam went straight to the dance floor. Georgie had to work, despite his Friday misadventures, left alone with his laptop and his bandaged thumb. When Maggie offered to stay behind, Mac looked at her with those curious green eyes. Eyes that seemed to compel her: *Come with me.*

And so she did.

He stopped her as they walked inside. "My knee's feeling sore, actually," he said, voice loud to challenge the music's volume. "Want to sit outside instead?"

Maggie nodded, feeling a blush creep up her neck.

He looked relieved. "Awesome, I'll get us some drinks. Grab a table?" She nodded again, but this time Mac flashed a smile. "Be right back," he said, before turning toward the bar.

She weaved her way outside to a two-seater facing the bay. A dozen boats were tied to the dock, cast in the moonlit glow of the Fire Island night sky. Settling down, she tapped her fingers on the glass tabletop, noticed they were shaking. She opened her Notes app:

Butterflies, I think it's happening again. I feel reckless and young, like all those summer movies foretold. My heart wants to throb. He and I, we've danced this routine once before. I think I still remember the moves.

She felt her stomach tighten a bit.

But why can't I remember how it felt when we first turned off the music?

Maggie sighed, and then she startled. Her phone was still on airplane mode.

After her fight with Liz, Maggie had spent the afternoon hidden upstairs, writing. She filled her phone with mistakes she'd made, the apologies she'd never said to Liz, for abandoning her at NYU so rashly, for not flying home immediately when she'd heard about her mom. For letting so much charged silence spread like weeds between them. She'd written it all while on airplane mode. No wi-fi, no service, the best way for Maggie to throw herself into her words.

Now she hovered over the settings, but she didn't feel ready to reconnect, to reawaken her phone to any missed texts or calls. For tonight, she didn't want to be accessible.

She only wanted to be here.

"Writing a poem about me?" Mac said with a smirk, placing an ice-cold gin and lemonade on the table.

"Like the good old days." Maggie smiled, tucking her phone away. "Thanks for the drink."

"Thanks for letting me skip out on the dance floor." He

bounced his knee up and down in the chair next to hers. He was forever the athlete who couldn't sit still.

"I'm sorry again, about your knee," Maggie said. "That must have been terrible."

"I got through it."

"Still. I wish I'd known. That you'd told me about it sooner."

"You weren't here. What could you have done?"

"Well, I'm here now."

"I can see that. How's it feel being home?"

"Like I'm an overgrown middle schooler?"

Mac laughed. "Be serious."

"Like I wouldn't want to be anywhere else."

"We've missed you, M. I missed you," he said, voice lower. "It feels right to have you home."

"I'm starting to agree with that."

Mac looked at Maggie and it was like he was staring into her soul. He had seen her through it all. Through the drama of growing up, through the drifting away of her parents. He'd been a classmate, a teammate, a best friend. Before they started dating and turned from schoolmates into something more, Mac had always been there. And now he was sitting an inch away from her, under the Fire Island stars, staring at her like she was the brightest one of all.

Mac leaned in. Maggie leaned closer.

She tilted her head, inhaled, and with a shortness of breath, she shortened the space between their noses. Was this happening again?

Should she let it? Why not?

Then she heard a cough.

"Maggie?"

She turned around.

It was Ty.

His face fell. "Sorry, I didn't realize you two . . ."

"It's fine," Maggie said, her tone probably too curt, too tight, but she was caught off guard as she watched a blush take over Ty's face. Guilt panged as she watched him stand there silently, staring at her. She could feel Mac's annoyance vibrating off his skin. "What's up?"

"Um, sorry." Ty recalibrated. "I just wanted to congratulate you, on the new Kurt Robinson project."

Maggie deflated. "Oh, Ty—"

"Just saw the *Deadline* announcement, sounds like it's going to be his next big hit." Ty's voice was earnest. "Congrats."

"Oh." Maggie frowned. "There's nothing to congratulate me for. I didn't work on it," she started, knowing she needed to confess about her firing, that she wasn't part of Kurt's team anymore.

"Oh, really?" Ty's eyebrows were crooked. "I figured you had, because it said the movie takes place on Fire Island. Why else would you be here?"

Maggie felt nauseated as a lump grew in her throat. Ty's words were like bullets, but he didn't even realize he'd pulled the trigger.

She felt like she could faint.

"I have to go," she said, running off the Matthew's deck and onto the street before the scene could explode in front of her. She heard Ty calling after her, but it didn't matter. She needed to get out of there, to find a quiet spot.

Falling onto a vacant park bench, Maggie turned her phone off airplane mode.

Three missed calls from Kurt. A voicemail she couldn't bring herself to listen to.

What did he want from her? What could he possibly want? It had been a month since she'd walked out of his office, humiliated and defeated and alone. Was he simply bragging about some new script sale, like Ty said? Why? She'd told him she would honor her NDA, like she had any choice in the matter. She'd returned her parking pass, turned in her company phone, shredded any scripts she had left over at home. She had driven miles and miles away. Couldn't he just leave her alone?

But then Ty had said Fire Island.

Maggie knew what this meant.

She started to cry hot, angry tears. The kind she never usually let herself feel. The past month, the past six years catching up to her. She felt like gravity had left her. Her center beginning to fall.

She was resting her forehead in her hands when she heard his voice.

"Mags, are you okay?"

It was Mac. He had followed her. He took her in his arms. She couldn't help it, she eased into him. Her brain couldn't think, her mind in shambles; she just wanted someplace solid. Something familiar when everything else was crumbling. Any respite from the recollection of all that had ruptured in LA.

Maggie rested her head on Mac's shoulder.

"Do you want to talk about it?" he asked, his brow creased.

"Do we have to?"

"Of course not," Mac said. "But for what it's worth, whatever it is, whatever's happening that's got you so upset . . . I know you'll get through this. You can do anything. You're perfect, Maggie. You always have been."

Maggie turned her head, looked up at Mac. There he was, with those kind eyes. The arms that had always cheered her up, the hands that had high-fived her, applauded her, held her for a year, those arms were wrapped around her body again, tight and close. Limbs touching limbs. It was like a blanket, the safest, warmest, oldest blanket in the pile. It smelled like home, and Maggie wanted to stay inside his embrace forever.

She didn't want to be alone. She pulled his body closer, leaned right up against him, and kissed him. He kissed her back, breathed her in, then rested his forehead against hers.

"I've wanted to do that since you came home," Mac whispered.

Maggie swallowed. "Me, too." It was the truth.

He kissed her again, his teeth on her lips, his hands squeezing her waist. Pent-up pressure, bodies closing in. But this time, it felt too sudden. Too much at once. Something missing while moving too quick. A piece that was missing, that had perhaps always been missing. A calculation that didn't fit.

The math was wrong: He was drunk. She was drunk.

He was rebounding. She was lost.

They were friends. Better as friends.

The sudden clarity hit Maggie like lightning. Bright and terrible all at once.

She pulled away, trying to put space between them. Trying to close Pandora's box.

"I love you, M," Mac said instead.

Maggie's heart broke. This wasn't right. None of it felt right.

She saw a flash of Robyn, eyes pooling, suitcase packed.

She heard a spiral of Liz's words, echoing in her brain.

This was all too familiar. Maggie had done it again, ruined things.

Had she just been messing with Mac's head?

And for what?

Her mind flooded with all the other memories she'd (willfully? Wistfully?) forgotten since moving home. That she'd somehow subconsciously locked away.

The magic of a new relationship had carried them through the spring and summer. There was something inherently intoxicating about holding a hand you'd known forever, about stealing a kiss in familiar places, looking at an old friend in a fresh way. With graduation around the corner, it had seemed like their entire grade had coupled up. Mac and Maggie had gladly answered the siren call.

But when they were alone in his basement, behaving the way they thought they ought to, Maggie had to admit it felt quiet. No fireworks, all tension gone. No heat, at least not in her heart. The anticipation, the mystery, the romance had been caught up in the longing. Once they had each other, the wanting was replaced with the reality and so much began to extinguish.

NYU brought distance that Maggie never minded. She'd reunite with Mac every other month or so, homecomings during the holidays. But she knew it didn't feel right. It didn't look like a plot from a movie, didn't sound like a love song. It wasn't anything like Liz and Cam's relationship, and Maggie hated what that meant.

So when she transferred to UCLA, she blamed long distance for their inevitable breakup. She told Liz that was why she and Mac couldn't last. It was too far, too bleak a statistic to even attempt.

Maggie blamed long distance because that was easier than the truth: she and Mac just didn't fit in that way. Not like Cam and Liz fit. Not like the ever afters in the stories. Maggie didn't want to hurt Mac's feelings, or Liz's feelings, either. Liz, who had been so excited by the news, who had always wanted to be sisters.

Cam was Liz's forever.

But Maggie and Mac were only meant to last a moment.

How could she have forgotten all over again?

Maggie was practically professional at blacking out the pain, at blocking out the harder memories. At hiding away everything that didn't go according to her master plan. It's what had made her a great assistant to Kurt, the trait that had let her persist through all his infuriating demands.

Now she shook her head. Such naivete, focusing again on the idea of Mac, and not the actuality of *being* with him, of holding him, of being held by him, that she'd once known all too well.

Now she remembered, but it was of course too late.

She'd led him here, she'd led him on, she'd come home and couldn't get him out of her brain. Liz was right.

Everything Maggie did was wrong.

"I can't do this. I'm so sorry, Mac." Maggie stepped away.

"Wait, M, stop."

"What is wrong with me?" Her eyes were welling. "Why can't I do anything right?"

"Maggie, what are you talking about?" Mac tried to get closer, to erase the space between them, but she put her arms out. She needed to keep him away. She didn't deserve him, she didn't deserve anything.

"I'm so sorry." She turned around, tears rising, and saw that Liz was standing right next to her.

Liz. Maggie couldn't handle her right now.

"I'm sorry," she whispered, before pivoting and racing away. Her flip-flops could barely keep up, her feet speeding back to the house. She tried to outrace it but she couldn't.

Liz's disappointment had been on full display.

Had Maggie thought she could erase the past simply by moving home?

Her world was crashing down all the same.

Chapter 18

iz had been watching them from the bar. Waiting for the crash. Like a doomed and underpaid babysitter, she kept one eye on Cam and one eye on Mac.

Liz willed herself to relax. To let PJ twirl her, to bump hips with Brenna, let Cam serenade her with each verse of the bar's sing-along soundtrack. For the most part, the bachelor-bachelorette party had been fun; the weekend was moving along. She just had to get through each day until she found out her future.

The more she let the fantasy of Milan form in her mind, the more she savored its possibility for escape. Liz had lived her entire life in New York—Long Island, then Manhattan. Milan scared her in the best way. A new language. A new culture. A new map. She could get lost.

Liz realized that maybe, this time . . . she *wanted* to get lost.

It had just taken the ring, the official engagement, for her to finally admit it.

Then a commotion of movement outside caught her eye. Through the back windows of Matthew's, she saw Maggie jump up from the patio table where she and Mac had been sitting. A new person had approached them, the same guy whose frisbee found Maggie on the beach back in June. There were pained looks, some exasperated faces, and then suddenly Maggie took off, racing out the bar's side exit. In her wake, it looked like Mac said something to the guy, who then shook his head and walked away.

Liz watched as Mac looked around Matthew's, face forlorn, until his eyes landed on her, their gazes meeting through the window. She raised her hand, beckoning him inside. Back to their friends, back to their lives.

He turned and went after Maggie instead.

Liz breathed in but her emotions were unsteady. Why did she care what Mac did? He was a grown adult. He wasn't her responsibility.

And yet.

Something about Maggie's exit, the worried expression with which Mac followed . . .

Something was wrong.

Liz followed them.

She shouldn't have, but she followed. She listened to their breathless words and hated herself for eavesdropping. She just wanted to make sure Mac was okay.

Liz heard them kiss, their voices silenced, the sounds of

clothes colliding, bodies intertwining, and knew that was her cue to leave. Maybe the mess would come in the morning, or months from now. Or maybe never. Maybe this was how it was always meant to be. Liz and Cam and Maggie and Mac. She couldn't help but smile, just a little.

She had wanted that fantasy as much as, if not more than, any of them. She'd always wanted a sister. Why not have your best friend become your sister-in-law? They could sign their future children up for the same ballet classes, backyard dinners on Sunday nights. Liz had rooted for this. She had wished for it on shooting stars. Couldn't she root for it again?

And then the crash came. She heard Maggie's stuttering apology, snapped out of the daydream. It had never been real. A pretty story, nothing more. Liz grimaced through Mac's confession, Maggie's rejection.

She felt the colors blurring, her emotions heating up. She couldn't just listen silently as one of her best friends—her future brother-in-law—had his heart ripped out all over again.

Liz intervened, stepping out of the shadows, but as soon as she saw Mac's face, she knew it was the wrong move. He looked at her with guilt and embarrassment and annoyance, but more than anything, with sadness. By being there, Liz would only make it worse.

"Why did you follow us?" he said. "We were just—"

"She's just using you, Mac!" Liz couldn't help it; her frustration, her emotions from this entire weekend couldn't be bottled up. Maggie was back and it overwhelmed her. Filled her with hurt over everything they'd lost. That Liz had lost. That Liz would never get back. The words spilled out. "She's messing with you like always."

"That's not true," Mac said.

"She comes to you when she wants attention. And you just give it to her—"

"You don't know anything about our relationship."

"What relationship, Mac? She hasn't been home in years. You may be drunk but you're smarter than this."

"I can handle my own shit, Liz."

"I was just trying to help—"

"Well, you're not my mom, okay?" he snapped.

Liz felt like her heart had been ripped out through her throat. "At least you have one."

He winced. "Liz, that is so unfair."

"Just forget it. Go after her if you want. What do I care?" Tears filled her eyes. She didn't care about acting sensible, measured. Anger took control instead.

Mac stood frozen, a deer in headlights.

"Just go," she whispered, the tears now loose and falling down her cheeks.

Mac shook his head and followed Maggie home.

Liz sank down onto the ground.

White, she thought, looking down at the cocktail napkin she still had in her hand, wet and clinging like a needy lover to the drink she'd run outside with. Ripped up into tiny pieces. She paired it with a memory.

White: the hospital walls she had stared at for months on end.

She could close her eyes and still see that hallway where she'd waited. Sitting on the floor, sobbing in Cam's arms. The cancer had come back at an aggressive level, and now her mom was gone.

The second-worst day of Liz's life had been nearly five years before, the awful Wednesday morning in October of freshman year at NYU, when Nancy first called with the news.

Her doctor had found something.

Cancer was something that happened in books and TV shows and movies, thought Liz. To other people, to other families. Not to her. Not to single parents who were also best friends of their only children. Not to a woman a town counted on. Not to Nancy.

And yet, here they were.

Liz had rushed home immediately. Together, they read and reread the pamphlets and printouts about Nancy's ovarian cancer, the next steps, the recommended plan. It was so scary, so serious. Liz was too angry to cry.

Those next months, she was with her mom at every appointment, or she covered shifts at Grey's Garments. Liz helped the business endure through a school year's worth of graduation and sweet sixteen dresses, weddings gowns and more. For a decade, Nancy had put her clients' deadlines above everything else. Now she needed to focus on herself. Liz would do anything to help carry the load.

Her mother made Liz promise to keep the extent of her diagnosis a secret. It felt too personal, too private, and she didn't want their community getting worried. Nancy could picture the fuss, the too much attention. That was typical Nancy, never wanting anyone else to hurt just because she was in pain. It was bad enough that her daughter was sacrificing so much of her freshman year to be by her mom's side, she said. Nancy was already a single mom, a working mom. She'd long ago reached her quota of knowing, pitiful stares.

It had killed Liz, not telling Maggie the truth about what was happening with Nancy, but she had to respect her mom's wishes. All she was allowed to say was that there was a health issue, that Nancy was going to doctors and Liz would have to spend more time than usual helping out at home. Deep down, she tried to telepathically beg Maggie to ask more follow-up questions, to insist on not taking "She should be fine soon" as a satisfactory answer. To come back to Long Island with Liz just once, to see Nancy herself. But Maggie was on a different planet those days. Liz couldn't reach her.

It would be okay, though, Liz had told herself as the chemo progressed and her mom responded well. They were on the right side of statistics as they watched Nancy's numbers count toward hope. It went as well as it could. Nancy was in remission.

It was nearly the end of spring semester when Liz could finally breathe.

One week later, Maggie sat Liz down with an announcement of her own. The news that she was transferring.

Liz was devasted, but also oddly grateful that Maggie's timing somehow—maybe instinctively—aligned with Nancy's remission. Liz had only momentarily stopped drowning. The pain was still familiar, but numb. No, if Nancy had still been sick, if Liz had still been treading water when Maggie abandoned her for LA, Liz wasn't sure she'd have ever risen to the surface again.

She learned then and there that people wouldn't stay. Her dad first. Up and gone. Now Maggie, too.

Maggie left and Liz was reeling, but she managed to stay afloat. She managed five years of relearning to swim, of trusting the waves, of daring herself to float on the surface, to let the sun kiss her face. To celebrate, to cherish that she had her mom.

Then came the worst news of all. Five years of peacetime, erased with one terrifyingly too-late scan. The cancer was back with a vengeance. Nancy and Liz stayed calm as they levied the troops and prepared for the second round of war. But they were outnumbered. And they were unlucky.

The cancer had spread to her liver and lungs.

Six months later, Nancy was gone.

Liz knew then that it had all been some mirage. A trick of the light, a knockoff daydream she'd naively hoped would come true.

Nothing could last forever.

Cam stepped in. He was the only person she had. They were two years out of college and found themselves reviewing her mother's will. Selling the house, packing away Liz's childhood. Her heart broke each and every day.

There was nothing left.

There was no one else left.

There was only Cam. Liz burrowed into him like he was the last safe space left in the world. He was there. Mac was there, too. The entire Peters family was there for every second, every day, Liz remembered. They built her back up bone by bone. Slowly, excruciatingly, Liz found her way.

Since then, she'd had to hold them all tight and close. Suffocating and desperate, the only option. She had to protect them, she had to repay them.

She had to make sure they never slipped away.

"Lizard? What's wrong?"

She looked up and saw her fiancé's face, Cam's eyes shining with concern. She let out a sob, rushed toward him, hugging him as tight as she could. She needed to escape, to burrow back into him, to be rescued and swept away.

"It'll be all right," he whispered.

She nestled her head further into the curve between his shoulder and his neck. She wanted to forget everything, to fall asleep right there.

Then she looked down on the ground and saw his phone.

The screen was facing up, the display completely shattered.

"Cam, what did you do to your phone?"

He winced, caught and guilty. "It slipped," he said, but Liz recognized the lie. She heard the sadness in his voice, the tiredness in his throat. Something had happened to Cam to-night, but this time she didn't feel like dealing with it.

She didn't have the energy.

She was exhausted. She was empty.

She could only look around and see how far from perfect they'd fallen.

Chapter 19

H er, on his pillow. Birds chirping. Sunlight breaking in. Like everything in Mac's life, it was almost perfect. But the mascara stains streaked across the pillowcase were a reminder that nothing was as good as it seemed.

Mac woke up to the sound of Maggie's gentle breathing pushing toward his ear. Her eyes fluttering, dreams dancing behind her eyelids. Her hair tossed in every direction like a pair of jeans crumpled on the floor.

There were no discarded clothes on Mac's carpet, though. Maggie was fully dressed, still in her Saturday night outfit. Denim cutoffs and a tank top. Mac had changed into a pajama shirt and gym shorts—it was his room, after all—after Maggie's tears had transitioned into a steady, sleepy rest. He'd tucked the comforter around her, turned off their TV show, and whispered good night.

Mac liked to fix things. Georgie teased that Mac's preferred pastime was to play the hero. Mac knew his tendencies to help, to problem-solve, were probably wrapped up in some narcissistic Superman complex, but he didn't care. He was the kind of person who renewed his CPR training every year, even though he hadn't used the skills even once since he was seventeen and a lifeguard at the town pool. He obtained his wedding officiant license to help out a coworker whose original presider had come down with food poisoning the morning of the rehearsal dinner. He fostered dogs regularly. Cats, too.

The feeling of taking charge and watching the pieces fall into place, the look on his teammates' or his friends' or his coworkers' faces when he stood up and showed them where to go, told them that everything would be okay.

That was magic to Mac. Total magic.

Ever since his eighth minute of life, he'd been a big brother. That's how long it took for Cam to join him earth-side, to follow his twin out in the world. Mac felt like their natural leader, their ready-made captain. Cam was generous and wise, but he was naturally shier than Mac. Until Liz came along, Mac felt like it was his duty to make sure Cam was having a good time. He loved feeling like he was the reason that Cam smiled. His little brother happy meant everything was in place.

Mac liked consulting for that same reason. Being a leader, a melder, a problem-solver. He liked to fix things, to feel like he was among the *best* of the fixers.

Mac didn't like learning that not everything could be repaired.

Mac didn't like learning that magic could fade.

His knee ached. The injury had shaken him more than he cared to admit. The reminder of fragility and decay, something so far out of his control. A wrong kick, a wrong slide, and now he was stuck on the sidelines for good. He hadn't even stretched his knee in weeks.

PT was the first class that Mac had flunked. When had he become this person? Someone who couldn't nurture, couldn't lead, couldn't heal even himself.

He wanted to pull himself together, but he was scared. His soccer team was gone. Cam was getting married, committing officially to a new half. Liz looked at him like he'd morphed into some kind of fool. Robyn wanted more from Mac than he knew how to adequately give right now. She was disappointed in him constantly it seemed.

But Maggie?

She felt like a reset. She reminded him of the before.

Last night, Mac could feel himself coming on too strong, moving without a sensible plan. He regretted the words as soon as he whispered them—it wasn't even the truth. He *had* gotten over Maggie years ago, despite what Liz so obviously assumed. It was surprising, of course, seeing her back here. In this house again. He wasn't sure how best to proceed, how to slot her into his new life. How to grapple with the disconnect between how she used to make him feel and how disappointed he now was in himself.

Robyn had left and Mac was alone and, well, this summer

had been the hardest one yet. Maggie reminded him of how easy it had all been, back when they were teenagers. But last night he said those dumb words and he didn't even really mean them, and she rejected him again.

Where did that leave Mac?

Alone.

It was like Robyn had said. Before she left Ocean Beach, before she slammed her suitcase shut and stormed toward the ferry terminal, she accused Mac of being afraid of being alone. She said he surrounded himself with people and placeholders so he wouldn't have to face his own disappointment.

Mac had tried to brush it off in the moment, to consider it one of Robyn's hyperbolic platitudes. When they first started dating, he'd loved how she was so opinionated and perceptive, always making big declarations and assessments, like how representatives of Congress should be required to answer their constituents' direct messages on Instagram within six hours of receipt. Mondays called for a meatless diet, whereas Thursdays had to begin with caviar and cocktails (preferably at a restaurant that required a jacket). A night's sleep soundtracked by jazz guaranteed the most fruitful dreams. She believed in and then pursued what she wanted, and Mac found comfort in following her lead.

Now in the Sunday morning light, something about Robyn's analysis of Mac's recent behavior, of their breakup, stuck with him like a piece of gum on his shoe. He replayed her words over in his head. *Macky, I love you, but I think you're afraid of being alone.*

Afraid of being alone.

Was she right?

Mac reviewed the past few months, the mistakes and the cracks rising to the surface. He'd lost sight of so much, forgotten how to move, it seemed.

One thing was for certain: he had so much growing up to do.

He needed to get out of there. His limbs itched to run but his knee, his knee, his stupid, damn knee ruined it all again.

Maybe just a walk on the beach to clear his mind. To figure out what to do next, one step at a time.

Life was just bandwidth, right? His endurance would expand.

Mac leaned off the mattress, gathered his socks and sneakers as silently as he could. Before heading out, he glanced back at Maggie.

Maggie on his pillow. She looked perfect.

But it wasn't meant to be.

He turned the knob as softly as he could on his way out the door.

Chapter 20

Liz woke up to the sound of a door closing down the hall. She heard Cam shift his body, twisting closer to her side. He slipped his arm around her waist. His fingers traced her hip bone. She felt heat under the comforter. He was definitely awake.

"Morning," Liz whispered, her eyes still closed.

"Morning yourself," Cam said, kissing her neck. He pushed his body closer, immersing Liz in his warmth. She loved mornings like this, pressed like pieces of a puzzle, hitting the snooze button, ignoring the sun.

How long could they manage to stay tucked in their room this Sunday morning? They'd planned on taking the three p.m. ferry to Bay Shore. She only needed ten or so minutes to throw her things back in her bag. Take a quick shower. Maybe they could get away with a few hours, hidden from everything, just the two of them. They could fix Cam's phone screen back in the city. Liz could call Mac, apologize for interfering with his love life, smooth it all over when they got home.

For now, Cam and Liz could soak in each other's warmth. They could ignore the world together.

"Can we stay like this forever?" he asked, reading her mind and making her melt.

"I wouldn't mind moving into the Serendipity House for good. Permanent renters."

"Full-time Ocean Beach residents." Cam smiled. The sun shone through the window and landed right on his pillow, shining against his face like a highlighter.

Liz felt her stomach pang with guilt. She hated lying to him. She hated that she wasn't even sure why she had decided lying to him was the best path forward. There was the fear that he might not support her dreams. The shame that she wanted to run abroad as soon as a ring had been placed on her left finger.

Yet Cam had spent a decade proving that he was someone trustworthy, who could catch her upon a fall.

He had spent the past year picking up her pieces.

The first year without her mom had been painful in the missing. The first Memorial Day barbecue missing her famous coleslaw side. The first birthday, missing her signature three cards (one funny, one punny, one sweet). The first dozen times Liz went to call or text her mom and remembered that there was no one waiting on the other side. The advice, the stories, the dreams—all with no one to tell them to. She wished she'd had more time, more opportunities to imprint her mother's brain into her own being, so she wouldn't have to live one more day wondering what her mom might do or say.

The silver lining was that she had Cam.

Last night, when Liz needed a sturdy place to call home, Cam was there. He was outside, holding her, kissing her hair and her neck and her cheeks until the tears were dry.

The daybreak brought new clarity, which Liz hated to realize she'd been lacking. She was ready to tell Cam about Domus. About how a program in Milan might factor into their future.

Then both of their phones buzzed at the same time.

In an instant, Liz glanced at two notifications that sent her gut spiraling to her toes.

The first was from Roseanne. Liz's heart sped up as she read it, skimming the incoming gray cloud.

Phrases like "family heirloom" and "sick with sadness" and "utterly disappointed" popping out like bullets.

The ring.

"You—you told your mom that I lost the engagement ring?" Liz stammered, throat suddenly dry, heartbeat preparing to race. "We said we would deal with it when we got back home. Together."

Cam covered his face with his palms. "I'm sorry. It was a photo."

"What are you talking about?"

"Last night. I sent the group photo of all of us, with the decorations. She wanted to see how it turned out and I wanted to thank her, but then she realized your ring was missing."

"She realized last night?"

Cam nodded. "I feel like such an idiot. She's so upset, of course."

"You talked about this with her last night?"

He just motioned to his phone. Through the cracked screen, Liz picked apart the text messages between Roseanne and Cam, the sadness she expressed over the lost engagement ring. She was disappointed, of course. Angry. That's why Cam had come outside, to get some air, to process the tricky situation his fiancée had put him in. When that didn't work, he told her, he had thrown his phone in frustration.

"This is why *I* wanted to tell her," Liz said, her voice tight. "I would've gotten flowers and promised to pay her back, messaged it correctly."

"I'm sorry, I didn't realize she'd be able to tell from the photo."

Emotions overwhelmed Liz. She felt suffocated and trapped and foolish and sorry. How could she have been so rash to have lost the ring in the first place? Why had she thought it would be okay? Why hadn't she called Roseanne and confessed immediately?

Why was Liz making the wrong decision at every turn?

She'd lost her sense of navigation. It felt like Liz and Cam's official engagement had morphed into something she didn't recognize, like a sculptor had thrown the base out the window and started, lopsided, from scratch. Roseanne had always been loving to Liz, welcoming, always calling Liz her bonus daughter, gifting her hand-me-down designer clothes. Roseanne was strict, sure, but once you made it into her circle, she was fiercely loyal. She was a front-row kind of mom. A read-articles-about-your-job-industry kind of mom. A brag-about-you-to-the-cashier kind of mom. Everyone in town was constantly kept up-to-date on Cam's and Mac's and Liz's successes.

Liz used to love that. Now she wasn't sure where she stood. The ring was inexcusable, a huge mistake. But it felt like a bigger change was brewing beneath the surface. Was Roseanne annoyed that Liz wasn't better at wedding planning? Was she upset with her for some other reason? Or was Liz simply reading into everything, feeling more sensitive to it all, because of her own loss?

Had she made a terrible mistake?

Then Liz let herself read the second email. The second announcement that had buzzed on her phone and threatened to ruin everything.

It was from Domus.

To Elizabeth Gray,

Thank you for your application to the Domus Fellowship. We received an unprecedented level of qualified applicants and it is with regret that we are not able to offer you a spot at this time. You have

been added to a wait list and if there are any subsequent vacancies, you will be promptly notified.

Liz couldn't read the rest. *Wait list.* Tears rose up in her eyes. She felt crushed, her options eviscerated before her. It was almost worse than a flat-out rejection. The hope, she knew, was futile. What were the chances of a wait list turning into an acceptance? Who in their right mind would turn down a dream like Domus, would let Liz walk their path instead? It would never happen, she knew. She resigned herself to the reality: Milan would not be for her.

Did she still have to tell Cam? What would she even say? *Oh, I know your mom is royally mad at us, but also, I secretly applied to a master's program in Italy and I didn't even have the chops to get in.*

She was stuck. With these shifting relationships, suffocating forces.

She looked at her fiancé and was taken aback by the level of sadness in his eyes.

Why make this morning worse?

He didn't need to know. Not yet.

"It'll be okay, right?" Cam said, pulling her against him. "We'll be okay?"

Liz didn't know how to answer honestly. She hadn't been honest all summer, so why start now?

"Sure," she said. When they were teenagers, she'd teased Cam about how *sure* was her least favorite word. It was so noncommittal, so laissez-faire. Now she couldn't manage anything more than the world's smallest promise.

"I'm gonna take a shower," she said, feeling her morale sinking. "Clear my head."

She grabbed her toiletry bag and towel and tiptoed through the house. Past the sleeping bodies hungover on the couch. PJ and Georgie, surrounded by empty beer cans and Nintendo 64 controllers. Liz had to smile—at least someone had a fun summer night.

Still, their summer ease felt in sharp contrast to her own heartbreak. She loved these people. What did it matter that she'd spend another year at home with them?

A smaller voice couldn't help but wonder. Would her mom have wanted her to expand her horizons? Would her mom have been disappointed to see that her daughter didn't even have what it took to get in?

Liz wished she could call her.

The showerhead in the outdoor shower let a steady stream of water fall onto her shoulders. She couldn't help it. She started to cry.

Then she heard a voice that made her eyes open wide.

Chapter 21

Maggie groaned and opened her eyes. A headache banged on her skull to the tune of nearby birds singing outside the window. Reaching for her phone, she typed the voice of her nightmares:

If wine gets better with age, then why do hangovers only get worse as we get older?

She was awake in Mac's bed, fully clothed, alone.

She was mortified.

Last night was a disaster. Ty's delivery of the Kurt news. Her old boss was haunting her, his face flashing behind her eyelids each time Maggie blinked. He was a ghost she was determined to outrun.

Ocean Beach was suffocating. Her mind was swirling. She needed to get out.

She checked the homebound ferry schedule—surely she could make the 10:40 A.M. boat back to Bay Shore? Hop on the next LIRR after that? She'd handle the apologies in Manhattan. Explain everything later.

For now, she needed stable ground.

Maggie crept out of Mac's bedroom and exhaled. Thankfully no one was in the wood-paneled hallway; no one else even seemed to be awake. Where was Mac? She couldn't let herself wonder. Instead, she tiptoed down the hallway, to her and Brenna and Quinn's room. She opened the door as slowly, as silently as she could, eager not to disturb her sleeping roommates. Maggie threw her belongings into her faded purple duffel bag, a hairbrush and miscellaneous makeup. She spied a spare condom at the bottom of the bag, embarrassed to remember how she'd packed one in case the weekend brought unexpected romance. Maggie cringed at the reality. She had spent the night in someone else's bed, but the circumstances couldn't have been less sexy.

As she zipped her bag and tiptoed downstairs, she remembered Mac's worried face as he'd walked her home last night, as he let her cry in his bed, not wanting Brenna and Quinn to come home early and see her in such a state. They settled on his mattress, Maggie under the comforter, Mac on top, as he angled his laptop out so they could both rewatch episodes of *How I Met Your Mother*. She was too exhausted, too hurt, then, to wonder if he was swallowing the same memories. The reminders of the last time they'd been in that very bed together.

Instead, she'd spent last night silently screaming about all that had happened, all that irreversible damage since they'd moved from the category of friends to lovers to exes.

She'd let the show's laugh track lull her to sleep.

Now, as she slid the Serendipity House's kitchen door closed behind her, morning birds chirping their familiar tune, Maggie wondered what it meant, how Mac was there like a shoulder to fall on, right when she needed him most. He was always thinking, always caring, always doing, yet she couldn't ignore how their chemistry had extinguished like a flame doused with water when his lips pressed against her own last night.

The summer in New York had felt like endless round-peg-square-hole syndrome, relearning a rhythm that rewired her roots. Would she ever be able to fit into Mac's life again?

Then she heard movement from the backyard, the porch door swinging open.

Maggie looked up and saw him.

"Mags, I was just coming to find you," Mac said. He held two coffees in a travel tray.

"Hey." She felt her cheeks warm.

"You're leaving?" He clocked her duffel bag.

"I, uh, yeah. I don't feel well," she said—not quite the truth but not quite a lie.

Mac tilted his head. "Is this about last night?"

She bit her lip.

"Can we sit for a second? Talk?" He placed the iced drinks

on the outdoor table, but it only made Maggie want to run. Her blood started racing, her stomach swirling. She generally loved the spotlight, but she hated confrontation, especially when hungover. Especially when so much was at stake. Guilt poured through her, but she knew she couldn't handle a repeat of last night.

She couldn't take another one of Mac's love-soaked confessions.

"Thanks for the coffee," she said, rolling on the balls of her feet, itching to escape. "But I should get going."

"Just one second—"

"Mac, come on, let's not—"

"I dare you, M." His eyes widened, his face serious. "I dare you to tell me what's going on. Why did you move home? Look. Last night—"

"I can't do this again," Maggie said, pained. The reminder of their broken adolescence only made her regret crystallize. "I can't give you what you want, Mac. I know that now. Maybe Robyn should've stayed—"

"Robyn?" He looked stung. "This isn't about Robyn, this is about us."

"There is no *us*, Mac." Maggie's voice was a whisper.

"I know, let me explain—"

"Mac, please, please, don't make me say this all again."

"Really?" He shook his head. "You know, I was doing fine until you came home. Robyn and I were solid. I was good. And then you came and messed with my head and—"

"Ruined everything?" Maggie said, tears brimming involuntarily. "It's what I do. Liz. My parents. My job. Now you. I
broke your heart all over again."

"Christ, Mags." Mac grimaced, running his hands through
his hair before standing up. "I want to be your friend right
now. But do you ever stop and wonder if not everything re-
volves around you?"

It was a punch to the gut. "What is that supposed to
mean?"

"That came out wrong." He winced. "I'm just trying to say,
I've always been there for you. Sometimes I just wish you'd
return the favor." With that, he shook his head and walked
back inside the house. The untouched coffees sat where he'd left
them.

Maggie was too stunned to reply, to call after him, to explain herself. She was mortified, speechless.

Had she misread everything with Mac from the start?

She needed to get out of there, but then she heard another
sound that fixed her feet, frozen.

"Just like that?" a voice called out.

She whipped around and saw Liz, towel wrapped around
her body, the outdoor shower door closing behind her.

"Just like that, you're leaving?" She was staring at Maggie's
duffel bag, shaking her head. It looked like she'd been crying.
"You're leaving all over again?"

Maggie was tongue-tied. "I, uh—last night—"

"Did you ever care about us at all?"

Maggie's whole body went cold. It was like the wind had been knocked right out of her. But before she could reply, Liz swallowed a sob and ran back into the house.

"Of course I did," Maggie whispered, but it was too little, too late.

Her heart sank. How could Liz think that Maggie cared so little? About Mac, about all of them?

That she had only moved home to break their hearts?

Liz, gone again. Liz, the worst casualty.

It had been Liz first, always. Even before Cam and Mac. Liz hadn't just been Maggie's next-door neighbor or best friend. She'd been the closest thing she'd ever had to a sister. Mac was kind and a worthy runner-up, but Liz had always been that support system she craved, that sense of home and peace and place.

Maggie had let flashbacks of teenage hormones and misguided romance get in the way of what had mattered most all along.

She couldn't believe how wrong she had been. How much growing up she still had to do. She had sacrificed her relationships in pursuit of success once before, and she wouldn't do it again.

Ocean Beach blurred by as she walked through the town square to the ferry. The streets were already buzzing with tourists and beach lovers, merriment and day drinking at the ready, but Maggie's mind was racing with apologies and explanations. All her regrets and missteps. And for what? For Kurt? For the embarrassment of a lifetime?

She plopped onto a bench, her heartache in stark contrast to the cheerful foot traffic circling her every which way. She knew it was time to listen to Kurt's voicemails. To read the messages that had poured in, the ones she couldn't handle until now.

She owed her friends the truth about what had happened out in LA.

But that meant being honest with herself. And how could Maggie explain that she had given up her life, her family, her friends, her free time to work for a maniac like Kurt? It was humiliating, embarrassing—for her, for everyone who had hoped for her success. He hadn't needed to use his fists or fingers to harm her. Sometimes, in the worst moments, she'd wished he would hit her. Throw a stapler, like those mailroom horror stories in the past.

Instead, Maggie was subjected to the twisted, slow-burn power of words. Kurt was a yeller, leapt at any opportunity to scream or to scold. Like the days she'd ordered his usual salad, only for him to accuse her of intentionally ruining his diet. Didn't she know he was no longer consuming dairy? he'd shout. Kurt Robinson refused to listen to excuses. He said excuses were just mistakes dressed up as hand-me-downs: useless and in poor taste. If she tried to explain, Kurt would say denial only made her look even uglier than she already was. He told her she needed a nose job, and she'd need a new job, too, if she made a mistake like that again.

Maggie put up with it—the personal tasks, the particular orders, the perennial commands—because she'd convinced herself that this, all of this, was simply what it took. She swallowed the discrepancy between Kurt's slate and the monster behind the scenes. She was working for a visionary. Of course it demanded perfection. It demanded that Maggie chip away at herself day after day, let verbal abuse roll off her back, all with the promise of mentorship. It demanded being on call every waking hour, all in hopes that one day, he would read her scripts. He'd mold her writing, maybe even angel-invest in or help produce her films. She'd be on her way.

Kurt had seen her scribbling in her notebook, sneaking her laptop out in every corner. Opening to Final Draft any second she could get. He knew Maggie's endgame was to make movies of her own.

After two years of Maggie working for him, Kurt called her into his office.

Write something new, he told her. *Give me something.* If it was good, they'd talk.

His voice thick with honey so Maggie hadn't known it was a trap.

She wrote. She barely slept until she'd finished *The Come Back Comeback,* a story about mothers and daughters and friends. Family that never left you behind, that you could always find your way back to again. It was everything she wanted to say to her mom, to Liz, to everyone she'd abandoned when she fled to LA. She was a coward in real life, sure, but in that script . . . she said it all. She set it on Fire Island, the beach community of her youth that still glowed with hope. The perfect backdrop for a rewrite.

She emailed the script to Kurt on a Sunday night, glowing brighter than her laptop screen. It was the best thing she'd ever written, her favorite story yet. It had fallen out of her fingertips like an April shower from the sky. The sweet release, the rush, the pride.

Only, a week passed, and then a month, and Maggie still hadn't heard a word from her boss. It was impossible to focus on her assistant duties when she didn't know what Kurt might say about her writing. It was vulnerable, terrifying.

Finally, she plucked up the courage to ask. *Have you read? What did you think?*

Maggie's career nightmare followed.

He'd hated it, Kurt said. It was one of the worst scripts he'd ever read. The characters were undeveloped, the dialogue felt like Maggie hadn't ever spent time with a real human being. *Do you even have any friends?* He had ridiculed her. She'd never cut it as a screenwriter, he said. She was a pretty good assistant, though, so he'd let her stick around. But there was only so far a girl like her could go in this town.

Maggie spent the next few weeks going through the motions. Was any of this worth it if she couldn't write?

Part two of the nightmare began the following Monday morning, when Kurt added a new project to the status report of his slate. *The Come Back Comeback.* Kurt's next project. Maggie found the script printed on his desk; half of the pages were hers, the other half were butchered with his rewrite.

Maggie's name was nowhere to be found.

Surely it was a mistake. There'd be an explanation. She

deserved a cowriting credit if anything. Weren't those the rules?

Kurt laughed at her when she asked him. He actually laughed. Did he look like someone who followed the rules? She worked for him, didn't she? So technically anything she wrote while in his employ belonged to him. Hadn't she read the fine print in her employment contract?

Maggie could handle the trips to three different restaurants when he couldn't remember which offered his favorite brussels sprouts. She could do the weekly car washes and take the impossible reservation requests in stride. She could do the constant reading, the constant working, the constant tracking, the constant coverage, the constant grind.

She could not do this.

When she threatened to report him to the WGA, he dismissed her out of hand. Who would believe her? Who would care about her? He wasn't afraid of the Writers Guild. He was *Kurt Robinson.* Her name meant nothing.

He fired her after that.

Maggie hadn't cried until she was in her car. Then the realization dawned: She was done. Exhausted, broken. At home, in bed, lying there silently, she wished that she had fought harder. Maybe if she'd had the energy. If she had slept the better part of the past few years.

Then Brenna and Quinn had posted on Facebook that they were looking for a roommate.

It was the final sign. She needed to get out of there. Her

dreams were over. She didn't want to work in LA ever again. She drove back to New York in the next three days. Head hung low, she prepared to face everything she had been most afraid of. Failure. She wasn't special. She wasn't strong. She wasn't cut out for anything interesting or different or big.

She was just mediocre, boring Maggie.

Now, on the park bench in Ocean Beach, she saw the proof in the pudding. The *Deadline* announcement of how Kurt had sold his new hit script. The premise of the movie was the same as hers, but her name had disappeared like sidewalk chalk after a storm.

She listened to Kurt's voicemails, resigned herself to reading his texts. They were all threats, reminders of her NDA, of her contract, of how little she could do about any of this. Maggie was simply a loose end. Kurt wanted to make sure that she was on the same page, that she understood that he was doing this without her. Then he never wanted to hear from her again.

On the park bench in Ocean Beach, Maggie sank her head into her hands.

It was over. Her story had been taken. Her career was gone.

She had never felt more alone.

Then someone tapped her shoulder.

It was Ty.

Despite the still-early hour, he had ice cream from Scoops in his hands.

Ty was the last person Maggie wanted to see right now. A

concrete reminder of how misguided her professional pursuits had been.

Yet his face didn't seem ready to gloat, or to pry. He looked concerned as he sat by her side. He must have seen her through the window of Scoops, walking into town, because he had a second spoon tucked into the cup of mint chip.

"The best thing about ice cream for breakfast is that it tricks your body into thinking the hard stuff is over. That it's already time for dessert," he said, offering Maggie a spoon. "I'm sorry if I interrupted anything last night or said something that made you upset. I didn't mean to."

Maggie swallowed some ice cream, took a good look at Ty. She didn't know why, but she felt a resolve building. She wanted to do things differently. The past wasn't working; she needed to bring about a change.

She had to.

"I haven't been honest with you. About why I'm here, what happened with Kurt," she said.

Ty turned toward her. She watched as his eyes grew wide, his face smoldered, as she told him the truth. All of it. Walking through the history gave clarity to the amorphous, forced her to pull her previously hidden thoughts to the surface. Surprisingly, it felt good, in a weird, foreign way. To bring someone into the fold, to have her hardships heard. He gave appropriate responses when warranted, "I'm so sorry" or "No fucking way," but for the most part, he simply listened.

By the end of her monologue, Ty had a small smile slightly

outweighing the scowl that had previously weighed his face down during her story. "Do you know what I think?"

"That I'm a total pushover loser hopeless talentless poseur who never was cut out for LA in the first place?"

"Dear god, no." Ty laughed, nudging her shoulder gently. "The farthest thing from it. I think you're a rock-star writer who survived one of the worst bosses on the planet. And even Kurt—a monster, who, by the way, we aren't going to let win this—couldn't deny it. Your writing is good, Maggie. It's more than good. Your script sold. And even someone who was determined to keep you broken, lying helpless on the ground, couldn't deny that you have something in you that shines."

Maggie felt her eyes start to tear up ever so slightly.

"And to let him keep you down? Well, then he wins. I definitely don't like that ending. And the rom-com-loving Maggie I know? I have a feeling she'd agree."

The horn of the inbound ferry blasted as Maggie bit her lip. Next to her, she caught Ty staring at the town's bulletin, his eyes drifting toward a flier. The Fire Island Film Festival was next month.

The final weekend in Ocean Beach.

The final chance to change her story. With Liz, with Mac. With herself.

Suddenly, Maggie knew what she had to do.

~~~~~

To: maggie.may.monroe@gmail.com

From: admin@fireislandfilmfestival.org

Congratulations! We are pleased to announce that your short film *Summer of Second Chances* has been accepted into the Fire Island Film Festival. It will be screened at the final awards ceremony on Sunday, August 13th, located at the Ocean Beach Village Community House. The festival will begin at 1:00 p.m. Please see the attached document for a full list of finalists and run time. See you there!

~~~~~

~~~~~

Liz: Hey, sorry, it's been a weird couple of weeks.

Liz: Can we talk Friday in Ocean Beach? Just us?

~~~~~

WEEKEND THREE

~~~

August

Chapter 22

As the temperatures skyrocketed into August, Liz felt like she was walking on progressively thinner ice. For the past month, she had tentatively tipped through the motions, half-hearted yet hyperaware of her untrustworthy ground. It felt like all it would take was one wrong step for everything to shatter.

After the July weekend in Ocean Beach, she reached a tentative truce with Roseanne—the wedding dress shopping fiasco negated by the engagement ring disaster—but Liz was anxious, nervous about future mistakes. She was sure more mishaps lay waiting around the corner.

Meanwhile, Cam flung himself full force into the engagement party planning, playing second assistant to Roseanne and Meghan. Liz had invited a few distant relatives and co-workers and the college friends she'd interacted most frequently with on Instagram, but the majority of the engagement party would be populated by the Peters family. Liz wasn't surprised by that roster; she knew her circle was small. But still, it felt hard to lean into the allure of a party that could have practically been thrown in honor of Cam and [insert fiancée name here].

Tucker, the event coordinator at Maguire's, had welcomed Cam and Liz right off the five thirty p.m. Friday ferry with two complimentary glasses of champagne. Cam and Liz had their arms filled with party decorations, candles for the tables, and twinkling lights for the walls, which they gladly plopped down at Tucker's request in exchange for the bubbles.

The space was gorgeous and distinctly beachy. Massive windows punctuated rich wood walls, decorated with various antique Ocean Beach signs and nautical netting. A large white deck had tables facing directly onto the bay, where the sun was beginning its sparkly descent. It was casual yet sophisticated. Fire Island charm.

It would have been perfect if everything between her and Cam hadn't felt so fragile.

If Cam noticed Liz's recent retreat from the engagement party enthusiasm, he didn't draw attention to it. Over the past few weeks, she had kept her conversations with him light and easy. She'd seen flashes of his anger, his pain, their previous weekend in Ocean Beach. He was struggling, but Liz told herself that all would be better if they could make it past the party. Maybe smiling for the happy relatives would make them happy, too.

The thinnest ice of all was the Domus Fellowship. No changes in application status had occurred, despite Liz's hourly refreshes on the program's website. She would log on to the site each morning as she sipped her coffee, and then again during lunch, and lastly right before bed. No matter the time of day, the answer remained the same: wait list.

Liz hated that she couldn't let her Italian daydream die and be buried, but she didn't want to tell Cam yet and risk breaking their rocky peace over nothing. Over a rejection she knew would come any day now.

Instead, she had boarded the ferry to Fire Island and slapped on a happy face.

"And your mother mentioned someone will be recording the big night?" Tucker asked them now, interrupting Liz's thoughts.

"Yes, our friend Maggie," Cam said.

Maggie. She had texted Liz all month long. Words of encouragement, memes, jokes. Liz didn't answer but Maggie kept them coming. It was her way of apologizing, Liz presumed, of begging forgiveness. Her wish to be let back in.

Liz hadn't known how to answer. She could practically hear her mom in her ear, telling her to forgive. To make space for Maggie again in her life. To at least give her another chance.

Yesterday, Liz finally texted Maggie back, asking to talk in Ocean Beach. She'd rip off the Band-Aid. If Maggie was staying in New York for good, they had to figure out some way forward. Either a blowup or a makeup. It would be either a blessing or a disaster.

Nancy would have known exactly what to do. She had always led with kindness, with grace.

Liz just wasn't sure that she could ever be as strong, as forgiving, as her mother.

"Leave the rest of the decorations right over here for now, we'll make sure everything is set up perfectly before tomorrow." Tucker gestured to the office down the hallway, toward the kitchen.

There, Cam dutifully organized the welcome signs, the banner, the signature cocktail napkins, carefully placing everything on a table, a chair, the floor. As he did, Liz caught sight of a tube of toothpaste poking out among the bags.

It was Frozen Mojito Fresh—one of Robyn's signature flavors.

In all the unexpected moments from this summer so far, Robyn's "goodbye gift" was certainly up there with the most surprising. A few days after Liz and Cam had gotten home in July, and Mac had solidified his breakup with Robyn, a care package arrived at their door. Inside was a sampling of Robyn's start-up prototypes and free products, as well as a card thanking Liz and Cam "for the life experience." Cam had held up the toothpaste and grinned. "Now *this* we could actually use at the engagement party." They'd include it in the bathroom baskets at the venue, along with a warning label: alcohol very much included.

"That should be everything," Cam said, taking stock of the decorations. "Next up, we party." He flashed Liz a smile. His cheeks were tan, his hair even blonder after a summer of weekends in the sun.

"What, something in my teeth?" he asked.

Liz smiled back. "Nah, just checking you out."

"Tomorrow is going to be perfect." He grabbed her hand, twirled her around him. She had no choice but to smile. He still sent butterflies in her stomach, even when she was stressed. "I can't wait to celebrate you, to dance all night."

"Save one for me?" Liz said.

"How about all of them?"

She couldn't help it. She swooned.

"Last order of business. I promised my mom I'd take a photo of the space so she's mentally prepared for tomorrow."

"Easy enough."

"Can I borrow your phone, babe? My screen still looks like a construction site."

Liz rolled her eyes—Cam had been putting off replacing his damaged phone screen for weeks—but acquiesced.

"Thanks, Lizard. Be right back."

He went to record the space, leaving her with a quiet sense of hope. Maybe they could do this together, rechart their way. A party wouldn't be so awful. Surely she could put away her worries for the weekend.

Yet when Cam came back to her, his face pale and angry, she knew she'd been sorely mistaken.

"Can we talk about this outside?" He angled Liz's phone screen back toward her view, toward an email he had no doubt opened and read.

It was from the Domus Academy.

A notification that had rolled down her home page while her phone was in Cam's clutches.

The timing couldn't have been worse.

The subject line was clear as day: **Congratulations on your acceptance—see you in Milan!**

She got in.

But now Cam knew what she'd been hiding. He'd caught her red-handed.

Liz followed him outside, excuses spiraling through her brain, her blood pressure climbing to the sky. "My professor from NYU recommended me for this program—" she started, hoping to explain in the best course, but Cam cut her off.

"Have you been lying to me all summer?" His voice was at once confused and worryingly empty.

She tried to backtrack. "I wasn't sure I'd get in, I didn't want to risk—"

"How does that change anything? You still kept this huge thing from me."

"I wanted to tell you. I just didn't know how. You've been so excited about wedding planning, and this would change things and—"

"Sorry I'm excited to marry you, Liz! Didn't realize that was a crime."

She wanted to get closer to him, but he flinched back when she took a step toward him.

"That's not what I mean. I just, I knew you'd be upset. And the acceptance rates are so low—"

"So what? I still deserve to know you're applying to some-place halfway around the world. You're my *fiancée*, Liz, we are getting *married*!"

"You're right. I'm so sorry. Really. There's no excuse. I'm just saying—"

"And you knew I'd be upset because it's the wrong thing to do."

Liz felt like she'd been burned. "The wrong thing to do?"

"We're engaged. We're getting married. We're building our life together and now you want to run away from it all? Go to Italy for some random program? I didn't think grad school was a thing in the fashion world. How is this even necessary?"

It was the exact reaction she'd feared. "You don't know anything about it. How could you say that?"

"Why do you need to run right as things are getting good?"

"You think this is good?"

"We're planning a wedding! *Our* wedding!"

"*You're* planning a wedding. You and your mom. I know she's a professional, but do you really think this is making it any easier for me?" Liz yelled, sick of biting her tongue. Cam had struck a nerve, and everything fell out of her. "A proposal next to your parents' apartment? A wedding picked out by your mom? An entire engagement party planned practically just for your family? Do you, do *either* of you ever stop for one second to think about if this is what I want? To ask yourself if I even can do this—do any of this—without *my* mom?"

"Liz." Cam moved toward her, but this time, it was Liz who backed away.

"No. I tried to smile and go along with all of this. Do you have any idea how hard this is with you guys throwing your happiness in my face? I love your family. I want to be a part of your family. But this? This is hard for me. Without her."

It was everything Liz had spent the past two months feeling in the deep, dark corners of her heart. Everything she'd tried not to dwell on in order to move through the day. She missed her mom more than anything, and even though she knew Nancy would want her to celebrate, to be a glowing bride, Liz couldn't. The grief hadn't shrunk, it had grown into some new body part, a limb of its own. She took it with her wherever she went, and though she tried to hide it, swallowing her sadness when she could, Liz had reached her limit.

Wedding planning had made it clear. For the rest of Liz's life, her mom wasn't going to be there.

"Liz," Cam said again, walking toward her once more.

"Stop. I don't want to look at you."

"You don't have to," he said, pulling her into a hug. "I am so, so sorry. But Italy? All these lies? I mean, is that really what's going to help us right now?"

"I don't know. Maybe? I'm sorry I didn't tell you, but I just feel like I don't know anything anymore. Nothing is making sense," she whispered into his shoulder.

"We make sense though, right?" Cam's voice was low.

After considering for what seemed a lifetime, Liz wasn't so

sure. "I think I need to be by myself for a little. Can we talk about this later?"

Cam's face was pained, but a part of him must have felt the same. The part that felt betrayed by her lying, by her secrets. By her wanting to escape to Italy, to leave him behind.

"Okay," he said. Without putting up any more of a fight, Cam grabbed their bags and turned to walk toward the Serendipity House, alone.

Liz shakily pulled out her phone and didn't exhale until she heard the voice answer on the line. "Any chance you're ready now?"

Chapter 23

Maggie hadn't been exactly ready for her world to come rocking, but she was starting to see the bright side to a tectonic shift. Back in Ocean Beach in July, Ty had unlocked a monumental reframe in Maggie, one so powerful she would've been jealous of his insight if she hadn't been so grateful for his words. Because he was right. Maggie had spent years tying her self-worth to her career, seeking external validation from toxic people. Kurt had tossed her over a cliff, straight to rock bottom, but now she had a ladder. She could climb her way out, one rung at a time.

First, she'd attempt to process the only way she knew how: by writing.

When Maggie walked into her Murray Hill apartment back on that Sunday afternoon, she opened her laptop and started to work on her short. It was breathless, restless, but it had to be. She only had three weeks to prepare something in time for the Fire Island Film Festival's deadline. With Ty's surprising encouragement, she suddenly knew that she had to enter, to see if she still had it in her, this dream she'd spent all summer attempting to forget.

By the time Brenna and Quinn had returned home from their Sunday evening ferry, Maggie had a sense, an outline, of the movie she wanted to shoot. *Summer of Second Chances* would be about two best friends in New York, finding their way back together after years adrift. Brenna and Quinn accepted their starring roles before Maggie could finish her request.

Then, Maggie opened up to them about what she'd endured in LA. About how Kurt had continually berated her, then stolen her words, then had been checking in on her surrender, sending threatening texts and emails to make sure she kept the truth at bay.

They hugged her tight for what felt like a beautiful eternity before Brenna extracted herself to research labor laws and studio HR policies and WGA credit arbitration processes. Quinn looked up a series of cross-continental hexes that might work faster, just in case.

Even though the harm was done, and Maggie knew she wouldn't let him get away with it, the relief of sharing the truth, of being honest and vulnerable, was instant. She cursed the June version of herself who'd been too proud and stubborn to trust that anyone might catch her from her free fall. Brenna and Quinn had proven the exact opposite. For so long, Maggie had felt like her corner had been covered in cobwebs, having soldiered through so much alone. It felt good to look around and see some furniture, a painting or two. She was so lucky to have them.

Those next weeks of filming in New York City had been exhilarating. Riding the subway with her equipment, going from a water scene on the East River Esplanade to an exterior FiDi café in a matter of blocks. Coaching Brenna and Quinn on their lines, laughing through it all. Maggie even took the Staten Island Ferry (for free!) to cover her establishing shots. The sunset behind the Statue of Liberty. A sunrise over downtown.

She loved it.

When she found out *Summer of Second Chances* had been accepted, she sent Ty the *Breakfast Club* fist pump GIF and tried to ignore how the thought of him made her stomach tighten, just a little.

Now Maggie hoped she'd make it to the festival to see their hard work presented on a screen.

Assuming Liz didn't send her packing from Fire Island first.

Liz's and Mac's faces had gnawed at Maggie like a pit in her stomach the past few weeks. She hated how she'd left things with them, hated more the cold shoulder they'd both sent in her direction since. She knew it was what she deserved. She'd been selfish and self-centered. For weeks, Maggie had been convinced that Liz and the Peters family were going to disinvite her from the engagement party entirely. They hadn't officially asked her to stay back yet, to skip the final Ocean Beach weekend, but Liz hadn't answered a single text that Maggie had sent all month. Maggie could read between those lines.

Until her phone pinged yesterday.

Liz: Can we talk Friday in Ocean Beach? Just us?

Maggie was all too familiar with the Judgment Day trope in movies. The grand retribution, the payback for all the protagonist's flaws. Maggie knew what was coming in hers. The *Hey, soooo we don't actually need a videographer, and maybe you should just stay home entirely, and let's never try being friends again* talk. She spent the entire ferry ride over coming to terms with it.

She was never going to be welcomed back by Cam, Mac, and Liz.

Settling into her room at the Serendipity House, Maggie realized this could be her last day here. After Liz officially ended their friendship, Maggie knew she'd have to leave, to give Liz her space. She was grateful that at least she'd hopefully still have Brenna and Quinn. That maybe Georgie and PJ would still meet her for pizza and Bud Light towers at Cornerstone Tavern if she asked nicely. She plopped onto the rental's trundle bed and tried not to cry.

Then Liz called.

Her voice was shaky when she asked if Maggie could come talk now. Originally, Liz had suggested meeting at the bay for drinks after her and Cam's meeting with the Maguire's event coordinator. Maggie figured the meeting had ended early. Liz probably wanted to get their awkward conversation out of the way.

It felt like a date. She smoothed her hair and quickly changed her outfit three times and her earring choice once before racing out the door.

Maggie wrote as she walked:

I have no eloquent words, no observations, no poems. I only have one wish: please, please, please, let this go well. I miss my best friend.

As Maggie turned onto Bay Walk, she saw Liz standing in a beam of sun, such perfect lighting that it felt like a set. The best views on Fire Island were here, on the bay beach, where the water sparkled and the sky looked like a painting. Liz's red hair was longer than it used to be when they were kids, but Maggie's mind still flashed with a scrapbook of photographs from their youth. Girl Scout camping trips and bowling birthday parties, the soccer summer league neither should have signed up for. Afternoons picking flowers and singing songs on the sidelines instead of following the ball or learning offsides.

Now in Ocean Beach, Maggie felt herself taken aback. What was it about friendship that made her heart swell? Liz was more than a friend, she was a sister.

Maggie had risked losing it all.

She rushed up to Liz now and felt tears bubble in her eyes. The apologies, the explanations that Maggie had rehearsed sat on her tongue, but suddenly, nothing was enough. Instead, she pulled her friend, her best friend, into a hug. She cried.

And Liz laughed. Her signature avalanche. "Are you okay?"

Maggie laughed back at herself, at her tears. "I don't think I've been okay for a while."

Liz grabbed her hand. Her face was furrowed, too. "Me either."

Maggie and Liz spoke at the same time.

"Liz, I'm so sorry—"

"You remind me of her."

Maggie raised her eyebrows. "I remind you of who?"

"My mom," Liz said, and Maggie felt goose bumps spread. "She'd be so proud of you, you know? And it hurts to think about the things she *would have* been."

Maggie shook her head. "I've been awful."

"You've been tough," Liz said. "Brenna and Quinn told me about what happened in LA. They knew how much it was weighing on you. I'm so sorry you had to deal with that."

"It's no excuse to be a terrible friend."

"I haven't been much better," Liz said. "I just, well. I don't think I was prepared for how much you remind me of her. Of my mom. Of everything we've been through."

"I do?"

"It's like I see it everywhere now that you're back. All the memories. Us as kids, as teenagers. You remind me of a happier time, and I guess I just . . . I haven't really wanted to let myself feel happy. And I think I blamed you for that. For all the things you make me think about that I don't have anymore."

Liz's lip quivered as Maggie let her friend's words soak in. An engagement was supposed to usher in the happiest moments of someone's life. A celebration and a promise of the shared life ahead. Yet Liz's happiness was still shrouded in the sadness of the missing. Of course it was. Maggie hated that she'd been absent for so many opportunities to take her friend's sadness in stride, to shoulder it, to share. That she had moved when Liz needed her most.

But Maggie could be here for her now.

She traced her fingers in the sand. Before she knew what she was doing, she held a clump of the fine grains in her palm, and she spoke. "I'll never forget Nancy's smile, or the smell of her kitchen. Those bright yellow walls popping against her orange hair as she whipped up cookie dough and let us carve out chunks with spoons. The crunch of the chocolate chips between our teeth like secrets just for us. Nancy's stories, her Brooklyn accent, her advice, her reliability. She was there when I needed her, a family that I chose, a family that she graciously let me share." Maggie's voice cracked but she persevered. "Nancy, I promise to carry on your spark, to laugh and smile and cheat with chocolate dough. To always care for those who need it most. I miss you, I love you. Forever, forever."

In an instant, Maggie raised her arm and tossed her

handful into the bay. The sand hit the waves with a shimmer like raindrops or sprinkles from the sky.

"To Nancy," she whispered.

When she looked over at Liz, she was surprised to see that her friend had gathered up her own handful of sand. Liz joined her at the edge and lifted her fingers one by one, the sand trickling down into the depths of the bay.

"I miss you, Mom. So much. Thank you, for everything. I hope I make you proud."

Maggie grabbed Liz's hand and squeezed. "I bet she's laughing at us somewhere, you know. 'Those two girls, always so *dramatic*,'" Maggie said, in her best Brooklyn accent.

Liz cackled. "She totally is laughing at us. And she wouldn't be wrong. I've been pretty dramatic."

"So have I."

"And pretty mean."

"So have I."

"I'm really sorry."

"I'm so sorry, too. So, so sorry, for it all. I never meant to hurt you. I just wanted to make you all proud."

"We'll always be proud of you, Maggie. Even if you do nothing at all. You're one of ours."

Maggie nodded, letting herself believe Liz's words.

"Let's never do this again?"

"Promise," Maggie swore.

"Promise. Are girls the worst?" Liz asked.

"They're the best," Maggie said.

As the friends sat down in the sand, crisscross-applesauce style, like the postures of their youth, Liz let her head rest on Maggie's shoulder. "Sisters are even better," she said with a sigh, and Maggie felt her stomach pulse with a pit again.

"All that Mac stuff, I'm sorry if I made you—"

Liz sat up straight. "Mags, I didn't mean it like that."

"As much as I'd love to be sisters-in-law, I don't think there's ever going to be a real future for me and Mac," Maggie said. "I'm sorry to let you down."

"No, I'm the one who's sorry. For putting pressure on you guys. I think I just wanted you to be as happy as I was," Liz said. "But we don't need the Peters boys to be sisters. We were sisters way before they even joined our bus stop, remember?"

"Don't let Cam hear that. He still insists they single-handedly supplied the street with a 'whole new energy,'" Maggie said.

At the thought of Cam, though, Liz's face looked pale.

"What's wrong?" Maggie asked.

"That Milan program I told you about?" Liz's chin crumpled. "I got in."

Maggie leapt up. "Liz! What? That's incredible! Congratulations!"

Liz pulled her back down to where they'd been seated. "But Cam found it out in the worst way possible. Just now. We fought about everything and I don't know what to do." She groaned, leaned her head again on Maggie's shoulder. "What do you think?"

Maggie softened. "I know I've been gone for too long, but the way he looks at you, Liz? It's like you're both still seventeen. You're meant to be together. I know it in my bones. Give him a chance to see what you see in Milan. And if you need to cry or scream or vent or just eat chocolate chip cookies for an hour, you know where to find me. This time, I'm not going anywhere."

Maggie meant it.

t was one of those overused platitudes, but Cam *really* meant
it when he said he didn't like change.

Cam had eaten the same lunch every day from kindergarten through twelfth grade, a turkey-and-Swiss sandwich.
He'd worn the same hairstyle since he was eleven. Despite the
overt security risk, he'd had the same password, ringostarfish96,
for every internet account from the time he downloaded AIM
and was in a big Beatles phase.

And ever since the very best day of his life, he'd had the
same girlfriend. Well, until she became his fiancée.

When Cam signed his fellow East Meadow classmates'
yearbooks with the words *Never change* in bold, he took his own
advice and was sure to follow through. He stayed close with his
family and friends. He remained at the top of his academic
classes. He put everything into his relationship with Liz. He

liked order, familiarity. He felt duty-bound to be reliable and counted on. To stay as close to the same as one humanly could.

But adulthood brought changes that Cam couldn't avoid.

Like Nancy.

When Nancy's cancer came back, Cam held tight. To Liz, to anything that could make her happy. But he also tried to keep all the other parts of their life the same, to give Liz a small source of comfort amid the unthinkable chaos. He still kept their apartment clean and made all her favorite meals and even maintained a running list of funny tweets and adorable dog photos to show her when she needed a smile. He still came home with flowers like he did every Thursday after work. Cam held Liz tight and didn't let go. He wanted to wear her pain for her, to inhale it and paint it on his body in a desperate prayer that she might be okay. He wanted to be her armor, keep her safe.

When the worst of it was behind them, when they'd made it through that first awful year without Nancy, Cam felt an inner itch toward the next step. An engagement. A promise to make Liz his permanent family. To be her armor, forever.

It was funny, because proposing to Liz *should* have felt like more of the same. Cam figured it would mean more dances, more of their favorite weekend rituals, like picnics in the park. More of the promises he'd always made, to never leave her side. More Cam and Liz. The two of them. Only now it would be officially forever.

But the moment Cam told his parents that he wanted to

propose, he felt the energy around him change, like a tilting of some fundamental axis. Especially when it came to his mom. He loved his mom, he and Mac owed everything to her. But it was clear from the beginning that bringing Roseanne into the engagement fold brought her into their relationship, too. Cam felt that the two roles he'd always played to perfection—loyal son and loyal boyfriend—were suddenly at odds when it came to all things wedding planning. His family dynamics were being redefined and it was like each day-to-day had a whole new instruction guide. One that was in a foreign language, one that he could never understand, one that he failed and failed and failed.

His relationships didn't feel the same, and that made Cam so sick. He'd spent the summer almost constantly nauseated. The anxiety infected his bloodstream, and he knew he was making bad decisions because of it, that he was disappointing everyone. How could he tell his mom to scale back when her passion for planning was also her new profession? Would she hate him forever if he admitted that he didn't want to be her client, he only wanted to be her son?

He couldn't be honest with his mom, but he couldn't be honest with Liz either. How could he complain about his mom and her over-the-top involvement to someone who'd spent the past year mourning her own? Instead, Cam would drink too much just to escape his own brain, but he'd regret it immediately. He lashed out. He kept secrets.

He hated how much everything had changed.

This afternoon at Maguire's, it was like Cam was seeing some bizarre, distorted reality of his life. Liz had lied to him all summer, too. How had he not been able to sense that she was keeping something from him?

Now she was talking about Italy, about moving away. The biggest change yet. What would they do?

Cam knew that he couldn't control everything. Life would exist outside his purview, and he'd have to adapt, to relent.

But Liz, his favorite person, had never belonged to that category. The girl he'd fallen in love with on the playground and the school bus, the friend turned soul mate turned fiancée, had stayed by his side for as long as he could remember. Why did this feel so different now?

Cam looked around the Serendipity House as he walked inside, greeted his friends with false enthusiasm, and headed straight to the room, a quiet space where he could collect his thoughts, rest his mind.

He hadn't noticed it back in June, but he realized now that there'd been changes to the share house since their after-prom weekend, too. The coffee machine had been updated, the once-peeling wallpaper in the bathroom redone. The hallway floorboards still creaked and the armchair still sagged, but there were differences, too.

The Serendipity House hadn't stayed exactly the same.

Had any of the people currently living inside it? He thought about his friends hanging out downstairs and their various new jobs, new hairstyles, new hobbies over the years. Quinn had learned a new language, Brenna had switched to a new career, PJ had moved to a whole new city after UVA. The list went on and on.

Could anyone stay the same? Cam wondered, as he laid his head down on the pillow and closed his eyes. Was change the only constant?

He wasn't sure, but from the comfort of the Serendipity House, the wind blowing in gently from the opened window, he let himself slowly consider the possibility.

Change was all around him, he realized, as he let his breathing rock and slow. Had it always been?

Suddenly, Cam's eyelids burst open, and he woke up from his afternoon daydream with an idea.

He needed to call his brother.

Chapter 25

When Maggie woke up on Saturday morning, her mouth still tasted like margaritas. Friday's taco night dinner at the Serendipity House had left her with a hangover, but there was a lightness to it, a brightness that hadn't been there yet this summer.

PJ's signature guacamole was spicy, Quinn's signature margaritas were sweet, and Maggie felt balanced knowing she could look around the room and not be afraid to make eye contact with Liz, or worry about accidentally sitting next to her on the couch, hoping Liz wasn't hating her guts.

It felt like rolling her shoulders down her back, unclenching. Maggie had spent so much time worried about Liz, their silence. Holding a grudge was a chore in and of itself. Yesterday was a much-needed course correction, back on the track they'd laid as kids.

During last night's pregame, the friends told stories and sipped cocktails, played games and gave dares. Brenna obliged and took a tequila shot out of the refried bean can, the residual legumes tinting the liquor with flair. When their favorite We The Kings song from tenth grade came on, they even remembered their choreographed dance. Well, a few moves from it, at least.

As the sun set and the stars appeared, the friends took their party to the streets. It was their last Fire Island weekend and they wanted to kick it off in quintessential Ocean Beach bar-hopping fashion. First was Albatross, a dive bar where they ordered a round of Rocket Fuels. Per tradition, Brenna and Liz took turns swinging the squiggly shaped lamps that dangled from the ceiling whenever the staff weren't looking. The lamps hovered low over the bar counter and would wave like pendulums. A row of dartboards lined the back wall, and when PJ won the round, Maggie signed "Serendipity" in loopy scrawl on the dart blackboard. The Island Mermaid was their second stop; the restaurant right on the water was soundtracked in the evenings by a live band. They ended the night at Housers, which turned into a nightclub, and the friends danced and took shots. Georgie and PJ bought a round for a pair of brunettes at the bar while Maggie, Liz, Brenna, and Quinn formed a dance circle they didn't break for a sweaty hour.

It was the summer night a friend group dreams about, when nothing matters except the laughter and the memories and the music. When you feel like, together, you could take on anything.

As long as you didn't harp on what was missing.

Mac and Cam.

Cam had stayed back for the night, in very un-Cam-like fashion. Liz told the friends that he was coming down with a headache and wanted to sleep it off, at the risk of it bleeding into the engagement party day. But on the walk home, as Liz and Maggie drunkenly stumbled past a couple of deer lying in the park by the town hall, an Ocean Beach trademark, Liz told Maggie the truth. She'd overheard Cam earlier on the phone with Mac. He seemed stressed, which made Liz stressed, too.

Before they left for the bars, Liz had tried to talk to Cam about Domus again, but this time he was the one who pulled away. He claimed he needed to figure out a few other things first.

Liz was nervous.

Maggie promised her that it would all be okay, but what else could Maggie do?

She stood by Liz's side, tried to distract her with a night out. But Maggie was nervous, too. If Liz and Cam broke up, would it be the end of their East Meadow friend group? Would the guys and girls fissure, the group puncture back to the way it had been in middle school? Was this the dawning of the end of an era as they knew it?

Rubbing the sleep out of her eyes, Maggie yawned, donned a bikini and cover-up, and headed down to the kitchen, where she found her roommates. Brenna and Quinn were flipping pancakes, scrambling eggs. Maggie grabbed a yellow Gatorade from the fridge and checked the large farmhouse clock.

There was another Peters boy to fret about first.

Maggie had half an hour until Mac's ferry arrived. He'd decided to come in Saturday morning with his parents and his grandma, to help load their car with supplies and make sure they were settled in their own rental for the weekend. She needed to talk to Mac as soon as he got to town, to smooth things over before the rest of the house exploded.

"Order up." Quinn's voice shook Maggie out of her thoughts as she slid a pancake-covered plate down the counter. "You ready?"

"Define 'ready,'" Maggie said. "I think he'll maybe hate me forever."

"Maybe," Brenna said. "But you still have to give him the chance."

"Chances, shmances," Maggie said, mouth full of banana-chocolate-chip pancake, but she knew Brenna was right.

"And you and Liz?" Quinn said. "Last night felt like old times."

"Which we're happy about," Brenna added.

"Me, too." Maggie smiled. "Here's hoping this is the summer of forgiveness."

"Starting with my body forgiving my brain for those shots," Quinn laughed.

"Last weekend out here, gotta end it with a bang."

"More like a *splash*," Georgie suddenly shouted as he

barged down the stairs. He had a portable speaker in one hand and timed it so that right as he entered the kitchen, "Surfin' USA" blasted through the house.

Maggie cocked her head. "Have you been standing there waiting for a good cue?"

"Nope! Just lucky timing." Georgie did a little dance in his board shorts.

"This is actually doing wonders for my headache," Maggie said with a laugh.

"Okay, Georgie. What's going on?" Brenna asked.

"I met a girl."

"Ah," Maggie said. "The beginning of every great story."

"I met a girl last night and she told me that there's Jet Skis at the marina. For rent. We're doing it." Georgie turned the music up even louder, causing PJ to appear in the hallway behind him, pajama-clad and hair askew, but smiling.

"I surprisingly don't hate a musical wake-up," PJ said. "Where were these all summer?"

"Two words, people. Jet. Skis. That actually might be one word. I'm not sure about the hyphen status. Let's go."

Before long, in a moment of beautiful spontaneity, the group had changed into appropriate water-wear and were walking to the marina. Everyone except Cam and Mac, that is. Mac was on the inbound ferry with his parents, and Cam had gone straight to his family's rental house to make sure everything was set for their arrival. He'd said it was a one-man job, no reason for Liz to miss out on the fun.

The sun was hot already, and Maggie could hear her friends drafting a text for Georgie to send to the girl from last night. They debated verbiage and punctuation, the strongest starting word.

For Maggie, their voices went in one ear and straight out the other. All she could focus on was attempting to settle the rubber-band ball of nerves in her stomach. The anticipation of seeing Mac again was just as terrifying and as electrifying and as annoying as it had been when she first moved home.

The friends got to the dock as the ferry pulled in, shouting greetings as the deckhands tied the boat to the dock. "The Peters have arrived!" "Hi, Grandma Peach!" "Mr. and Mrs. Peters, you made it!"

Mac's face was tan, his hair longer. He smiled as he helped his grandma down the ferry's steps, as he piled their bags into their folding wire cart.

Maggie snuck out her phone as she looked at him, over-whelmed with words.

I love how he helps his family. How he always helps us all. He's a prince and he's charming, but I know by now that he'll never be mine. I'm not in love with Mac, but maybe I did love the story. A fairy tale, friends to lovers. But it was only ever fiction.

She felt her hands shaking as the Peters family approached.

"Maggie, it's been so long. I was pleased to hear you'd moved back home," Roseanne said, pushing her sunglasses to the top of her head. She was beach casual chic, cream linen culottes and a simple black tank. Roseanne was nothing if not put together.

"And how lucky for us, to have you record tonight's party, too," Mr. Peters chimed in.

"I really can't wait," Maggie said. "Thanks for inviting me."

"Of course, dear. Well, we better get going. We'll see you tonight—make sure your dancing shoes are ready, kids!"

Before Mac could turn to head off with his family, Maggie made herself speak. "Hey, Mac, could I talk to you for a sec?"

He looked quickly at his mom, who nodded. "I'll be at the house in a few. This won't take long," he said. Daggers to Maggie's confidence, but she powered through. She had to say this now, before she ruined anything else. The final apology.

"So, what's up, Maggie? What do you want to talk about?" Mac's voice was light, but she could tell it was only because he was trying to make it sound that way. They hadn't spoken since July.

"Can we walk?"

He looked over his shoulder in the direction of his family as they shrank from view.

"It'll be quick, promise," Maggie said.

Mac shrugged, relenting, and followed her down Bay Walk. When they passed Rachel's Bakery, the quaint yet delicious coffee shop and pastry store, Maggie suggested they stop for a quick iced coffee.

"I really don't have much time, Maggie."

"Just one coffee."

"Fine," Mac agreed, "but only because I slept at my

parents' last night and my grandma wakes up before dawn. The TV has been on since three a.m., I swear."

Maggie bought them two iced coffees, trying to bolster her nerves. She wanted to call attention to the extra-large piece of crumb cake with M&M's on it right next to the cash register, ease the tension, but she resisted.

Sitting down outside the bakery, she braced herself for the potential end of M&M.

"I don't know if you remember this, but when I first floated the idea of transferring to UCLA, you immediately told me to go for it. No questions asked. I remember being so stunned that you'd be so easily supportive of me moving that far. To a whole new time zone and everything. But you never made me feel guilty. Never made me feel less sure."

"Sometimes you have to go far to get close to your dreams," Mac said, and Maggie ignored the familiar instinct to tease him for saying something so cutely clichéd. Maybe once they were friends again, they could return to their rhythm.

She kept going: "I can't apologize for leaving you guys, for breaking up, for moving to LA. But I never should have led you on when I came back."

Mac stared at his knees. "I always liked you, Maggie. You didn't lead me anywhere."

"I liked you, too. It was scary back then. I didn't want to mess it up. You were Mac Peters, for Christ's sake. *The* Mac Peters. The freaking king of Long Island," she teased, a dare now just to see if he would smile.

He did.

"And it could have been perfect," Maggie went on. "Me and you and Liz and Cam. But then it fizzled, remember? And yet after I had gone, I always missed you. Missed what you represented here. What might have happened if I stayed. So, when everything turned sideways in LA, when I felt like I was at my lowest, I wanted the closest thing I'd ever had to perfection. I wanted you."

Mac took a sip of his coffee, the ice cubes rattling. Maggie couldn't stop now.

"I'm sorry that I confused things. I used my own quarter-life crisis against you, to twist things up that could have just been simple. It was selfish. I never wanted to get in the way of things with you and Robyn."

"Robyn and I weren't meant to be."

"I sadly don't think we are either. Not anymore. I'm so sorry, Mac. I just miss you. Our friendship. I hated life without you in LA. I hate life even more without you here. I think I wanted to see what would have happened to us, for us, if I stayed. But now I wish I could take it all back and just start over. I'm so afraid that if I lose you, I'll lose all of this, too."

Maggie realized that was why her bones shook when she saw Mac. Why her stomach tossed and turned.

She'd thought it was because she still had feelings for him.

In reality? Maggie shook because she was afraid of him. Afraid of what life would look like if he vanished from it again.

If *all* of her East Meadow friends did.

Mac had been her most recent rock, her home base, her way back into the group after things went sour with Liz. Maggie had taken him for granted. No wonder Liz had held it against her for so long. When Mac had given Maggie nothing but kindness and love and friendship, how had she repaid him? All of them?

By falling out of touch. By throwing it away.

Now Maggie was throwing it all back to Mac at last, and she just hoped he'd catch her. It wasn't a typical profession of love; growing up in the same town as someone didn't mean you had to be soul mates. She knew that now. It was okay if that sort of love didn't last forever. There was room to change and grow, to morph into something new.

Maggie just hoped that Mac would want that, too.

He sat silently, and she braced herself.

But then he did the unthinkable. He turned toward her, and he kissed her on the cheek. "I love you, M. You're the best. But you have to know by now, after this summer especially. You don't need me as your boyfriend to have a home in New York." Her breath caught but he continued. "I'm sorry, too. I wasn't welcoming either when you first came back. I needed space from you when I was with Robyn. Then she left and, well, I guess I'd been deluding myself a bit, too. It felt easy to think you were the answer, plopped back in my life when I needed it most." Mac shook his head.

"What do you mean?"

He inhaled. "I was mad at you for not being honest with

me, but I haven't been all that honest with myself either. I've been feeling off these days, too. Like, nothing I do is right. With Robyn, my knee, my job. When you came home, it reminded me of how things used to be. Of the person I used to be. The person I used to love being."

"I know the feeling."

"It's not so easy, this growing up thing, is it?" Mac gave her a smile, smaller than his signature one but just as kind, just as caring. He looked straight into her eyes.

"It's definitely not. But we'll figure it out together," Maggie said, trying not to let her voice crack.

He laughed, wiped his own eyes. "All right, enough dramatics. Sheesh, Maggie, welcome home. You haven't changed a bit." He teased, she laughed, like old times again. "How about you buy me that M&M crumb cake and we call this whole thing even?"

She grinned. "You've got a deal."

Chapter 26

Brenna and Quinn didn't need a Jet Ski to feel like they were living on the edge. The ups and downs of the summer, the deal-or-no-deal drama of their friend group, had shocked them plenty already.

When the marina saleswoman told Georgie that there weren't enough Jet Skis available for the whole of their group, Brenna and Quinn opted out within seconds. They'd had their eyes on the tennis racquet rentals from the moment they'd walked into the shop.

Brenna and Quinn had been second-string doubles partners on the East Meadow tennis team from eighth until tenth grade, when they'd both been cut from varsity. They'd still played after school, in the bubble at Club Fit, or over long weekends and breaks between semesters when they were home from college. It was harder to find court time in the city unless you woke up at four a.m. to try your luck for a Central Park court, which neither Brenna nor Quinn had any interest in doing.

Now they'd happily settled into the rhythm of a rally. The Ocean Beach court looked right onto the bay. Salt air filled their noses as they alternated serves. Their thoughts moved easier to the sound of a tennis ball flying over a net. They always had.

Brenna and Quinn had been best friends ever since their moms signed them up for the same baby music class when they were just eight months old. Quinn was an only child, and Brenna was the youngest of six, all older brothers. They found each other before their brains were even fully formed, but even then, they had clung hard to each other.

There was no denying they were different from each other. And their differences only grew with age. By middle school, Quinn was sarcastic and dry, often wearing exclusively black clothes. Her long dark hair was always in two braids down her back like Wednesday Addams. Meanwhile, Brenna's brunette hair never grew past her shoulders, dancing at the collar of her signature denim jacket decorated with a smiley-face patch on the back. Its wide grin couldn't compete with Brenna's own.

Yet Brenna and Quinn were inseparable because of everything they had in common. They unabashedly loved Broadway shows and musicals but were terrified of clowns and circuses. The only exception ever made was for *The Greatest Showman*, though it was no secret why. Two words: Hugh Jackman. They loved spicy foods and baked goods and going thrifting for antique furniture they could never afford. They'd always create fictional stories about who had owned them and discarded them and why, before moving on to explore and inspect the next armoire or old tufted couch.

Above all else, though, Brenna and Quinn were inseparable because they both loved friendship. More than anything. It was simple: they got a kick out of each other. And they got a kick out of their friends.

Nothing had been better than their East Meadow group.

For most of the summer, for the high points at least, there was nothing better than their friends, together right now, at age twenty-five. Sweet, sweet twenty-five.

Some people cried when they turned twenty-one, or when they graduated college and entered the real world. Quinn and Brenna? They loved their midtwenties. They were energized by this singular time of life. Finally, they had disposable incomes and autonomy. They had the streets of New York City, the TKTS booth, twenty-four-hour karaoke, and Levain cookies. They had all their friends back in the same neighborhood, living along Second Avenue. They were together again, but older, better. It was perfect.

The youngest of Brenna's brothers was five years older than her, so she'd seen countless times firsthand how this age—this twenty-five-year-old magic—didn't last. Twenty-five and twenty-six were the beginning of a turning point, a tip toward a change that Brenna and Quinn weren't yet ready for. The second phase of adulthood, when everything went from loud and wild to quiet and contained.

Marriage, kids. They might be far-off plans right now, but Brenna and Quinn knew they'd be there in a blink. It would be a cycle that began, a wheel that would get going and wouldn't pause again until they were in their thirties. By the time it stopped, by the time they got off the carousel ride and looked around at each other, so much would have changed.

Liz and Cam were already engaged. They'd probably be married by next summer. How much longer would they still squeeze into vacation rentals with eight high school friends? How much longer would someone be willing to crash in a bunk bed or pass out on a couch before backs started hurting or boyfriends and girlfriends and partners were added to the equation and twin beds just wouldn't cut it?

How much longer until all their calendars started to fill with weddings and showers, bachelorette weekends and plans? How much longer could they all find three weekends in one summer alone to commit to nothing but friendship? No work—well, except maybe for Georgie—no parents, no weddings. Just each other.

Brenna watched her brothers' friend groups dwindle as they each paired off, got married, and settled down. Mortgages and business trips. New jobs in new cities. New priorities, new plans.

She watched as the big group trips, the friend group trips, went the way of the dinosaurs.

Still, Brenna wasn't afraid of that, no matter how existentially dread-prone her spiral became. She knew it was a part of life. She recognized and respected the rules of growing up.

It just made her even more determined to make the most of what she had now.

Twenty-five and free. The buzz of it all. Her friends together. A summer, all here. She'd always do whatever she could to make them happy. Even if sometimes that meant meddling when they didn't know they needed a little Brenna-and-Quinn push.

They were her best friends for a reason.

"Quinn?" Brenna said, as she hit the ball across the court.

"Yes?" Quinn said, returning the rally.

"Can you hear me?"

Bounce.

"Yes?"

Bounce.

"I love this summer."

Volley.

"Me, too."

Return volley.

"I love being twenty-five."

Bounce.

"Me too. It's the best."

Slam. Point, Brenna; 40–15.

"Okay so I've been thinking," Brenna said, tossing the ball in her hand for a quick break. "We have to end this summer right."

Quinn took a sip of water. "I'm listening."

"I think I have a plan."

Quinn tracked the gaze of Brenna's eyeline over to the street, where she'd caught a glimpse of a figure walking by. She'd recognize those shoulders anywhere.

"I love a good plan."

Chapter 27

iz was careful not to hit her shoulder with the curling iron. She had an hour and a half until the engagement party, and like with most special occasions, she'd decided to do her own hair and makeup. In the runway shows of her collegiate fashion days, she always did the glam for her models, styled to match her handcrafted designs.

Her engagement party would be no different, though her hand certainly shook more with nerves today than it ever had when displaying her design capsules. Given the oceanic backdrop for tonight, she opted for loose, beachy curls. She'd found some small shells on the way back from the Jet Ski outing, and she braided a few into her hair. It felt earthy and grounded, like a promise to the beach forces: please, please, please let this go right.

She'd barely seen Cam all morning. At first, Liz was

worried that he might wake up and cancel the entire party after yesterday's fight. But his alarm went off early, and he was soon up and racing to check his family's rental, to make sure everything was smooth before his parents and grandma arrived. The party was happening, and Liz wouldn't be the one to object.

Cam needed to spend the rest of the day running around, he said, getting everything set up at the venue, helping his grandma iron her dress. Every time Liz texted, asking if she should be there, if she could lend a hand, Cam told her to enjoy the day. It was the last Saturday in Ocean Beach. Why should they both lose out on the final beach day because his family insisted on a party?

Liz bit her lip. It was rational, but Cam's behavior still felt suspicious. Was he avoiding her because he didn't want to crush her Domus dreams in front of their closest friends and family?

Looking in the mirror, Liz focused on applying her makeup in a natural style. A lip gloss that glittered in the light, a greenish eyeshadow that made her brown eyes pop. That would match nicely with Cam's green suit. It was meant to be an ode to their prom outfits, all grown up.

Only this time, Liz wouldn't be wearing green.

Instead, she carefully pulled a white dress out of the closet, slipping it from its garment bag like a knight taking off his shield.

It had been one of Roseanne's suggestions. In the week following the wedding dress shopping debacle, Roseanne had emailed Liz late one night, or actually early one morning, with hyperlinked articles listing different ways to honor a deceased loved one on a wedding day. Their initials could be sewn into the fabric of a dress or a suit pocket. A piece of their jewelry could be wrapped around the ends of a bouquet.

Their own wedding dress fabric could be incorporated into the bride's day-of ensemble. Her engagement party ensemble, too.

Liz had gasped when she read it. First, from the sheer shock of her future mother-in-law emailing at three a.m. But mostly because Liz couldn't believe that she hadn't thought of it herself. Her mother's dress. Her gorgeous mother's gorgeous dress. Safely tucked in storage. *Of course*, she realized.

Ever since her mom had passed away, Liz had felt her creativity siphoning off. The colors had faded and left her one-dimensional and dry. Black and white and sad all over. But just because things felt broken, didn't mean they had to stay that way. She could remember her mom while repaving her way.

Like most artists, Liz sometimes struggled to feel genuinely proud of her creations. Impostor syndrome a too-tempting headspace. Yet as she stepped into her engagement party dress now, a redesigned version of her mother's gown, she had no qualifiers or caveats.

She had nailed it. The dress was perfect.

A knock at the door made her jump. Was it Cam? What would he say?

"It's just me!" Maggie's voice called.

Liz eased. "It's open."

"Just wanted to wish you luck before I go set up," Maggie said as she walked in. "Holy shit! You look like a mermaid—no, a princess. A mermaid princess."

"Is that a good thing?"

"Of course. I love it. And oh my god." Maggie paused as she admired Liz's dress. "Did you make this?"

Liz nodded. "From my mom's."

"Are you kidding? I literally just put mascara on. Please don't make me cry. Nope, I'm crying."

"I think she'd like it. It's so different from hers, but still sort of the same."

"It's incredible. She would be so proud of you, Liz. She is so proud, I know it."

Liz looked at Maggie and smiled. "I know, too. Finally, I know."

Liz found herself daydreaming in hypotheticals these days, thought experiments brought on by *What would my mother do? What would my mother say?* Her mom had been unpredictable and spontaneous, but she was consistent when it came to being kind. She was always forgiving. She believed in making room for everyone, despite their mistakes.

Nancy had known that Maggie had moved to LA, that the girls had lost touch the way so many childhood friends do in college, after college. But if she had known that Maggie had since returned and Liz wasn't letting her in with open arms, that she wasn't the one to be kind, to forgive—that would have broken Nancy's heart the most.

Liz was grateful she didn't have to worry about that anymore. Maggie was back.

And three seconds later, Quinn and Brenna were there, too. They hadn't even bothered to knock, barging in with a bottle of champagne and pleas for Liz to curl their hair, quickly, if she had time, before they were all due to head to the party. In exchange for zipping up the back of Liz's dress, she sat each of her friends down and shaped their hair.

It was something out of a Louisa May Alcott novel. Something Liz imagined all mornings would have looked like with sisters running around in her house. Shared bathrooms, shared clothes. Shared laughter and dreams. When it was half past five, Brenna, Quinn, and Maggie heaped side hugs onto Liz (her dress was one thing, but her hair had to stay perfect), and departed for the venue.

In the momentary quiet, Liz heard a tap on the window. Followed by another tap.

Peering through the pane, she saw Cam down below in his green suit with a handful of pebbles.

She searched his face as their eyes met across the distance. Her heart nearly jumped out of her chest. Some love requires hyperbole. A love that can move mountains, or a love that can fling you to the moon, to orbit Earth and never come down.

Liz and Cam's love was plain and simple. It was unwavering. It was true.

How could she survive if he changed his mind?

She tried to control the pace of her pulse, the beating of her heart, as she walked downstairs to meet him. She was nervous and scared but also so deeply in love, she would have run right into the ocean if he'd asked her.

Instead, he picked her up and lifted her straight toward the sky. The best part of dating your high school sweetheart was the ability to drop into any memory, any emotion, at any moment, together. Right now, it felt like they were seventeen again, hearts unabashedly on fire.

"You look amazing. You *are* amazing," Cam whispered, breathless.

"I missed you today," Liz said into his cheek. He smelled clean and fresh.

"I missed you, too. I love you, Lizard," he said, after taking a step back to really look at her. "I love your dress. I love your hair. I love your brain and your patience and your kindness and your laugh."

"I love you more."

"And I love your talent. This dress! I love your smile. I love your hands." He pulled her close now, her fingers held in his own.

But then, Cam was kneeling. Kneeling on the ground.

"Hold on. What's going on?" Liz's heart skipped a thousand beats.

He put his hand up. "Let me say this, before I forget. I've been practicing it for hours."

Suddenly, he pulled a new ring-size box out of his pocket.

Was this what he'd been keeping from her all day?

She didn't have time to think or to process or to worry. She could only listen as Cam cleared his throat and started to speak.

"Liz, this past year has been remarkably hard. This summer hasn't been much easier. Life is, well, it's changing fast, and I lost sight of what to do. But I know that I never want a future that doesn't have you in it. You inspire me every day, Liz. You make me think bolder, live bigger. I used to think we worked so well because we were always the same, but I realized this weekend, that's not it. Not quite. Some parts of us are the same, sure, but we're perfect because of how we've managed to change so perfectly together. How we've grown and ebbed and flowed in a lockstep of our own. And Liz, I never want to not be growing with you."

"Me either," she said, eyes wet.

"So, if that means you spend a year studying in Italy, then *andrai a studiare Italia.* I think I memorized that correctly but I'm not sure. The point is: I'm so sorry for how I reacted yesterday. How shaky this whole summer has been, with planning stress and my mom and all of our missteps. But more than anything, I hate that we lost focus on us, on how good we are together. So, I know we're technically already engaged and everything, but I think we could both use a fresh start. Let's do a redo. Will you agree to marry me? Again?"

Cam opened the box and Liz saw the most perfect ring. It

was a rose gold band, with interlocking leaves and small diamonds throughout. It was exactly what Liz would have designed herself. Something beautiful yet simple at first, stunning when she had a chance to study it, when she saw it for what it was. Just like Liz and Cam.

The two of them had been through hell and back. Relationships are easy when everyone is happy, they learned. It's not hard to get along when loved ones are healthy, when jobs are fulfilling, when paychecks reliably come through. It's when life falters that relationships turn real. Turn true. Together, Cam and Liz had learned what couldn't be taken for granted. They wouldn't waste their time fighting, only forging ahead. The answer was obvious.

"Yes, Cam. A thousand times yes," Liz said, breathless, pulling him up and into her arms, kissing him square on the lips. "I'm so sorry, for everything. I should never have kept the program from you. I haven't been acting like myself this summer. I just know I love you, I can't wait to marry you. I'm so sorry."

"Me, too, babe. Me, too." He kissed her hair.

Liz thanked every star above for planting the most patient, generous, loyal human right around the corner from where she'd grown up. She knew it again in that moment. How lucky she was, to never know a life without Cam.

"No more lies, I promise," she whispered.

"I promise, too."

She would hold tight and never let him go.

"I have one more thing to ask you, then," he said, his eyes suddenly picking up a mischievous dance. "Mac? Think we better get this show on the road."

"I believe it's technically a wagon, not a show." Mac suddenly appeared, calling out from down the street. "Sorry, I wasn't eavesdropping. Not the whole time. Beautiful stuff, guys."

Liz and Cam both laughed, blushing. "What's the wagon for?" Liz asked.

"We weren't sure if you had on a fancy long dress or something that you wouldn't want to walk in," Cam explained.

"The towels?"

"In case of dirt?"

"That's so complicated and confusing and so thoughtful. I love it. I love you both."

Mac beamed. "You guys are seriously so perfect for each other," he said. "But you are also both so perfect for me. It hasn't been easy, these past few years. But I'm finding my place. I haven't missed PT in a month. Last week I signed up to coach an intramural soccer league at work. And that's because of you guys. You inspire me to be better. You're the greatest siblings a guy could have."

"Mac, we just want you to be happy. Always," Liz said as she squeezed his shoulder.

"I'm sorry if I ever made it feel like I wasn't grateful for your help, or appreciative of your advice."

"You couldn't make us think that even if you tried," Liz said.

"Love you, brother," said Cam.

"Love you, too. Both of you," Mac said. "Now, Cam. Ready to tell her your big plan? The real reason I'm standing here like some sort of proposal stalker?"

Cam's eyes glistened as he flashed Liz the biggest grin she'd seen on his face all summer. "I think I have the perfect idea."

Chapter 28

There was no more perfect sight to Maggie's eyes than the bright red recording sign of a camera flashing on. Signaling showtime, ready to begin.

It had taken some getting used to, picking up her camera. It was also powerful, to reclaim something she'd sworn she would never touch again after everything that had happened in LA. No matter how broken Maggie had felt, there was no denying that making movies, storytelling, was her passion. Her favorite thing in the world. Kurt had ruined so much for her, taken her words, her energy, her years, not to mention the unpaid overtime. She didn't need a job to prove what she knew to be innate. She didn't need Kurt's support. His stamp of approval was worthless; she could see that now.

Maggie was filming again, and it had never felt more right.

Glancing at the Maguire's entrance clock, she saw that there were still a few minutes before Liz and Cam were due to arrive. Guests trickled in, greeted by champagne on trays and appetizers passed with tiny napkins that read, *Liz and Cam—#BaesByTheBae.* Who knew Roseanne Peters approved of a hashtag?

Maggie opened her Notes app:

All around me, guests grin in anticipation of a night we're sure to remember. A kickoff to kick-start a celebration. The precursor to the wedding is almost more exciting than the ceremony itself. An opportunity not to witness any change, but just to cheer and marvel. To rev each other up. The pomp will come in due time. Tonight, we are here to party.

Maggie was elated to be a part of that party.

She just hoped that Liz and Cam had worked through their recent rough patch.

Then Maggie looked at her phone screen and felt her heart skip involuntarily.

1 missed call from Ty

She hadn't seen Ty in person since that Sunday morning in Ocean Beach, but they'd spent the past few weeks texting. Sharing movie and TV show recommendations, live reactions during HBO's Sunday night programming. But then notes continued into midweek check-ins on each other's day. It always made her smile, she couldn't deny, to catch his name on her phone.

Was he thinking of her now? Did he want to meet up, to hang out? Did she want to?

She did.

Maggie went to return the call, to click on his name, but then she heard the doors to Maguire's opening.

If all was to go according to plan, Liz and Cam were about to walk in.

She'd try again later, Maggie told herself as she confirmed that the sound was ready and peered into her camera's view-finder.

The display showed Mac's eager grin before Maggie really registered what was happening. It wasn't strange that Mac would walk in first, she reasoned, but was it weird that he was clearing his throat, and standing front and center, and making a sudden announcement?

"Can I have everyone's attention, please?" His voice boomed through the space, quieting the guests down. "At the request of our party honorees, Liz and Cam, could everyone please take a seat?"

The crowd murmured as it obliged. Then all faces turned their attention back toward Mac. "Tucker, my man. You ready?" The event coordinator gave Mac a thumbs-up, a grin.

"Everyone, we are honored to welcome you today to the *wedding* ceremony of Cameron Peters and Elizabeth Grey."

And just like that, there were tears in Maggie's eyes. Liz and Cam hadn't simply found their way back. They were committing fully to their future.

Maggie knew she couldn't miss a moment.

The room gasped as music began to play through the speakers. The doors opened and in walked Cam. He had the biggest smile she'd ever seen as he moved down the center of the room, a makeshift aisle, and stood in front of the windows that overlooked the bay.

Maggie picked up her camera and moved closer to the action. She tried to keep her hands from sweating.

This was a wedding.

Her best friend's wedding.

She normally would be one part of a videography crew of two or three, all helping capture the night from every angle. The faces of the crowd, the bride's entrance, the groom's wonder as the love of his life walked in. Luckily, she had filmed details of the flower arrangements and the party signs, exterior shots of the restaurant, the sun as it began to loosen its hover in the sky. For the rest of the night's coverage, Maggie would just have to give it her best.

She could do this.

For the next twenty minutes, she delicately tiptoed through the crowd. Liz looked stunning, simply stunning, as she walked down the aisle in her mom's dress, Nancy's spirit so present for this moment.

Cam's shoulders danced the entire ceremony, whether with laughter or with tears. He and Liz held each other's hands, welded together, greedy with luck and love.

Mac was the officiant, but it was a surprise for everyone

else, his own parents included. Maggie could tell from Rose-anne's fake smile that she wasn't fully elated by the unexpected event.

But she could also tell from the way that Cam and Liz looked at each other that nothing else would matter. No one else's expectations, no one else's promises. It was the two of them, forever.

Mac's ceremony was perfect. Short and hilarious, gracious and gentle. Everyone in the room knew what Cam and Liz had been through. From neighbors to best friends, to soul mates and survivors. They built each other up with each hardship and came back stronger every time. Mac said he was a better human simply for having known them, and Maggie could see the entire audience nodding in agreement.

Maggie's heart skipped as Mac officially declared Cam and Liz the newest Mr. and Mrs. Peters. Guests cheered as they witnessed the newlyweds' first kiss. She captured everything with a steady hand, following Liz and Cam until they walked out of the room for a brief quiet moment. A breath to steal a kiss and grab a quick snack before greeting a room filled with family and fans.

As Maggie spun the camera to record the crowd's reactions, that intoxicating, awestruck moment between ceremony and reception, her lens landed on Roseanne Peters.

And Roseanne Peters did not look happy.

Maggie could tell from the arch in her brow, the scowl on her lips, that Liz's mother-in-law had been caught off guard by the whole ceremony. That she didn't like it, not one bit. Maggie hated the thought of Liz and Cam having to see Roseanne stressed out, of any anxiety vanquishing their moment of freshly vowed love. She had to help.

Luckily, a light bulb sparked. Maggie knew what to do.

"Mrs. Peters! Congratulations. You look gorgeous," she sang in her best parent-pleasing voice.

"Hi, darling, thank you," Roseanne said with a tight smile. "Is that thing on?"

"Always." Maggie lifted her camera in response. "I can't believe they're married. What a surprise! Do you have anything to say to the bride and groom?"

Roseanne coughed slightly and gave a polite smile. "I love you both. Here's to your eternal happiness. Congratulations." She lifted her champagne glass toward the camera, but Maggie could tell there was still a hint of pain behind Roseanne's eyes. She'd need to try something else.

"Given the nature of a surprise ceremony, I want to go around and ask everyone what their favorite surprise is, second to tonight's wedding, of course," Maggie said, her face still behind the camera, her mind and spirit praying this play would work. That she could switch Roseanne's focus to memories of the past, not the blip of the present. That she'd remember and proceed with the good. "So, Mrs. Peters, besides the beautiful ceremony we just witnessed—what has been your favorite surprise in life?"

Roseanne faltered for a moment, taken aback by the

question. She looked at the ceiling, as if searching for an answer, until something occurred to her. A half breath later, her eyes dropped down and met the camera's gaze. This time, Maggie could tell there was a layer of moisture beneath the surface. Roseanne's face changed, at once more raw but also more joyful.

"The day I found out that I was pregnant with twins. Mac and Cam were the best surprise I'd ever gotten. We had no idea what to expect, how to raise one kid, let alone two, and, well . . ." Roseanne's voice trailed off as her eyes found Mac in the room. They tiptoed next across the space to where Cam and Liz had just entered, already a crowd forming around them for con-gratulations and hugs. "Cam finding his soul mate in high school and being wise enough to hold on to her all these years. That was the second-best surprise. Thank you for recording this, Maggie. I can't wait to see the footage."

With that, Roseanne excused herself and made her way to sweep Cam and Liz into a massive embrace.

"Well done," Quinn said as she sidled up next to Maggie from where she'd been watching.

"Thank you," Maggie said, grinning, "but you aren't getting out of this Q and A that easy. Come on, Quinn. A word to the newlyweds, and your favorite surprise. Spill."

For the next hour or so, Maggie made her way around the party, recording answers from the guests and capturing the magic of the night. Everyone had warm wishes, but the sur-prises were the most heartfelt. The most spontaneous. Cam's uncle recounted winning five thousand dollars on a scratch-off he'd bought for two bucks at Amia's deli in town. PJ's answer was when his parents flew in for UVA's Parents' Weekend, after they had initially said they couldn't make the trip. Family friends Grace and Sam Sharp said their favorite surprise was when the power went out at their daughter's wedding reception, but everyone started singing a cappella instead. Mac's twelve-year-old cousin remembered a bonus onion ring that came in a stash of french fries, a small silver lining in a moment when he'd needed it most.

Maggie hoped Liz and Cam wouldn't mind the direction she'd taken, but she thought there was something magical about knowing what memories their wedding would help inspire. Maggie had had her fair share of surprises these past few months. Tonight, this celebration, was the best one yet.

After Liz and Cam's first dance, Maggie sat down to massage her feet. She'd forgotten the ache of being a heel-donning camerawoman. She loved it; she just needed a break. The party was going perfectly. Filled with those moments that felt like religion, the meaning of life, the purpose of all of this. Relationships were what mattered. These moments, together.

She took out her phone. Her fingers itched for her trusty Notes app, but instead, she opened her Contacts app to her mom's name.

Since moving home, Maggie had meant to visit her parents. They'd scheduled a few dinners, a Sunday barbecue, but her mom had a headache, and then her dad had to work, and then

Maggie had to reschedule, and nothing carried through. She had filled them in on a few major career and moving-related highlights via text—most recently, the truth about Kurt. Typically, she was met with the bare minimum response, but Maggie hoped there might be room for more this time.

Now she typed out a message:

Hi Mom. Miss you. Can we talk?

She almost deleted the words. But then, before she could change her mind, she pressed send.

Maybe this would be the next surprise in store.

The music switched to a popular Earth, Wind & Fire song as more guests filled the dance floor. Maggie stood to record the scene and panned the lens through the crowd, but she nearly dropped the camera when she saw his face.

Ty!

Was that Ty?

She experienced an all-too-familiar feeling of shivers as she extended her head over the frame to confirm with her own eyes, but before she could find Ty's face again, she felt a tap on her shoulder.

"Can the videographer spare a dance?"

It was Mac.

"Don't worry. Just as friends."

Maggie tried to slow her breathing. Why was Ty at Liz and Cam's party? Why did he keep showing up? Why did it keep having a strange and sudden effect on the alchemy in Maggie's bloodstream?

"Just one dance," Mac pled. "Purely platonic. Please, I can't handle my Grandma Peach pointing at every girl in here, asking which one I'm dating."

"You want me to lie to Grandma Peach?" Maggie faux-gasped, one eye still looking for Ty.

"What she won't know won't hurt her," Mac said. His smile was as kind, his eyes as convincing as ever. Maggie considered it, until she saw a whir at the venue's entrance, a door creaking closed, a figure walking away.

Her heart, once again? It skipped.

Ty had left.

Chapter 29

When Ty left LA, there were a lot of things he knew he was leaving behind for good. His apartment's terrace, which had the perfect afternoon lighting. His early morning surf club. The fusilli alla vodka at Jon & Vinny's. And that girl from the mailroom who he couldn't get out of his head.

Maggie Monroe.

He had never felt that way around a girl before, that day he first met her. She sat next to him on a stool, listened as he worked. She took notes on every word he said. It wasn't the attention that he liked, though—who wouldn't like to be on the receiving end of her perfect stare? There was just something about her energy. She had a sharp tongue and fast brain. She smelled like flowers and made him smile the entire afternoon.

From then on, he did anything he could to see her. Whenever he needed a floater to cover his desk, he put in a request with HR for Maggie. He made up that his boss had requested her, that Maggie was the only one trained to know Ava's quirks. But really, Ty craved the look on her face when she rounded the corner of the third-floor kitchen. Her brows were furrowed, and she was so serious but so happy at the same time. He cherished the headset handoff, when sometimes their fingers would graze.

Ty would laugh at night when she'd pop up again in his brain. His phone would ping with texts from other girls at the agency who wanted to grab drinks after work or inquire about his Saturday night plans. He knew he was handsome, he knew he was smart. And he knew Maggie didn't like him like that one bit. He would shake his head. *Of course, I fall for the girl who doesn't even notice me.*

New York called to Ty like a song he couldn't get out of his head. His family was there, most of his friends. He could still work in documentaries, he could still surf, though only a few months of the year, all the way out at Rockaway Beach.

The only thing he'd really miss was Maggie.

And then he saw her. In Ocean Beach, of all places. The beach, then the ferry. He kept seeing her.

He never wanted to not see her again.

After Maggie told him the truth about Kurt, when he realized how awfully she had been treated, Ty went home and cried. He was devastated to realize what he had done, who he had inadvertently connected Maggie to. Where he'd guided her down the wrong path.

How would she ever forgive him now? How could she ever look at him again?

Sitting on the corner of Bungalow Lane, the sounds of Liz and Cam's party still swirling in his ears, Ty realized it was over. Her friends had been nice to invite him. It was sweet of them to think that maybe he had a chance. They said it was impossible not to notice how Maggie brightened whenever he texted her. They wanted to help her end the summer in a perfect way.

Ty knew they were wrong. He'd probably never see her again.

Then he smelled flowers.

In his vision, a figure bloomed up like a rose. Maggie was there, like a ghost or a hallucination. A dream. She was running.

"What's going on? Are you okay?" Ty asked, thinking maybe she was being chased or she was scared. How else to explain this girl sprinting with that crazed look on her face?

Instead, she ran right up to him. And she kissed him.

Before Ty's brain could catch up, he found that his mouth was kissing her back. She wrapped her arms around his neck, he pulled her in tight.

"Hi," he said, when their mouths broke apart.

"Hi yourself." Maggie smiled.

"Sorry I showed up unannounced, back there. I didn't want to startle you."

"I guess I shouldn't have been so surprised, considering you practically followed me around all summer long," she teased. "Popping up whenever I least expected."

"This time, I had an actual invite. Your roommates."

"I should have known." She grinned, and Ty swore he felt goose bumps on his skin.

"Sorry I left," he continued. "I thought you and Mac—"

Maggie displaced his worries with a simple shake of her head. "I'm glad I found you, then."

"You're a pretty fast runner."

"Well, you're a pretty handsome finish line."

"Oh, Maggie," he marveled, taking in the sight of her. The scent again, of flowers and the sea. "Things are only getting started."

Chapter 30

The next morning, Liz started her day, once again, to the sound of Cam's snoring. But there was something new this time: the wedding ring she was twisting around her finger. She was married.

"Wife" felt easy to say, like butter on her tongue, unlike "fiancée," which had always seemed so clunky. *Married*, Liz said in her head.

She was married to Cam.

The night had been magic. Complete and utter magic.

From the moment Cam started outlining his suggestion on their walk with Mac to Maguire's, Liz knew it was what they should do.

The new ring, the re-proposal plan, had been in the works since Liz lost Roseanne's diamond back in July. Cam said a small part of him had instantly regretted giving Liz a ring that never felt very "Liz-like," and this was a silver lining, the chance for a second try. An opportunity to make the process feel more like them.

The surprise wedding idea had come to him late Friday night, when the other friends were out barhopping and Cam was alone with his thoughts and fears, his anxieties about change and the future. He called Mac to talk it out, and the brothers thought of it together. Mac, who had gotten his officiant's license years prior for his coworker, would perform the ceremony. They spent all Saturday in secret, writing everything out, fine-tuning the details, on the chance that Liz agreed.

They had really hoped she'd agree.

Luckily, Liz loved the idea from the second she heard it. She had been struggling through the wedding planning, unsure how to celebrate a day that her mom wouldn't witness. She had known that Nancy couldn't be there. That there were countless moments still that her mom would miss. Their first house, their first child. But they would cross those bridges when they got there. All Liz could do was take one decision at a time, and this was the easiest one she'd made in months.

An impromptu wedding in Ocean Beach, with all their friends and family already gathered.

There was no point in waiting.

She said yes. Then she said I do.

Once the shock had worn off of Roseanne's face, once Cam pulled his mother aside to quickly explain their motivations, the crowd eased into celebration, too. Surely not for nothing, their happiness aided by the realization that no one had to save the date for yet another wedding weekend on their calendars next summer.

Nancy would've loved the spontaneity.

Now, the morning after, Liz listened to Cam snore for a few breath cycles longer before rolling over to check her phone. She pulled up the acceptance letter, words she hadn't let herself embrace for fear of Cam's disapproval. It read:

Dear Elizabeth Gray,

Congratulations! We are thrilled to offer you a spot in our inaugural Domus Fellowship program. Your classmates hail from over fifteen countries, forty cities, and we can't wait for the worldly perspectives to blend in one inventive, inspiring student class all focused on how to change the fashion industry, and the planet, for the better. Over the next few weeks, we will send enrollment information, class selection guides, and travel details to prepare you for the October semester to begin. For now, congratulations. See you in Milan!

Liz soaked it in. She would accept her spot now that she had Cam's blessing. They'd talked it over last night, when they'd gotten back home, feet sore from dancing, cheeks sore from smiling. As Liz's voice picked up, explaining the courses and the potential, Cam immediately saw what she loved about it, why she'd applied in the first place. He knew it was something she needed to do.

Liz would quit her job. The program didn't start until October, but she would spend the time preparing. Resetting her brain. Finding inspiration, so she could hit the ground running once she'd made it to Italy.

Cam offered to find a way to transfer his job to somewhere in Europe, to find a new job in Milan, too. Liz told him not to be silly. They'd been through worse than a year of long distance. Instead, they'd book his flight for Columbus Day weekend. They'd go to Florence for the holidays. They'd meet in Paris for spring break. They'd upgrade to an international phone plan so they could call each other as often as they wanted without any fear of hidden fees. They'd do whatever they could to make it work.

All of that could wait, though, Liz knew. She'd start making plans, tell the East Meadow friends later today. For now, she curled up against her husband (her husband!). She kissed his cheek as her foot found his. Cam's eyes fluttered open.

"Morning, handsome." She smiled.

"Good morning, beautiful wife," Cam replied, yawning. "You know, you might look even more beautiful today than you did yesterday."

"Are you going to say that every day of our marriage?"

"I just might."

Liz kissed his cheek again and then her lips found his mouth. She never minded Cam's morning breath, even though she hated her own. From the feel of him under the covers, she could tell he didn't care one ounce about the dryness of her mouth. Only that her lips stayed against his.

She curled up close to his chest, they breathed each other in like perfume. Morning sex was their favorite. Morning-after-the-wedding sex? Liz felt a wave of excitement between her legs. They pushed closer, as if there was any room to spare, desperate to close any distance between their limbs. Hands began wandering, reexploring familiar territory, the same bodies feeling somehow brand-new after the novel promises of last night.

Until they heard a creak on the staircase, and Georgie's voice shouted out, "Mimosas are ready!"

Cam pulled away with a groan. In a rental house shared with their best friends from high school, it was unlikely that they'd get much further. "My first regret of marital life: not getting a hotel room for last night."

Liz laughed, throwing her face under the covers. Their friends would likely cut them some slack, laugh it off if they heard a rocking bed, but it was probably safer to avoid the prospect entirely.

Not that considering the safety made it any easier.

"I want you," Cam whispered in her ear. Liz let out a soft murmur.

"Then I guess it's a good thing that you have me forever."

"Can't wait to get home," he said as he wrapped her up in a hug, rested his chin against her forehead.

"One more day of Ocean Beach. I can't quite believe it."

"Then home? In bed?"

She kissed his nose. "Home. Bed. You. Me. Forever."

"Forever," he promised.

"I said—mimosas! Bloody Marys, too." Georgie's voice once again ricocheted down the hall. Liz could hear doors opening, bare feet creaking down the stairs.

The Serendipity House was awake.

"For now, our final day," Liz said, pulling herself and then Cam up and out of bed. She threw him a T-shirt from the floor, then found a white bikini in her drawer. She knotted a white sarong at her hip. Bridal morning chic she'd packed coincidentally for the occasion.

The kitchen was soaked with morning light, a table decorated with bagels and spreads, pitchers of mimosas and Bloody Mary cocktails, even a plate of scrambled eggs. The friends gathered, toppling on chairs, perching on windowsills. The house full and alive in the very best way a rental could be.

"Friends, I have an announcement." Georgie raised his glass to prepare for a toast. "First of all, congrats to Liz and Cam. Epic night. You're married!"

"They're married!" Brenna cheered.

"Congrats again, guys," Maggie said as they all clinked their glasses.

"Okay, Georgie, the spotlight is yours. As requested." Liz nudged him in the ribs.

"I, George 'Georgie' McHenry, have officially quit my

job," he announced. The room was stunned into silence. "I repeat. I have just *quit. My. Job.*" From a speaker carefully tucked by his feet, "Free Fallin'" by Tom Petty started blasting through the kitchen. "And from here on out, I'd like to be called just George!"

"Let's go!" PJ stood up and grabbed George in a bear hug.

"Just George!" Quinn teased.

"Proud of you, man," Mac chimed in. "No more late-night door slams, thank God."

"They didn't deserve you, buddy. Here's to the next thing," Cam said.

"Any idea what you have in store next, Just George?" PJ asked.

"I think I want to get into the vacation rental game," George said.

"Maybe you just need a *real* vacation," Quinn said.

"To Georgie's vacation!" "It's just *George*!" "To Just George!" The group chimed as a collective chorus.

Liz fell heavy against Cam's shoulder. She smiled across the room at Maggie. She took in the view. She loved being here more than anything.

The bagel tasted like cloudy heaven in her mouth. "This is the best bagel of my life."

"This is the best weekend of my life," Cam echoed.

"So, our favorite newlyweds," Maggie said, falling into the spare chair next to Liz and preparing a bagel for herself. "What's next? Honeymoon plans?"

"You *have* to go to St. Lucia," Brenna suggested.

"Or New Zealand!" Quinn said.

"Maybe we'll take the ferry down to Kismet. Get another Fire Island rental for the week." Liz smiled.

"Anywhere will be perfect if I get to go with you," Cam said, which prompted PJ to throw his un-schmeared bagel in the newlyweds' direction.

"Can we eat before you guys make out all over each other?" George said.

"Roseanne Peters has something better in mind, sadly," Liz said. "We have to leave in ten or so, brunch with Cam and Mac's parents."

"Well, I'll wait to start eating again until then, just to be safe," PJ laughed.

Fifteen minutes later (a few of which Liz and Cam admittedly spent making out, upstairs in their room with the door securely closed), Liz, Mac, and Cam were walking once again toward the Ocean Beach town square. Five minutes after that, they were seated at the Landing, facing Mrs. Peters, Mr. Peters, and Grandma Peach, ordering their second meal of the morning.

But before sipping her mimosa, Roseanne cleared her throat. Liz felt like she was bracing for a schooling from a particularly stern teacher, ready to be chastised for tardiness or talking in class.

They were married now. Yes, it had been a big stunt. A huge secret they'd kept from her in-laws.

But could they really still get in trouble with their parents? Liz was afraid to find out.

Roseanne spoke. "Last night was certainly unexpected. When Mac made his announcement, frankly, I was a bit hurt. Why didn't they include me in this decision? After all the work I'd put into your plans already? Did they want to make me look a fool in front of our family and friends?"

"Mom, come on, it wasn't like that," Cam started, but Roseanne cut him off.

"I know, Cameron. I know that now. I didn't in the moment, but when I saw your mother's dress, Liz. And I heard your vows. And when I talked to your loving friends, too. I realized why." Roseanne reached across the table and placed her palm on top of Liz's hand. "Last night was beautiful. I am so sorry that your mother wasn't with us in person, Liz, but when I saw you in her dress, I felt her spirit fly in through the windows, I swear. I miss her, too. These past few months have been, well, not my best behavior. It's a strange feeling, watching your child make a family of his own, and wanting to help but not sure how best to do so from the sides. It's new, but it's for the most wonderful reason, and I'm so sorry for my missteps. But I love you, sweetheart. We all love you both."

"Welcome to the family!" Grandma Peach added with a smile. "Officially!"

"Thank you." Liz wiped her eyes, transmitting an apology back over the table to Roseanne. She was right, Liz knew, that it couldn't be easy, raising someone only to watch them make a new home, having to let a new voice in after being the one calling the majority of the shots for so long. But Liz also knew it wasn't that simple, it wasn't black-and-white. It wouldn't be some foolish winner-takes-all game for Cam's heart.

Together, Liz, Cam, and the entire Peters family would find new footing. They'd get into a new groove. She was grateful, more than anything, to have them as her family. Cam squeezed Liz's thigh underneath the table as their brunch plates arrived, but she was no longer hungry. At last, she felt full.

Mr. Peters broke that silence between bites. "But in all seriousness. Mac, if you get married without warning us, we will disown you." He grinned, and the family laughed.

"You don't have to worry about that. If and when I get married, I want the whole thing. Five-course dinner. Thirteen, no, fourteen-piece band. Three outfit changes. Mom, you can plan the whole thing."

"We'll see what his bride thinks about that," Grandma Peach croaked out.

"I always thought you'd end up with that Maggie," Roseanne said. "I can't wait to see her footage from last night! She's something special, that one. But we'll obviously adore whoever you choose, MacIntosh."

Liz found Mac's eyes across the table. Even if Maggie wouldn't be her sister-in-law, she couldn't wait to meet Mac's future bride. The more sisters, the better, in Liz's mind.

She smiled, squeezing her husband's hand. "Me, too."

Chapter 31

Two?!" When Roseanne Peters registered what the doctor was telling her that day, she cried. Right there in his examination room, twenty-six years ago, tears flooded down her face at the news. There were two.

Twins.

She couldn't believe it. She looked at Jeff and almost screamed when she saw that he was grinning. Beaming, really. The happiest she'd ever seen him in the twelve years that she'd known him. The five years that they'd been married.

"Twins!" Jeff marveled. "Can you believe it, Rosie? Two of them. Two babies. Two of everything."

"Two of everything," she whimpered. And then she started to sob. Two childbirths, two mouths to feed, two bodies to clothe. Two beds, two college tuitions.

Two of every risk, of every fight, of every fear.

Roseanne's tears had finally dried up by the time she held the tiny babies in her arms. They were early, in the NICU for three weeks, but they'd be healthy.

They were hers.

She named them Cameron, her father's name, and Mac-Intosh, after the farm where she and Jeff had gotten married.

"You can't name them Cam and Mac! C-A-M? M-A-C? They're palindromes!" Her mother, Peach, had shrieked at the idea.

"Technically, they're anagrams," Roseanne had replied. "But I think that's perfect. A perfect pair, just like them."

When they were babies, she tried to keep them on a schedule. Sleep at the same time, nurse at the same time. But they were so identical, and Roseanne was so tired, that once she mixed them up. She had to bring them back to the hospital, mortified, admitting that she'd forgotten which twin was which. The doctor laughed good-naturedly as he compared the foot-prints on file—*This happens more than you'd think*—but Roseanne didn't quite see the humor.

From then on, she held tightly. She wouldn't lose track of any more details. She'd never take her eye off the ball. Once the boys started walking, it somehow got worse and better all at the same time. They were so brilliant and so handsome, tiny people with entire worlds inside their brains. But they were also every-where, like high-speed bumper cars, with only one of her to protect them from any danger. Jeff was back at work, so it was up to Roseanne to keep an eye on their endless wanderings.

Even the most basic household items became a new danger. Everything scared Roseanne. She just wanted to keep them safe. Had to keep them safe.

Because what would happen if she dared let go?

From then on, she vowed to stay focused, to do her best. Carefully orchestrating and executing plans became her love language. Control, the most reliable solution for her worries. She gave them everything, every piece of her brain. But even as the boys grew older and became more independent, even when Cam was officially engaged, her mind still raced with fears. What if she'd taught him something wrong? What if she forgot something crucial about life? What if he was making a mistake?

What if he never came back to her again?

She tried to help through the planning, utilizing the tools she knew best, but she could sense Cam slipping, even still.

As Roseanne watched her son walk down the aisle, as she felt the crowd of family and friends give way to the unplanned wonder and love and cheer, she had a small moment of realization.

Perhaps she had come on a bit too strong.

Mac and Cam had grown to be hard on themselves, too. Like mother, like sons.

Motherhood was doing your best every day. It was getting up and trying to be a little more patient. A little kinder. A little more forgiving, of the kids and of yourself. Even if at the end of the day, your mind raced with regrets, if you made some mistakes, if you cried in the shower, you promised that tomorrow you'd do better.

Roseanne was still a little terrified, but she would never stop showing up for her family. For the people she loved.

Maybe she'd try to let go a bit. To let others take over some of the reins.

She could try to soften, in doses, in certain scenarios.

Like weddings, maybe. Or with grandchildren, God willing.

At the brunch restaurant in Ocean Beach, she looked at her sons. She'd done good. They were good. Look no further than the beautiful friend group they'd held on to. Such shining forces, such good people. Faces she adored to champion, cheer on.

She would hold all their hands and smile. Maybe she'd loosen the grip ever so slightly. Love with a little more ease. See where a looser plan might lead them. She promised to lighten her squeeze.

Chapter 32

The room went dark, and Maggie gave his hand a gentle squeeze. The same hand she'd held for the first time last night, under the moonlight. The hand she then begrudgingly dragged back to Maguire's when she remembered she still had a job to do.

Ty.

Maggie wasn't so naive as to believe this was the inevitable grand telling of their love story. She hadn't had an "It Had to Be You" revelation as she watched him walk out the door last night. She had, however, realized that he was there for a reason, he had shown up at her best friends' wedding, and she wanted to know why.

As she walked out the door, she'd also realized he'd dropped his wallet on the floor.

So, naturally, she thought, "To hell with naivete." She accepted that maybe she was in a love story.

She ran.

And as she ran, she remembered the way his mouth had curved upward when he taught her how to roll calls. How it had felt to sit next to him for an afternoon, the hint of a morning surf still in his hair. How her heart had waltzed down her spine every time she saw him on Fire Island.

She was tipsy from champagne, drunk from wedding joy, but that just made it easier to say yes to a romance that had been building all summer long.

Maggie kissed Ty and it was perfect.

The rest of the night felt like a starry dream. Back at Maguire's, Ty helped film the wedding so that he and Maggie could take turns on the dance floor, or refilling Liz's and Cam's never-empty champagne flutes. At one point, Maggie turned the camera around and angled it just so, to catch her dancing at Ty's side, a quick peck on his cheek. He pulled her close, tipped her face back toward his, and kissed her square on the mouth. Their own private spotlight, all on them.

She wouldn't put that in Liz's reel. Maggie wanted that memory only for herself.

They parted ways after the wedding with coy grins. Maggie hated to leave him, but she didn't want to miss the last night and the last morning at the house with her friends. There'd be more nights, and hopefully more mornings, too, Ty said. Another kiss goodbye—Maggie's lips had never felt so lovely yet so tired—and they left with a promise to meet outside the Ocean Beach Village Community House at one o'clock sharp the next day, right in time for the first film.

There were ten films total, all shorts of various genres and topics. The community house had been transformed by way of a custom black-and-orange step-and-repeat sign and a concession stand, even a makeshift marquee announcing the finalists' names out front. The host was a Fire Island resident, current Yale student and professional actor Jesse Ray Sheps. He'd impressively founded the festival as just a teenager, organizing it as part of a nonprofit fundraiser for St. Jude Children's Research Hospital.

Now Jesse stood in front of a podium at the base of a projector screen, kicking off the day. He welcomed the room of filmmakers and industry veterans, thanked the Fire Island community for its arts-loving history and sun-kissed support, and gave a special shout-out to his parents, beaming proudly in the back of the room.

And then, without further ado, he lowered the lights and Ty's film began to play.

Maggie couldn't stop smiling. One minute in and she knew he'd win. Ty had interviewed famous restaurant owners in the city, following as they each prepared their most popular dish, as well as their favorite one to make. They spoke about the history of their food, their heritage, what had gotten them into the fast-paced world of dining and hospitality in the first place. The stories all ended with hope, some tears. Groups of people doing what they felt they were called to, what they were meant to do. Maggie's favorite thing.

The pride bubbled off her skin like electricity, her gratitude for knowing him, for finding him again. For sitting next to him once more. She knocked her knee against his.

"You're amazing at this, you know?" she whispered.

"No talking during the movies," Ty whispered back, but she could tell he appreciated her words.

His film ended to thunderous applause. The lights turned on, and Brenna and Quinn immediately clapped Ty on the back. George and PJ leaned forward, too, shouting their congratulations from down the row. Almost the entire Serendipity House was here. The Bamboo House was also in full attendance, including Ty's younger sister, Talia, whom Maggie met this afternoon. Talia wasn't overly warm, but she wasn't completely unfriendly.

Ty had rolled his eyes afterward. "Ignore her. She thinks she needs to be some intimidating sibling to make sure you don't break my heart or something. She does this to everyone."

"Got it," Maggie said, cocking her head ever so slightly. "So, what you're saying is, there's been many of me before?"

"Actually, the opposite. There has never been anyone like you," Ty had replied. For a brief second, Maggie let herself sit back and swoon.

Now she was just waiting on Liz, Cam, and Mac. They'd promised they'd be at the festival, but Maggie knew she couldn't be upset if they bailed. Not after they'd granted her such generosity and forgiveness. Maggie would take what she could get until she'd worked her way all the way back. Maybe in a few months she wouldn't think this way anymore, finally, but she didn't want to take any chances too soon. She didn't want to risk this, any of this, again.

When Jesse announced a ten-minute intermission until the next film was set to play, Ty went to the concession stand to refill their Diet Cokes and popcorn bags. Maggie bit a loose cuticle. She was nervous—really nervous—for an audience to see her film, but also for something she knew might or might not appear on her phone screen.

"I'm gonna go stretch my legs," she said to Brenna and Quinn before walking out into the main hallway. There was a spare bench, the perfect place to momentarily collapse.

Maggie wanted to write, but she was afraid to check her phone.

She'd missed a call from her mom this morning. Maggie saw it ringing, surely an answer to the text she'd sent last night, but suddenly, she felt scared and anxious, nervous for all the things that could happen when she and her mom finally connected again. There was so much to say. Where would she begin?

Instead of calling back later in the day, she had sent her mom a photo of the festival program, bright orange paper with her name in bold capital letters among the list of finalists. It was daring, a risk she knew could wind up pushing her mom even further away.

Maggie had tried to give up storytelling. Her parents would have been proud, probably for the first time in years, she hated to realize. But no matter how hard it was to face what she'd been through, there was no silencing the voice inside her that demanded she write. That craved it. When she needed them most, stories were there to pick her up and wipe her face and encourage her to keep fighting. To trust again.

Ocean Beach had rocked her back to life.

She finally felt like herself again.

Now she took a deep breath in and turned her phone around.

1 new voicemail from Mom

Maggie felt every emotion swirl through her body as she dug for her AirPods, connected the Bluetooth, and hit play.

Hi Maggie. It's Mom. Sorry I missed you, just wanted to call . . . we hadn't realized you were in a festival. That's . . . exciting. Next time, let us know and we'll, uh, your father and I will try to be there. Listen, come over this week for dinner? We, uh, we need to talk about your awful boss. We want to help in any way. Maybe we can sue? And, well. To think you were alone out there, for so long. . . . We never want you to feel that far again. See you soon.

The voicemail ended and Maggie crumpled. It was years too late, she knew that. They had so much terrain to climb. But if she had learned anything this summer, it was that nothing could be rebuilt without a first brick.

Words swirled through her mind. She opened her Notes app, tears fully formed and falling down her cheeks. She went to type, to make sense of everything in the only way she knew how, when she heard a voice.

"Mags! Are you okay?"

She looked up and saw Liz's face. Sunglasses tucked up into her bright red hair. Sundress flowing to the ground, moving with the wind as she rushed to Maggie's side.

Wordlessly, Maggie transferred her AirPods over to Liz's ears and pressed play on the voicemail. She let her head fall against Liz's shoulder as she heard Liz gasp.

"Wow, Mags. That's probably the most emotion I've ever heard from your mom," she said, holding her friend until the sadness passed. Maggie almost laughed. Instead, she dried her face. "Everything will be okay," Liz whispered.

"There she is! Hollywood's finest," Roseanne's voice suddenly called out.

Maggie looked up and saw the Peters posse heading their way. "I hope you don't mind that we tagged along with the kids," Roseanne said. "We can't wait to see your film."

Grandma Peach held an extra-large, extra-buttery bucket of popcorn beside Roseanne. Her smile was fixed in a grin. "You know, I was cast as an extra in *Fame*. If you look closely, one hour and forty-eight seconds in, I'm there. Watching those kids dance in the streets! Swear to God. Boy oh boy, do I love the movies."

"Me, too," Maggie said, smiling.

"Everyone made it!" Ty rounded the corner with a grin, taking in the sight of the Peters family. "There's still a bunch of seats near us. I'll show you."

"So excited for you, Mags," Mac said with a wave.

"Break a leg," Cam added.

"You ready to go do this?" Liz asked, pulling Maggie up with an outstretched hand.

"Not even a little." Maggie laughed. "But that's my favorite part."

The friends found their seats, Maggie sandwiched between Liz and Ty. She held both of their hands, which rippled in a chain reaction throughout the row. PJ and George and Mac and Cam, Brenna and Quinn and Grandma Peach, too. Even Mr. and Mrs. Peters joined in, knees dancing and voices whispering with excitement. Hands interlocked and fingers squeezing in anticipation for Maggie, their returned friend. Their best friends, all one tier.

Maggie had to laugh. A group of adults, holding hands in a movie theater. Just like the spectacularly strange, loyal, perfect friends they were, that they had always been. Her parents might not be here, not yet, but maybe one day.

The lights dimmed, but Maggie had never felt brighter.

How could she have ever thought there was anything regular, anything mediocre, about finding her way back home?

Chapter 33

The floorboards creaked out in song as the friends dragged duffel bags down the stairs. They threw dirty sheets and towels over the railing and into the hamper, taking turns loading and reloading the wash. Music played as brooms swept floors, board games and decks of cards were tidied up and put away.

It was the end of a summer, the end of a vacation, and the Serendipity House was exhausted.

Maggie, Quinn, and Brenna lay on the stripped-down mattress, examining Maggie's certificate against the glare of the ceiling lamp as they waited for the last of the laundry to be done.

"Third place," Brenna said with wonder.

"Not bad." Maggie smiled. Normally, she would have beaten herself up for not coming in first. It came as no surprise when Ty was awarded the blue ribbon—his piece was masterful—but Maggie was genuinely shocked when they called her name for third. She didn't care about the prize. She had won so much already this summer.

"We lost our bet, though," Quinn complained.

"Something tells me Ty won't come calling for the winnings," Brenna teased, and giggles escaped their throats like they were young girls in the cafeteria again, trading notes about a grade-school crush in North Face jackets, doodling on each other's Converse sneakers.

Quinn nudged her. "You're welcome for that, by the way."

"Thank you guys. Again, and again. For everything," Maggie said. "My roommates. My costars. Now potential matchmakers? I'll never be able to repay you."

"Just take my turn vacuuming this week when we get home and we'll be fine."

"Deal."

"Knock, knock," Liz said, letting herself into their bedroom.

"Lizzy! Lie down," Brenna said, as Quinn tugged her arm. They lay folded on top of each other, magically embedded on a full-size mattress the way only best friends can fit.

"I wanted to show you guys my application portfolio," Liz said, opening her phone to a Google Drive presentation.

"How do you say 'congratulations' in Italian again? I keep forgetting," Maggie said.

"Complimenti!" Quinn sang in an Italian accent.

"Bravo! Bravo!" Maggie said, pulling the screen closer to her face.

She dropped it entirely when she saw the photo of Liz's final piece.

A two-piece set with a long and pleated skirt, all in a muted yet breathtaking pastel rainbow print. An ode to their shopping adventure, inspired by the memories of their big-hearted middle-school days.

"I couldn't have done it without you, Mags."

"Me either." Maggie and Liz had succeeded. A film festival, a screenplay. A wedding and a scholarship. These were some of their biggest dreams come true, but the best part was that they were celebrating here, heads on the same pillowcase. Reunited, again. "I'm so grateful for all you guys. Thank you for everything," Maggie said, grabbing Brenna's and Quinn's hands. A perfect friendship pile, together.

"This was my favorite summer ever," Brenna said.

"Mine, too," the girls answered in harmony.

Down the hall, George was bouncing up and down on his mattress so excitedly that he nearly hit his head on the bunk bed frame four separate times. He held his phone in his hands like a gold medal.

"Dude! She wants to meet up next weekend in the city!"

"Let's go! Awesome, my guy!" PJ said.

"Where should I suggest for drinks? Cornerstone Tavern?"

"Georgie—"

"Just George," he whined.

"Just George," PJ said. "I say this not just as your Ocean Beach roommate, but as your friend. If you want a second date, you sure as hell need to go someplace better than Cornerstone."

"I hear what you're saying," George said. "And I respect your opinion. But I dare you to find me a bar in New York with more style than Cornerstone."

"Dear lord, give me your phone. I'll help you pick a place."

As PJ and George searched for trendy date-night spots, Cam and Mac were in the kitchen emptying out the fridge. To ease the effort, they each had cracked open one final Montauk Summer Ale. They tossed what remained of a pint of blueberries, packed the leftover seltzers in a cooler for the journey back home. The ketchup and mustard would stay in the shelf with the collection of other condiments passed down from renter to renter.

"How does it feel? Being married?" Mac asked.

"So far? Pretty much exactly the same," Cam said. "I think I'd be scared if it felt any different."

"For sure." Mac grinned. "Mom's happy for you, you know. Even if she was surprised by it."

"I know. And she's happy for you, too. No matter what."

Mac coughed. "It's naive, maybe, but I guess I was a little nervous that it would feel like I was going to lose you?"

Cam took his brother by the shoulder. "That could never happen. We're forever. Promise."

"Promise."

Cam sipped his beer and smiled, too. "Man, remember when Robyn was here?" He couldn't help it. He'd always mess with his brother when he could. That's what twins do.

"I don't want to talk about it," Mac groaned.

"After all that, I miss her unusual business ideas."

"She was nice!"

"Pretty lucky you still got the big bedroom all to yourself this weekend."

"Yeah, yeah. Don't be jealous cuz you have to share a bed for the rest of your life, bro."

Mac didn't confess that he'd had the same thought, the same realization, at the beginning of this weekend. The small, silent hope that someone might end up on the mattress with him.

Now he knew it didn't matter. He didn't need the warmth of a body next to him to feel like he had purpose. He'd find it in himself. With Cam and Liz, yes, but also on his own separate plane. Not as a twin, not as a boyfriend, not as a teammate or a coworker or a best friend. Mac felt ready to find out who he was on his own.

He didn't tell Cam, but Robyn had texted him yesterday. She sent best wishes for Cam and Liz's party, and a recommendation for a therapist named Nina who might be able to help Mac find his way. Coming from anyone else, coming from any other *ex-girlfriend*, that would have seemed like an enormous overstep. But somehow, from Robyn, it felt like care. He was ready to make the call.

The brothers clinked their beers. It would be an interesting fall.

Before long, the friends made their way out of the house's doorway for the final time. One group of many in the ghosts of others who had rented before them. How many there must have been, who had left and learned and loved in an Ocean

Beach share house just like them, locking the door and putting the key in the lockbox, punching in the code like a final prayer.

Brenna's voice trailed through the air as the group walked into town. She was already planning a going-away party for Liz next month before she left for Italy in October. PJ's birthday was in two weeks; they were debating a new Brooklyn brewery versus a bowling and karaoke night. Maggie recommitted to seeing a movie once a week until Christmas, and promised she'd text everyone the weekly showtimes in case anyone wanted to tag along.

The friends may have been boarding a ferry, but it was clear they weren't going far.

Maggie slipped into a bench on the ferry's top deck. Ty sat down next to her. He watched as she registered a text message that had crept in from Kurt, still harassing her despite her silence.

"I'll never forgive myself for telling you about that job," Ty said, voice strained. "For putting you in his path."

"It's not your fault, Ty. Only his." With a few flicks of her finger, Maggie deleted the message and permanently blocked Kurt in her contacts for good. She'd figure out retribution with the guild, chart a course of action with her parents. She'd write and write and write until he was barely a footnote in the greater timeline of her career.

But she was done letting him control her through her phone.

Ty squeezed Maggie's hand. She squeezed back.

"I was wondering," she said, looking into his eyes as the ferry kicked off into the bay. "Want to hang out this week?"

"I thought you'd never ask." Ty grinned.

She let her head fall on his shoulder for the remainder of the ride as the Fire Island shoreline dwindled out of sight. They'd made it through the summer intact. It didn't feel like the bittersweet end of a vacation, the end of a trip. Maggie didn't have any nostalgia for the roller coaster of emotions Ocean Beach had left in her bones.

For now, she simply had promise. She had hope for the first time in a long time. She felt like herself again. Driven and eager and bold.

She couldn't wait to get home.

The David Bros. shuttle bus was waiting in the Bay Shore parking lot by the time they'd returned. They boarded like the weary travelers this summer had made them all. Maggie settled into her seat, rested her head against the window, but before she could get too comfortable, George called her name from down the row.

"The Serendipity House owner just asked if we could leave him a review," he said, voice bouncing with the wheels of the bus. "Mags, you're the writer of the group—can you do that for us? We should say something nice. Who knows? Maybe we'll want to come back for three more weekends next year."

"Sure," she said with a smile. "Maybe we will."

Then, Maggie started to write.

Acknowledgments

Hi! If you are reading this, I will let you in on a secret. I'm having a bit of trouble starting my acknowledgment section. You might say, "But, Becky, you wrote a whole second book! Surely listing the people who made that possible should be simple!" The truth is, dear reader, there is nothing simple when it comes to how I feel about this book or the people who helped me get here.

See, I wrote my debut novel, *Kismet*, in secrecy during the pandemic, tucked away on weekends. Plans were postponed, and friends and family were in lockdown, so I gave all my newfound free time and focus to *Kismet*. I am the luckiest person on the planet for all that it gave me in return.

Serendipity was born in what felt like an entirely new era. I wrote in the spaces between the world reopening, between publishing *Kismet* and working a busy day job and celebrating two of my quadruplet sisters (named Maggie and Liz!) getting married—all at the sweet-spot age when every weekend is a thirtieth birthday party or a graduation day or wedding event or another Big Life Moment that you feel so entirely overjoyed to be a part of. Aging is a privilege. Getting to grow up with your friends and family is, too.

At its heart, *Serendipity* is my love letter to this very gratitude I have for the way I was raised, surrounded by my big, caring, supportive family and our ever-growing extended Chalsen family-friend group, and all the countless weekends we spent packing in as many memories as we could.

Yet, in the course of committing to writing this book . . . I did not spend nearly as much time as I would have liked with the people who make me feel this grateful in the first place. I left early, or showed up late, or canceled at the last minute because of a publishing deadline. I filled my outbox with apologies and excuses, worrying they'd grown stale, that I'd risked and ruined everything to selfishly work on a project that no one had told me to write. Yet somehow, like magic, the replies were always the same: *Don't worry. Keep going. We're here, cheering, every step of the way.*

Being encouraged to follow my dreams, even if it meant sacrificing time spent with the very people who inspired me to dream in the first place, is what singlehandedly pushed me to finish this book. It has also now essentially rendered me speechless. There seems to be no proper combination of words to adequately capture this feeling, but because I'm still up against one of those lovely publishing deadlines, I will try.

First and foremost, my book family. Thank you to my sensational agent, Sabrina Taitz, whose fearless advocacy and fierce loyalty is nothing short of sisterly. I couldn't do any of this without you. (And thank you to Sab's real-life family, Eric and Isla, for sharing her with me.) To the brilliant WME book department—especially the great Ty Anania, Sam Birmingham, Caitlin Mahony, Carolina Beltran, Suzannah Ball, Tracy Fisher, Alicia Everett, and Jennifer Rudolph Walsh—thank you for being the best literary home. I've loved "growing up" in publishing with you.

Thank you to my dearest editor, Cassidy Sachs, whose keen wisdom and massive heart made this story better every step of the way. I'm so fortunate for our "again." To the visionary team at Dutton and PRH—John Parsley, Christine Ball, Caroline Payne, Hannah Poole, Alice Dalrymple, Susan Schwartz, Ryan Richardson, Melissa Solis, Christopher Lin, and Elke Sigal—thank you for welcoming my novels into your legendary lineage. It's the honor of a lifetime.

Thank you to my exceptional friends, who put up with the many aforementioned canceled plans it took to write this book. I am so grateful to have you all in my corner, especially Mary, Maddy, Jackie, Charlotte, Getsos, Farrel, Min, Alex, Danny, David, Kaitlin, and Connor, who endured the bulk of my flakiness. Thank you to Nicki and Dana, for your East Meadow tips and tricks. And a very special shout-out to my Bamboo House pals and our own epic Ocean Beach share house summer. Toasting a Rocket Fuel to you all.

To my in-laws, Debbie, Eddie, Craig, Brittany, Matt, and

Grace Schwartz, who have made space for me at their table and loved me like one of their own since I was seventeen. Thank you for welcoming me into your family, for teaching me all about the magic of Fire Island, and for always making me feel right at home.

To my siblings, Sam, Joanna, Maggie, and Lizzy, and their other halves, Katie, Jack, Brendan, and Bobby, who are my cornerstones. Thank you for being my biggest cheerleaders, my forever best friends and advisers, and for bringing to our family the most extraordinary type of love (and themed parties) imaginable. Growing up as a quadruplet with one older brother isn't simply the best fun fact. It's the best recipe for life.

To my parents, Chris and Georgine Chalsen, who have given me the world. Thank you for loving me wholeheartedly, for walking with me in lockstep through all the (well-researched) highs and lows, for encouraging every plan along the way. You have shown us how to live a life anchored by family, guided by hope, and comforted by loud laughter, daily aperitivo, and a healthy dose of color-coded systems. What a blessing it is to be your daughter.

To Zack, my brilliant husband, who inspires every romantic word I'll ever write. Thank you for being my favorite person since kindergarten, my harbor in any storm. If your patience and humor could be bottled up, I swear it would solve world peace. Thank you for transforming my daydreams into reality, for making me laugh without fail, and for evacuating our apartment during my marathon writing weekends. You are it, bear. The sweetest love story of all.

Lastly, to you, dear reader, thank you for taking a chance on *Serendipity* and spending three weekends on Fire Island with me. My wildest dream comes true every time you turn the page. And to anybody who might be holding this book one day, feeling like they are canceling too many plans, sacrificing too much, missing too many memories in pursuit of a dream of their own, to you, I say: *Don't worry. Keep going. I'm here cheering for you, every step of the way.* Thank you.